MW01531316

Rachel

Phoenix Born

Enjoy the series!

Laci

This is a work of fiction. The characters, incidents, and dialogue are drawn from the author's imagination and are not construed as real. Any resemblance to actual events or persons, living or dead, is entirely coincidental.

Copyright © 2017 Laci Maskell
Cover Design by Caedus Design Co.
Published in 2017 by Laci Maskell through Createspace

All rights reserved. No part of this book may be reproduced, scanned, or distributed in any printed or electronic form without permission. Please do not participate or encourage piracy of copyrighted materials in violation of the author's rights.

ISBN-13: 978-1542388610
ISBN-10: 1542388619

Phoenix Born

Laci Maskell

Also By Laci Maskell

Still Life Moving

So . . . That Happened

For my brother Andy, who everyday shows me the meaning of hard work and always expects the best out of me even when we don't share the same point of view. Someone who at times is my biggest critic, but whose praise means the most.

One

Do not go gentle into that good night. Rage, rage against the dying of the light. – Dylan Thomas.

Who seriously puts that in a birthday card? And what did it even mean?

I turned to Nash, my twin brother, who read the same card, with the same puzzled look on his face. Nash glanced at me and mouthed *What does it mean?* I shrugged my shoulders because I had no answer for him.

More confusing, was the fact that there was no name on the card. No giver of the card.

Nash and I both looked to our parents and I asked, "Do you know who this is from?"

My mom took the card from me, examined it, handed it

to my dad, who looked it over and they both shrugged. Oh well. It was just a birthday card.

We quickly forgot about it when our mom looked at our dad, smiled, and turned to us saying, "Are you ready for your gifts from your dad and I?"

Nash and I turned to each other, smiled, and ran for the door.

"Hold your horses," my dad called.

Nash and I stopped at once like characters in an old Acme cartoon.

"Where do you think you two are going?" our mom asked.

Nash and I slowly turned around to our parents. Nash said, "Come on, mom. It's our sixteenth birthday. We just figured you were getting us cars."

"Oh did you?" our dad chuckled.

"Well, yeah," I said, like it's obvious.

"And what if we didn't?" our mom asked.

Nash and I looked at each other and our shoulders fell, disappointed. "Oh," we both said together and walked back to the dining room.

"Well, now, isn't it a good thing we knew what you'd want?"

Nash and I immediately perked up and ran back for the front door. Nash got there first and swung the door open. It banged against the wall but we kept going.

In the driveway sat a shiny black crotch rocket motorcycle and a shiny black Dodge Charger.

Nash and I stood in the yard, our mouths agape.

"I think we did good," I heard our mom say from somewhere behind us.

"Good?" I asked incredulously. "You did amazing. I can't believe this."

Nash was still staring at his new motorcycle in awe.

"Now," our dad said in his stern voice. "You will wear helmets and you won't do anything stupid."

When neither of us said anything, he said, "Kids. They can both be taken back."

Nash and I jumped at his comment and said, "Yes, Dad. Nothing stupid."

Then Nash looked at me and said to my parents, "Can we take it for a ride?"

Our parents looked at each other worriedly, but smiled and said yes.

"Your helmets are in your car, Casslyn. Do not go far, neither of you have your license yet."

That's right. My car. I took the opportunity to run to my car and examine it. Instead of just ogling it. I opened the door and slowly slid into the driver's seat. The interior was all black, the cloth seats, the dash, the floor mats. It was glorious and it was all mine. I wanted to take it out for a ride but I knew Nash really wanted to take the bike for a spin. We could take my car out once we were back.

I looked in the back seat to find two black motorcycle helmets. I grabbed them both, got out of my new prized possession, and headed for Nash and the bike.

We pulled the helmets over our heads and were about to climb onto the bike when our mom said, "Go get your coasts, it's March for goodness sake. You'll catch your death." Our mom, the ever overprotective doctor.

Nash and I begrudgingly marched into the house, put on our coats and headed back outside.

We actually got on the bike and Nash started it up when our mom yelled, "Maybe you want to try it out another day."

"Mom," we said exasperatedly.

Our dad said, "Honey, let them go."

Nash said, "We're just going to drive around town a bit, go show it off to Xander and Tucker, then we will be back. An hour tops. Don't worry so much."

"Alright," our mom said. "Just be careful."

Nash always had a way of getting our mom to comply with his wishes. It was one of the very few things our twin bond didn't share.

"Ready, sis?" Nash called back to me.

I held a little tighter around his stomach and said, "Ready."

Nash pulled on the clutch. He gave the bike some gas. It roared and vibrated underneath us. He let off the clutch and pulled slowly away from the driveway.

It felt freeing to be riding on the bike. Not terrifying, like I'd imagined it would. We buzzed around a few blocks and through the center of town before Nash pulled over and asked if I wanted to drive. Before I knew it, I was letting off the clutch, giving the bike some gas and driving the motorcycle. I drove slowly and listened to Nash give me directions and pointers.

When I'd had enough, I pulled over into the city park. It was decently cold outside, so there were no children at the park.

"You know, that card was weird," Nash said.

I hadn't thought about it much since opening it, but now it came back to me. *Do not go gentle into that good night. Rage, rage against the dying of the light.*

"It was weird," I told him. "And the fact that it didn't have a name on it was too."

"Yeah. What was that about?"

I tried to think of an answer for him. Maybe it was just a mistake. Maybe it was really not as weird as we thought it was.

Before I could answer him, Nash said, "How jealous is everyone at school going to be?"

I smiled and said, "Oh, I know. Your bike is sweet. But I love my car more."

Nash playfully shoved me. I shoved him back. Within seconds we were on the ground, horsing around and laughing till our stomachs hurt. We stopped fighting but continued to lay there.

Nash turned to me and said, "Happy birthday, sis. I know I don't say if often and I'm not trying to get all mushy on you, but I love you."

The truth was, he never had to say it. Nash and I were so in sync, our bond so strong, that we often didn't need to speak to know what the other meant. Nash was my best friend. And I was his. We had never fought, had never been separated, and had never truly known someone the way we knew each other.

"Happy birthday, Nash. I love you, too."

"Hey, I got you something," Nash said, reaching for his pants pocket.

"I got you something too," I said, "but it's at the house."

"That's fine. But I want to give it to you now." He dug a little deeper into his pocket and pulled out a fisted hand. He held it out to me and opened it, palm side up.

In his hand was a bracelet. It was a red cord with a round metal pendant strung on it. I picked it up to examine it. On the pendant was carved what looks to be the Roman numeral two.

"Thank you," I said as more of a question, with my eyebrows raised.

"It's the Gemini symbol, I know our sign isn't Gemini. But, in Greek mythology, the Gemini were twins named Castor and Pollux. The Gemini is the symbol for twins. I thought about just getting you a yin yang pendant but I thought this was cooler."

"Thank you," I said with more conviction this time. "That's awesome. I love it. Help me put it on."

Nash tied the bracelet to my wrist and I stared at it until Nash said, "We should probably go show the bike to Xander and Tucker before mom calls a search party."

I looked at the pendant for a beat longer before I said,

"You're right. We should go."

It just went to show how similar we were. At home, in a box, sat a watch for Nash that had a face plate of a yin yang.

We put the helmets back on, Nash started the bike, and off we went.

We went to Tucker's house first because he lived closest to the park. He was happy for us, but was more impressed with my car than Nash's bike. But Tucker's sexual preference wasn't one that appreciated a fine motorcycle as it did a fine car. When Tucker told Nash, Xander, and I he was gay, we didn't even flinch, because Tucker is our best friend, that's who he was, and you accept your best friends for who they were.

Nash and Tucker went on a short ride, one which Tucker actually enjoyed and then we went to Xander's house, Tucker following us in his mom's minivan. Nash and I were the last of our friends to turn sixteen, but Tucker had yet to get a car of his own. Xander was so jealous of Nash's bike. Xander got a mustang for his birthday, but he really wanted a motorcycle. Nash and Xander went for a ride, Xander begging Nash to drive it, while Tucker and I sat and talked.

When they got back, Xander was smiling from ear to ear. His mom came out to wish Nash and I happy birthday and happened to be carrying a camera.

Xander said, "Mom," in that drawn out tone that said *I'm not a kid anymore, you don't need to document every moment of my life.*

She lowered one eyebrow while raising the other and

said, "Humor me, kids."

Tucker, Xander, Nash and I lined up in front of the bike, linked our arms together, and smiled for the camera. We were the four musketeers. Sure, the movie was called The Three Musketerrs, but there were four, because honestly, D'Artagnan was a Musketeer. Athos, Porthos, Aramis, and D'Artagnan. Four. The flash went off and Xander's mom smiled her proud mom smile.

I looked up to the sky which was now a darkish blue gray color. "We should go," I said, "before mom freaks out."

"You're right," Nash said, "Text her and tell her we're leaving soon and I'll start up the bike."

I did as he suggested, we said goodbye to our friends, and headed home.

Nash turned around to me and said, "How about we take the long way home?"

I smiled and nodded and Nash turned the bike so we were headed to the outside of town, instead of cutting through it.

"I want to open her up," he said.

"Oh great," I laughed. "It's a girl."

"What did you expect?" Nash's voice cut through the wind. We laughed as he drove.

We rode for a bit longer in silence, just enjoying the ride, the night, each other's company.

Nash turned his head slightly back to say something to me and in the hazy dusk that surrounded us, I squinted to see what he couldn't. A truck, with no head lights on, barreling down the middle of the road at us.

"Nash, look out," I yelled over the wind.

He turned his head back to the road and got as close to the side as he could without going off into the gravelly shoulder. Nash flashed his light at the oncoming truck, but the driver didn't seem to notice us. The truck started to swerve back into its lane then again into ours. Then it was on us. The driver of the truck turned its headlights on, the light blinding Nash and I both. Nash made one last swerve to miss the truck, but it was too late, the side mirror of the truck swiped the handle bars of the motorcycle and we were thrust into the truck and then bounced off of it. Everything was moving in slow motion. Nash was thrown from the bike, my pant leg was caught on the peg of the back tire and I couldn't get it loose. Then everything sped up and I was under the bike being drug along the road and gravel shoulder and I experienced a pain so excruciating, a pain I had never felt in my life.

Then the bike was on fire and I was on fire and my clothes were burning off of me and my skin was burning and I couldn't breathe. I tried to call out for Nash, but the smoke choked me and I tried harder but I couldn't breathe.

I choke and cough and then suddenly I'm back in third period ancient world history class and I'm not choking and I can breathe. I am clutching my throat, my pulse races. My eyes dart around the room. The whole class is staring at me. They don't laugh at me, like they would for any other student who fell asleep in class. They don't laugh because I'm still the girl whose brother died. I'm still the girl who is missing

9

half of herself.

I turn to Tucker, who gives me a sad smile but doesn't look away.

Mrs. Glass clears her throat, looks sympathetically at me and says, "Casslyn, if you could refrain from falling asleep in my class I would appreciate it."

"Sorry, Mrs. Glass," I say and put my head down. My hand instinctively reaches for the other one and gropes the cord bracelet that is still wrapped around it. I finger the pendant and try to calm myself. I would sing to myself, something that always calms me, but if falling asleep in class is a no-no, then I'm sure singing to myself would be construed as disrupting class. I pray for the hated memory to leave me but it plagues me, eating at me. I haven't had a dream about the accident for quite a while. For the longest time after it happened it was the only thing I could remember. I'm not sure how I survived it. I'm not sure how I still survive.

The police ruled it as a drunk driving accident. They still haven't found the truck, or the driver. But they found the mangled other half of my soul and I was too broken and medicated to attend his funeral.

I can feel the stares of my classmates, and am about to look up and tell them to mind their own business, when their gazes shift to the person walking through the classroom door. He's no one I've seen before. He hands Mrs. Glass a slip of paper. New kid.

Two

Only, the new kid is no kid. He's a guy. A man, even. He's huge. He has to be close to seven feet tall and he's got muscles bulging everywhere. There is no way he is sixteen, or even seventeen. Unless he is on steroids.

He is wearing dark blue jeans and a black zip up hoodie, the hood up.

Mrs. Glass says, "Class, welcome Logan Rivers."

The new kid, Logan, turns toward the class and stares directly at me. His hood shadows his face and all I can see is his eyes. Eyes so bright blue they look like blue fire. He continues to stare at me unabashedly. I'm still worked up over my dream and am not in the mood for some new kid to stare at me, or take any interest in me at all.

Mrs. Glass instructs him to take a seat. And which of the four empty seats in the room does he take? The one to the right of me. I am so not in the mood for this.

"Please remove your hood," Mrs. Glass says to Logan. "You will soon learn the rules here. One of them is that no hats or hoods are allowed while in class."

That's a rule I know well, and often break. Like so many others.

Logan slowly pulls down his hood. When he does so, he turns to me and smiles. This half side up devil grin that can only mean trouble. He winks and raises both eyebrows suggestively. And just as soon as it appeared, his smile is gone and Logan is glaring at me, his fire blue eyes ablaze.

A shiver crawls up my spine. This Logan is definitely no good. He's sure nice to look at though. Besides his height, his bulging muscles, and his intense blue eyes, Logan has jet black hair that lies just above his eyes and his skin is that permanent tan that means he's from a state with perpetual sun. Logan is not from Nebraska.

I turn away from him, my cheeks threatening to blush. This kid's been here for three minutes and already he's managed to upset me. I look to Tucker who is staring at Logan with a stupid grin on his face. I slap him on the arm which snaps him out of his trance and makes him turn back to Mrs. Glass. I do my best to keep my attention on her as well but my glance occasionally slips to Logan who is still intently staring at me eyes narrowed. The glare has slipped away, fortunately, but I find myself cowering in my chair and leaning away from him. Something about him has me un-nerved, rigid, on edge. He may be good looking, but he has me frightened. I'm not one to avoid people but I may have to make an exception for Logan.

I glance again at him, still staring at me. He raises his eyebrows again and then smirks at me. Yes. I'm definitely avoiding Logan.

I sit through the rest of the period staring straight ahead, unwaveringly. When the bell rings, I quickly gather my things and want to beat Logan out of the classroom, but with no book bag or other possessions, Logan has nothing to gather and beats me to the punch.

I get up from my desk and walk with Tucker towards the door. As quickly as I want to leave the classroom behind, Tucker seems to have the opposite wish. He walks slowly and I can feel him glancing at me. I stop and turn toward him.

Tucker looks at me with the sad, guarded eyes he's worn around me for the last six months. He knows I see the look and tries to rearrange his face. Luckily, Tucker is the kind of person who doesn't let things bother him, bring him down.

"Casslyn, are you-," he begins.

I cut him off, I know what he is going to ask. "Don't. I'm fine. Okay," I say walking towards the door.

"Honey," Tucker uses his puh-lease voice. "You are ten pounds of sad in a five pound sack."

I walk out the door to come face to face with my other best friend, Xander. Tucker and Xander are very different people. They act differently, talk differently, dress differently, and look differently. Tucker is a small, skinny, gangly guy with dark brown hair and sea green eyes. He is very nice looking and dresses to match. He wears very nice clothes; Aeropostale, American Eagle, the Buckle, and so on. Dark jeans, button up shirts, designer sweaters. Xander, on the other hand, has more muscle, more definition to his body with golden brown hair that reminds me of the hair of a lion, with eyes to match, light brown with flecks of gold. He most always wears jeans and a t-shirt of any kind. It doesn't matter, as long as it is a t-shirt.

"Thanks," I say, sarcasm lacing my voice.

"It's okay to be sad," Tucker says from behind me.

"Thanks," I say more sincere this time.

"So anyway," Xander says, "Who's the new kid?"

We all look down the hallway to see Logan walking further away from us.

"He's creepy as hell," I say at the same time Tucker says, "Isn't he yummy?"

"I asked who he is," Xander says, chuckling, "not what he is."

"I don't know," I say, trying to keep my voice level, unagitated. "Logan something. I think his last name had something to do with nature; creek, trees, forest. Something. Anyway, I don't want to know who he is. He's scarier than scary. Like I said, creepy as hell."

"It's Rivers. And he was only creepy to you," Tucker says, almost defensively. "What did you do, pinch him? I saw him glaring at you."

"I didn't do anything," I snap.

"Maybe he likes you," Tucker says with a smile but at the same time a frown.

"Maybe he didn't like your outfit," Xander says with a smirk.

I raise an eyebrow at him, daring him to make fun of my clothes. He tries every day.

"I love your outfit," Tucker says.

"Thank you," I say with a smug look at Xander. Today I chose the school girl look. Short green shorts, a white button up shirt, a black blazer, and a black, white, and green plaid tie. I am quite pleased with my look today. I even paired the look with long white socks, black boots, a high ponytail, and black reading glasses.

"You would," Xander says, "You're gay. Those are your type of clothes."

"Hey," Tucker says, feigning mock hurt. Tucker is proud of who he is and doesn't take offense when people make fun of him. Not that Xander was making fun of him. Xander would never do that. He just likes to get in playful jibes. Tucker does the same thing about Xander being straight. It's like we're characters in *Will and Grace*.

"But seriously, you don't think she looks hot?" Tucker says with a you-know-I'm-right look at Xander.

"I never said that," Xander says, quietly and turns away, his ears turning red.

I laugh, loop my arms through each one of theirs and

steer us towards our lockers. We discard our books and head for the gym for Rec sports. Along our way, we run into Ashley, Justin, and the rest of their crew. They all stand in front of us with their arms crossed, lips pursed, and their eyes shooting daggers.

As much as I'd love to skirt around them and avoid confrontation, they take up the whole hallway.

"Oh look, it's Flemming the flamer," Justin says.

"Real original," Tucker says.

When Tucker first came out, Xander got in many fights before he learned Tucker could fight his own battles.

"How's daddy, Casslyn?" Ashley turns her whip on me. "Oh, that's right, he doesn't live at home anymore."

"Says the one whose mommy moved out when she was born. Guess mommy didn't want her little princess," I snap right back.

"Watch it bitch," Ashley says.

"Did I hit a nerve?" I ask condescendingly.

Ashley steps forward like she wants to hit me. Xander moves to stand in front of me.

"Oh, look," Justin says, "Xander swoops in to save the day. Do you need him to fight all your battles for you?" Justin looks to Xander and says, "Have you slept with her yet? Or does she just let you stand up for her and give you nothing in return?"

Before Xander, Tucker, or I can come back with a retort, Justin, Ashley, and their whole posse are staring up and I feel a large, strong presence behind me. My spine crawls and I can only imagine who is behind me. I swallow a large lump in my throat and turn my head ever so slightly to find Logan standing inches from me, arms crossed, eyebrows furrowed, intensely intimidating.

The whole hallway is silent; we all look up at Logan. Stare. Wait for something to happen. He doesn't say a word, just stares back at us.

Finally, Justin clears his throat, an indication for his posse to pay attention to him.

Then Ashley says, "Whatever. I'm out," but there is a tremble in her voice.

The Sheek Squad hurriedly stocks off and Tucker, Xander and I are left staring up at Logan.

If he didn't creep me out before, there is no doubt he does now. I have never seen anyone scare someone, let alone Justin and Ashley, with so few words. Logan didn't use any words. Yes. He is that scary. In fact, I haven't heard him speak yet. Maybe he doesn't. Or can't.

My gaze is locked on Logan as if there is a magnetic field between us, holding my stare. Then, just like that, Logan winks at me, pivots on his heel like a soldier, and walks away from us.

When Logan is out of sight, my body decides it can finally move. Feeling liberated, it lurches forward. If it weren't for Xander and Tucker catching my arms, I might have face planted on the linoleum floor. I right myself and turn on my two best friends. I give them both a look that says, *I told you.*

"I don't like him" Xander says, in unison with Tucker

saying, "Isn't he gorgeous."

"You both saw that. He scared the crap out of them by standing there. He's creepy."

Nobody intimidates the Sheek Squad and he did it by standing there with a scowl on his face.

"I think you're overreacting, Casslyn," Tucker states.

"We'll see about that when I'm dead and buried. And what's with the winking at me? He's done it twice now."

Xander puts an arm around my shoulders and says "I've got your back, Cass. I won't let him harm a hair on your head."

"Thanks," I say to him, not too convinced.

We continue on to the gym. The tardy bell rings as we walk through the doors.

Three

The next three class periods pass fairly uneventful. I don't spot Logan again, or Ashley and Justin. I also don't fall asleep in class and have nightmares.

Two class periods left and I'm home free for the weekend. Of course, sometimes I'd rather be in school with Xander and Tucker than go home to one of two options; an empty house, or to a distant mother who thinks she lost two of her children, not just one.

Tucker and I walk in to homeroom and take our usual seats. He turns to me and whispers, "So, I found out that Logan is a senior."

My eyebrow raises and I say, "Then why is he in our sophomore history class?"

"I don't know. Maybe he got held back or didn't pass that class at his old school."

"Tucker, I swear there is something odd about this guy," I say as Tucker's eyes get bigger and he looks up.

I know, without needing to turn my head, that Logan has walked in the door. He has a presence that dominates whatever space he is in. I thought I was so close to escaping him. I slowly turn my head to look at him. He's taken a seat at the back of the room and is, again, staring straight at me with that devilish grin-smirk lighting up his features. I quickly avert my gaze, feeling my ears warm. At least he isn't sitting in the seat next to me this time.

Why today, of all days, the six-month anniversary of Nash's death, would some crazy creep of a guy have to come to school? I mean, it's Friday, couldn't he at least have waited until Monday? I should have just skipped school today.

I try my best to focus on my homework, find the degrees of this angle, name this bone in the hand, match debits with credits, but I can feel Logan's stare and it unnerves me.

The bell finally rings and I bolt for the door like a bat that sees the gates of hell open up before it. Tucker does his best to catch up with me and finally does so when we are at our lockers.

"Okay," Tucker says, "You may be right about the new kid. As cute as he is, he stared at you the entire period."

"He did what?" Xander asks, now joining us at our lockers. "Do I need to take care of this guy?"

"As much as I'd appreciate that Xander, he hasn't done

anything to me yet. He hasn't even talked. I'll just do my best to ignore him and maybe he'll get disinterested."

"Sure," both Xander and Tucker say together.

The three of us leave the main building and head for the Home Ec. building. Last period of the day.

"We almost forgot," Tucker says.

"Almost forgot what?" I ask skeptically.

"That we are kidnapping you for the weekend. You need cheering up and we know just the ticket."

"Xander, you're the one with the birthday in four days, and you guys don't need to cheer me up. I'll be fine," I say as convincingly as I can.

"We lost him too, Casslyn. He may not have been our blood, but we know somewhat of what you feel. Let us try to help. Let us try to heal each other. And if we can't, then you coming this weekend can be your present to me."

"Fine. Do I at least get to know where we are going?"

"Nope," Tucker says. He has been silent the whole time Xander berated me and I can see his eyes glisten but he smiles anyway.

We all pile into the tiny Home Ec. house and take our places at our kitchen stations. We started the year with an odd number of people and I got stuck without a partner. It suits me just fine. I love to cook. The process of it soothes me, calms me. Not having a partner allows me to be in my own world for fifty minutes.

That is, until the door opens and a chill runs over my body not caused by the weather.

"Ah, Mr. Rivers," our teacher Mrs. Sherman says. "Casslyn is the only one without a partner. Why don't you join her and we will get started."

I can feel my heart rate pick up and my vision gets spotty. How could I have three classes with him? How could he get paired with me in this class?

I work on slowing my breathing as I feel Logan walk up beside me and look down on me. With him this close to me he is huge. Way bigger than he looked standing next to Mrs. Glass. I'm not tall by any stretch of the word but I'm not short either and I don't quite reach his shoulders. His bulk seems bigger now too. He scares me.

I swallow a large lump in my throat and look up at him. He's already looking at me and winks when my gaze reaches his.

"I'm Casslyn," I say quietly.

"I know," Logan says with a smirk.

Logan's voice is so deep that it catches me off guard. A wave of warmth runs through my body at the same times as my skin rises with goose bumps.

Oh, I'm in trouble.

Not only is he gorgeous, massive, and ripped with muscles, but he has a sexy deep voice too. I definitely need to steer clear of him.

I snap my gaze over to Xander and Tucker's table. They both look at me with worried expressions.

I turn back to Logan and say, "How about you stop acting like a creep. Stop trying to freak me out and we'll get along just fine."

Logan leans down so he is looking at me directly and whispers, "Who says I want to get along?"

My body involuntarily shivers.

He's no good. He's no good. He's no good.

But damn is his voice sexy. His face too.

"Let's just . . . cook," I say, not knowing what else to say.

"Whatever you say, love."

My body tingles at his words. *Not good.*

"Don't call me that," I snap.

Logan grins and says, "You know you liked it. It stays, love."

My cheeks flush. I'm not sure if it's from pleasure or if I'm that uncomfortable. I pray it's not the former.

I turn away from Logan and assemble the ingredients and dishes we will need to make homemade pizza and get to work. I don't expect Logan to participate, don't want him to, and he doesn't. It's all for the best.

I make the crust and set it aside to rise. Then I brown the hamburger, cut up peppers, and mushrooms. Then I begin to assemble the pizza. I layer it like lasagna. A layer of hamburger and Canadian bacon, a layer of cheese, a layer of peppers, a layer of cheese, a layer of mushrooms, a layer of cheese. All the while, I can feel Logan's gaze on mine. Unwavering. After a time, it's not so unnerving as it is just there, a constant. By the time I pull the pizza out of the oven, Logan's stare is reassuring. But he still freaks me out.

I cut the pizza and serve it up. Mrs. Sherman gives Logan and I rave praise and a perfect grade for the day. Lucky bastard gets and A for sitting in a chair and staring at me. He doesn't even help me do the dishes.

When the bell rings and we make our last trip to our lockers, Xander and Tucker tell me to pack a bag, they will be at my house in two hours to pick me up, rather kidnap me, for the weekend. I step onto the bus, take a seat in the back, and jab my ear buds into my ears. It has been a long day and I need an escape.

Six months ago my twin brother and I turned sixteen. We both got vehicles. Mine still sits parked in front of my dad's house. We were both happy.

Now, I sit on a bus that takes me to a house that has never been my home. I'm not happy. And it's the worst day of my life, every day.

Four

I walk into our empty house, turning on lights as I go. Somehow, having a lit house makes it feel less empty.

I know no one is home, but I do a quick walk through-kitchen, living room, dining room-just to make sure. No one.

Mom and I moved into this house after I got out of the hospital and learned my parents were getting a divorce. My things were already boxed up. What a welcome home.

Our new house is an old farm house, shrouded by trees, set in the middle of nowhere ten miles on a gravel road. Our nearest neighbor is an abandoned house a mile down the road most people know as the old Melbourne Place. No one has lived there in over twenty years. Teens spend a night there on a dare. I've never been inside, but the outside alone is creepy enough to keep me out.

Our house is small. The floors and stairs creek. There is no cabinet space in the kitchen. The carpet was all old faded green and brown 70s style until we replaced it. The wallpaper was kittens, chickens, barns, and flowers, until we painted over it. There isn't even a full bathroom. It isn't my home, and never will be. It's the house that holds me until I graduate.

The old, rickety stairs groan as I walk up them to my new bedroom. I open my bedroom door, flip the light switch up, and walk in. Besides the essentials, I have not yet unpacked. I'm hoping that one day soon my mother will come to her senses and we will move back in with my dad. If not, then at least back into town. It's not likely, but a girl can dream.

I breathe in deep, blow it out through my mouth, and move through my room to get a duffel bag to pack a few things for this weekend. I have no idea where Tucker and Xander are taking me, so the few things will turn into a few more things.

I find my duffel bag in a box of random things that were hastily thrown into it. I don't know who packed my things while I was in the hospital but they didn't take much care. I don't even know what happened to Nash's things. I wasn't allowed to enter his room when I got home from the hospital. Then we moved and I haven't been back.

I throw a couple pairs of jeans, a few t-shirts, a sweatshirt, tennis shoes, and a few other weekend trip essentials into my duffel. Once I feel I have sufficiently packed, I run to the bathroom for those essentials; deodorant, hair ties, brush, the works.

Back in the kitchen, I open the cupboard above the fridge for the extra cash coffee can. Not knowing where Xander and Tucker are taking me, I grab a little more than is probably needed. Oh well, it's not like my mom will miss it, or even notice it is gone. The extra cash can is for me anyway; in case mom forgot to get groceries, in case I need lunch money, in case I need drug money. Scratch that. Just kidding. As much as I like to have my peers think I'm crazy, a bitch, or on drugs, I'm really not.

I have a half hour before Xander and Tucker are to pick me up and I really don't want to do any homework. I don't want to turn on the TV. And I don't want to sit in an empty house. But, I have yet to inform one of my parents that I will be away for the weekend. Calling my dad will resort in an *okay hun, do whatever you want*, which really means, *I don't care what you do, I no longer care that you are my daughter*. And calling my mother will result in pretty much the same way only an *oh Casslyn, is it Friday already? I'm working late, have fun.* Do I want the *I don't love you anymore*, or the *I've forgotten about you*? Either way, neglect is still neglect. But which of the lesser of two evils to pick?

I grab my duffel, purse, keys and cell phone from the house, lock up and walk outside, taking a seat on the old wooden swing that was here when we moved. I punch in the familiar number and listen to it ring, and ring, and ring. Finally, the other side picks up. "Casslyn, honey, why are you calling? I'm swamped here at the hospital. Can it wait till I get home?"

I pull the phone away from my ear, sigh heavy, pull it back and say, "I won't be home for the weekend. Xander and Tucker want to take a road trip."

"I don't know if that's such a good idea," my mom says. "This weekend is kind of a bad weekend."

"I know what weekend it is mom, I lived it!" I want to shout into the phone at her, but instead I say, "I know mom, but Xander's birthday is coming up and he really wanted to go and I can't let him down."

There is silence on the other end of the phone and I can tell my mom is thinking. "That's fine, Casslyn," she finally says. "See you on Sunday."

"Bye, mom."

She'd rather send me off than fight with me to make me stay home and deal with our problems. Maybe I should stay home, be here for my mom. Maybe she could be here for me too. She never left my side when I was in the hospital, but once I got home and we moved out here, she started putting all her effort into more hours at the hospital or fixing up our shitty new house. It was like she forgot about me, or like I became an afterthought.

When Xander pulls up in his mustang with Tucker, I look up and realize I have been scowling. My forehead hurts from doing so. I smooth out my features, pick up my things, and head for the car. I throw my stuff in the back seat then slip in after.

Xander and Tucker turn to me from the front seat. They both smile at me, although somewhat mischievously. Tucker looks to Xander then back to me and says, "Are you ready for this Sassy Cassy?"

I take a deep breath before answering then say, "Yes."

"Good," Xander says.

"Okay. So road trip rules," Tucker says.

"There are rules?" I ask, astounded, looking to Xander for help. He shrugs and looks away from me. Jerk.

"Yes. Now don't interrupt. We need to make good time. Rule number one, you have to wear the blind fold every time we say. And no peaking or there will be punishments. Rule number two, you must do everything we tell you, no matter what. Rule number three, you must have fun, no exceptions."

My eyebrows have risen, and I can feel my eye balls drying out from being held wide open. My mouth is open but I smile at Tucker's last rule.

Xander laughs from the front seat when I ask, "Blind fold?"

"Yes, ma'am," Tucker says, handing me a black piece of cloth folded several times. "Now put it on. And remember, no peaking."

I take the cloth in my hands, wrap it over my eyes and around my head, and tie it securely. My vision is taken from me. I can see nothing.

"How many fingers am I holding up?" Tucker asks me.

"How should I know? I'm blind folded. For all I know

you probably aren't even holding any fingers up."

Xander laughs again and Tucker says, "You so can see."

I laugh along with Xander and say, "Tucker, I swear I cannot see. It was by sheer luck you weren't holding any fingers up."

"Sure," he says.

Xander starts up the car and says, "You ready, Cass?"

"Yes," I tell him, then ask, "So how long have you both been planning this?"

For some reason I swear they must look at each other, then both say, "A while."

"Interesting," I say.

Xander puts the Stang in gear, backs out of my driveway, then turns right. After that, I can't follow any directions because Tucker makes sure to talk to me, blare the music, or somehow or other distract me. After a long time, I have no idea what direction we are going in, or how long we have been driving. Being blind folded is quite disconcerting. My other senses do kick into overdrive, but they also fight with my body's burning desire to see. You never know how badly you need something until it is taken away from you.

But the drive is fun. Tucker and Xander make me laugh. We talk about old times, stupid stuff our peers have gotten caught doing lately, things they should get caught doing, new times. For a while I forget what day it is, forget what my life is now, forget to think. For a while, without my sight, I just listen to our laughter and am content.

Eventually, my stomach starts to rumble. I didn't bring

any snacks with me and I have no idea how long until we will be stopping.

"Tucker, I am starving, are we stopping soon?"

"Patience grasshopper," Tucker says. I hear him rummaging through what sounds to be a backpack then am hit in the arm by something. I reach around for whatever hit me and open the package to a candy bar. I bring the candy bar to my mouth, not knowing what kind it is. It's like playing Russian Roulette with candy bars. Only, with one option, and one outcome.

We've been driving for a long time and I can tell we are slowing down, weaving through traffic. We must be in a city. Also, Tucker picks up his chatting again so we must be getting close to our destination.

Finally, we pull up to a stop and Xander turns the ignition off. I am about to take my blindfold off when Tucker slaps my hand away and says, "Ah, ah, ah. Don't even think about it."

"You're not really going to take me into wherever we are going blindfolded, are you?"

"Why yes, Casslyn, yes we are," Tucker says from the front.

"Ugh," I groan as Xander chuckles from the front.

I hear doors open and close, then the door to my left opens. I slide towards Xander holding my hand out to him. He grabs it gently and pulls me from the car. We walk away from the car in a direction I'm unaware of. I hear people and other cars. I feel awkward walking without being able to see where I place my feet, or without knowing what the closest thing to me is. I know Xander and Tucker won't let me run into anything, but it is still worrisome. A few feet later, we walk through a door and into a noisy room. I feel a bit conspicuous wearing a blindfold, but this is for my two best friends. What they want goes.

"You can take it off now," Tucker says from my right side.

I peal the blindfold away from my eyes and am overwhelmed by what I see. We have stepped into a restaurant decorated in a Hawaiian, beachy theme. The walls are painted with pictures of palm trees, beaches, the perfect setting sun, sail boats, crashing waves. Instead of being corny, it's actually quite warm and inviting.

"Welcome to Cheeseburger in Paradise. I can seat you. Is there just three today?" A very good looking guy who looks to be in his early twenties, presumably the host, smiles at us and turns around assuming we will follow him to our table. We take our seats, me on one side of the table and Tucker and Xander on the other, then the host places menus in front of each of us. "I'm Chris. Alex will be your server. Can I get you something to drink? Perhaps an appetizer?"

We go around the table giving our drink orders then Tucker says, "Can we get an order of the onion strings to start off?"

"Sure thing," Chris says and walks off.

"I take it one of the two of you has been here before," I say, eyeing the both of them.

"Yup," Tucker says. "My parents brought me here for my birthday last year. And this year. They have the best cheeseburgers you have ever tasted. And the onion strings- you know how I hate onions-are amazing. And they come with this dipping sauce that is so fantastic."

"So are you going to tell me where we are?" I ask.

"Nope," Tucker says with a smug grin on him face.

"You'll find out tomorrow, Cass. For now, could you just enjoy yourself?" Xander says.

I smile at the both of them and nod my head as our wait-ress walks up to the table with our drinks and a basket full of what looks like very thin fries. We place our orders and our waitress walks back to the kitchen.

"Dig in," Tucker says.

Xander and I look at each other skeptically. None of us like onions. But if Tucker says they are to die for, they must be good. I pull an onion string from the basket and tentatively place it in my mouth, biting down. Surprisingly, my mouth is enveloped in a flavor that is onion, but so much more than onion, and it is in fact amazing.

"Try the dipping sauce," Tucker instructs.

I do so and again my mouth is surprised and overjoyed by what it is tasting. Before I know it the basket is empty and Tucker, Xander, and I are laughing and smiling and happy. It's just like six months ago, with one exception, a fourth of us is missing.

When our food comes, Xander and I have to give Tucker props for his fine choice of dining establishments, for again, we are pleasantly surprised to find that, in fact, the burgers are possibly the best we've ever tasted. Though, in my opinion, a person can never go wrong with a bacon cheeseburger and fries.

When we are finished eating and pay the bill, Tucker makes me put the blindfold back on so I can't get any clues as to what town or city we are in. By now, I don't care about finding out where we are or what they have planned for this weekend. I only care about having fun with my best friends, getting back to a life where I can breathe.

I obediently put on the blindfold and let Xander lead me back to the car. We drive for what feels like ten minutes give or take. Then Xander parks, the doors open and I can hear the two of them open the trunk and grab the bags. Then one of them opens the right side door, grabs my bags and tells me to come out.

I take what feels to be Xander's hand and follow them a bit of a distance through a revolving door into another building.

"We'd like to check in," I hear Tucker say a few feet in front of me.

"You can take that off," Xander says. "Just don't look around too much. I don't want mom getting upset."

We both laugh and I take off the blindfold. Tucker is standing in front of a check in desk. I look around the lobby of the hotel. It's pretty nice. Tucker gets our keys and leads us to the elevator. When we reach the fourth floor, we get off and head to our room.

Xander, Tucker, and I share a king size bed, the boys on either side of me. I fall asleep feeling light.

***

I am awoken to Tucker shaking my shoulder and saying, "Wake up sleepy head. It's time to get up, Casslyn."

"What time is it?" I groan keeping my eyes closed.

"Seven thirty," Xander says.

"That's unfortunate." I say, my eyes still closed.

I feel a large body plop down on the bed beside me. "Casslyn," Xander whispers in my ear. "It's time to get up."

"No."

"Don't make me make you."

"Go away," I tell him, rolling onto my side.

"I warned you," Xander says before him arms are around me in a bear hug and he tickles my sides.

"Ahh, okay, I'll get up," I yell, but Xander doesn't stop.

"Stop, stop, please. I'll get up. I'll do anything," I plead.

I turn around in Xander's arms and come face to face with him. We are both still, other than our heavy breathing. Tucker opens the bathroom door and Xander and I bust out laughing. We fall away from each other. Xander does a tumbling move off the bed and escapes into the bathroom. I hear the shower start up. I roll out of the bed and grab my bag. I shower. We eat breakfast. Then I am blindfolded before we head out to the car. I don't keep track of turns. And I don't keep track of how long we drive. But eventually we park and get out of the car.

I follow the lead of Xander and Tucker until they come to a stop.

"Casslyn Evans," Tucker says, "Are you ready for your big surprise?"

I take a deep breath, trying to prepare myself for what is to come. "Yes."

"Are you sure you're ready?" Xander asks.

"Yes," I say, a bit impatiently.

"Okay. Take it off," Tucker says.

I want so badly to see what is before me, but I also want to savor the surprise. Finally, I pull the blindfold off, and I can't believe what is before me.

"You guys. . . I don't. . . I just. . . " I am rendered speechless, something that does not often happen to me.

I stand before one of my very favorite places ever. One of me and Nash's favorite places ever. I have no doubt I now know where we are. I stand before Omaha's Henry Doorly Zoo. My parents have brought Nash and I here once a year, every year, since we were two.

"Don't cry, Casslyn. Just enjoy," Xander says.

I didn't realize I was, but now that I am at attention, I feel the tears roll down my cheeks. Not many, but tears, plural, nonetheless. I didn't think I'd ever get to come to the zoo again, or want to, but now that I am here, I feel Nash here and I don't think I'll ever want to leave.

"Thank you," is all I can manage to say.

"You're welcome," they both say together.

"You've got two days, take your time," Xander says.

I start towards the zoo, Xander and Tucker following closely. We pay the entrance fee and march inside. I want to see it all and I can't wait. There is something about animals, no matter what animal, that I love. They calm me, they excite me, inspire me. I'm not sure if it's an animals' power, grace, fierceness, that does it for me, but whatever it is, I welcome it. I could watch Animal Planet or Nat Geo Wild all day. And I have before. Much to the chagrin of my family.

"Where would you like to start?" Tucker asks me.

"I want to see it all. Twice. We can go in a circle. Counterclockwise, starting with the closest thing. The Lied Jungle baby!"

Xander and Tucker laugh at me, then charge on towards the jungle. After the jungle we circle around to the Wild Kingdom Pavilion, then see the Gazelles, the Zebras, some exotic antelope, and so forth. It is still warm enough for most of the animals to be outside. I watch the animals, much longer than the people around us. Most people look and leave, but not me. I want to study the animals. Not that they do much. A lion sleeps up to twenty hours a day. That's only four hours a day that they are awake. What lazy animals. But what else do they have to do.

There is no attraction at the zoo that I don't like. I mean, giraffes, elephants, the Cat Complex, the gorillas, the bears, especially the polar bears, and the Aquarium. I could spend a whole week at the zoo and never tire of it. The only thing that doesn't hold much sway over me is the Simmons Aviary. I'm not the biggest fan of birds. Mythological birds, sure, strap wings on an animal and it's awesome, griffin, hippogriff, phoenix, dragon. Those are all awesome, but regular birds, I don't know, they just don't excite me the way other animals do. The more power an animal has, though, the more I like it, bears, lions, gorillas, horses, cheetahs.

The three of us watched the sea lions be trained and do the coolest tricks. Then we went to the Cat Complex to watch them be trained. That was nuts. As much as I love the animals, I would definitely be close to peeing my pants if I had to be that close to a lion, or a tiger, or a leopard. We went to the Red Barn Park and got to pet and feed the baby goats, and they had a mini donkey, and there was a calf and sheep. I felt like a little kid again. Then we went to this fossil dig that was cool. When we were dragging ass several hours later, we left only to come back the next day and do it again.

This is why I could never have any other friends than Xander and Tucker. They knew exactly what I needed. They knew that I needed not to forget about Nash but to remember him in the right way. They knew that when I didn't.

Five

"Kids, don't run too far," our mom said from a distance behind us.

It was our tenth birthday and we were at the zoo again. Me and Nash's favorite place in the world. My parents wanted to ride the train, not have to walk so far this year, but Nash and I wouldn't have it. If we were going to be lazy at all, we were going to ride the Skyfari chair-lift ride. But I had another plan. My parents took the seat in front of us. Their mistake. I was going to ride the Skyfari until we were over the Giraffes, then jump out of the chair into the pen. I told Nash my plan, thinking he would be on board and want to jump with me. Little did I know he would freak out, make me promise I wouldn't, and when I tried, hold me down in my chair.

"Nash, let go. I want to pet the giraffes," I said, struggling against him.

"No. You're going to kill yourself. You'll break every bone in your body," Nash protests.

Even at ten years old, Nash was looking out for me. I would have thought that a ten-year-old boy wouldn't even blink at the prospect of jumping out of a flying chair. Nash always jumped out of the swing when he was swinging, but no, a chair flying over all sorts of animals was out of the question.

When we got off the ride, though, Nash didn't say a word to our parents. He didn't rat me out. After our Skyfari ride, we went to the Red Barn petting zoo. We pet the animals, and when I tried riding them, Nash just laughed at me. Then we walked arm in arm, smiling and laughing with each other. My parents walked in front of us, smiling at each other, laughing at what the other had to say, holding hands.

Nash looked at me and said, "Happy birthday, Casslyn."

But his voice was far away. I kept walking, enjoying the moment. Nash and I were best friends. We had each other's back.

"Hey," I heard his voice again. "Casslyn."

"Hey," I snap to attention at his voice. I look my head away and swipe tears away from my eyes before I turn back to Logan. He sits a table away from me. I escaped to the library for some privacy. I should have known I wouldn't get any. More tears slip from my eyes and I hastily swipe them away. I want it back. I want to be back when we were ten years old, my whole family was happy, we had nothing to worry about, and I still had my twin brother.

I try to gather my things as quickly as possible, I do not need Logan seeing me distraught over a memory I had of my once happy family, but stop when I smell something familiar, and am almost paralyzed with sorrow.

I turn to Logan, try my hardest to keep a look of indifference on my face, and say, "You're not allowed to have lighters on school property."

Logan makes a show of looking around the library. When he is satisfied that we are alone, he turns to me and says, "I think I'll take my chances."

I turn back to my things, place my bag on my shoulder and turn saying, "Good luck with that," but when I look around, Logan has crossed the room and is standing inches from me. Maybe less. My breath catches. I back into a bookshelf without meaning to. Logan closes the gap I have made. My heart beats in my throat and I can't swallow. I try to steady my breathing, sure that Logan can hear my heart pounding, and will mock me, but fail.

"You don't scare me as much as you think you do," I say as confidently, as snarky as I can manage. But my voice quivers. I am still shaken over my memory, and Logan frightens me more than I like.

He grins that devilish smirk. He knows I'm scared and he likes it. He seems to revel in it. "Yes I do," he says.

I swallow hard against my heart pounding in my throat.

He thinks, and smirks again, "But you're not as cynical as you think you are. Or as much as you want people to think you are." His voice is so deep it catches me off guard. A wave of warmth runs through my body at the same time my skin rises with goose bumps. I've never been warm and chilled at the same time.

"Because you're an expert on me."

Logan takes the lighter from his pocket and lights it in front of me running his pointer finger and thumb through the flame.

I glare at him. I'm half tempted to put my hands on my hips, but decide against it because I am no longer twelve.

Logan grins, raises his eye brows, and winks at me.

I give him a look that says, are-you-joking.

His face falls and he says, "You're about as much fun as. . . well. . . nothing. You are not fun."

"Hardy har har," I say.

As he stands over me, his scent overpowers me. Logan smells like rain. Not the gross rain that smells like worms and dirt, but a pure rain, the scent they make candles out of. But he's not wearing cologne. Somehow I know that this is Logan's scent. It is all natural. He smells amazing. Intoxicating. It takes all of my will power not to lean closer to him. Not to take of whiff of him.

I brace my hands behind me, against the bookshelf, hugging closer to it, away from him. How can one guy be so scary yet so attractive? *I am in big trouble.*

I close my eyes, for clarity, balance, but am struck by

an image from my memory and again overwhelmed by emotion, longing, and sorrow. And suddenly I have lost my patience with Logan. He still stands over me. He leans one arm over me and rests it on the bookshelf beside me.

Logan still has the lighter in front of me and blows it out, in my direction. I have had enough. I am on the verge of tears and just want to go home.

"What is with you? You've been here a total of three days and already you're a psycho. Are you just trying to get a rise out of me? If so, mission accomplished. Now, you can leave me alone?" A few tears actually spill over the brim of my eye lids. Whatever. So he's seen me cry. That is the least of my problems right now. I give him a final, defiant look, skirt around him, grab my book bag, and leave without a look back.

But I can hear Logan say, "Nice outfit," from behind me.

I am impressed by my outfit today, a black mini skirt, leather jacket, white tank top, and black Chucks. Today is Xander's birthday and I was going to surprise him with it. He really doesn't like my clothes choices lately, so I knew he would hate this one. Unfortunately, Xander is not here today. Apparently he is sick, contagious, and can't have visitors. It would really suck to be sick on your birthday, but not to have visitors would suck worse.

I hate to leave Tucker, but I can't handle being in school any longer today. And I really want to see my dad.

I need to get into trouble. That seems to be one of the

only ways for me to be able to see him. If I get in enough trouble to be sent home, my dad has to pick me up because my mom works at the hospital and can't leave, and he works the night shift at Wilson Trailer.

Growing up a fairly decent kid, it took me a while to figure out how to get in enough trouble to be sent home. My clothes are bad enough, but the teachers and other authority figures gave up on sending me home for that a while ago. This being last minute and all, I don't have any way of getting any alcohol or weapons. Besides the point that I am way too chicken to bring weapons to school. Plus, I want to get sent home for the rest of the day, not forever. I could pick a fight with Ashley but I'm not really in the mood to make it very convincing. Either that, or she will piss me off to the point where I won't be able to control myself and will end up hurting her. Pulling a prank requires planning and attention to detail and enthusiasm. Not today. Swearing, continuously yelling something stupid or disregard for authority it is.

As I walk to my PE class I formulate my plan. Maybe fighting isn't such a bad idea.

"What are you doing?" I hear Tucker ask from somewhere in the distance, though he is walking right next to me.

"What?" I come to reality and say, "Oh. I'm getting out of school."

"You're leaving me alone?"

"I'm sorry. I just can't today."

"Alright, sweetie. Have fun with your dad."

I smile at him and continue to plot.

I dress for gym and come out of the locker room to find out we are playing dodge ball today. Perfect.

We divide into teams and begin to wage war on one another. I charge for the ball, knocking people, even my teammates, over. I don't go out when I am hit. I throw the ball, purposefully, at peoples' heads or their feet, knocking them on their asses.

It's a piss poor attempt at getting in trouble, but eventually Mr. Kneifl gets tired of it and my behavior warrants me a trip to the office where they call my dad.

I sit in the office and wait for my dad, smiling to myself. Reveling in my little victory. The secretary leaves me alone. She has better things to do. All is right with the world until, to my dismay, Logan walks through the office door. I don't know why I can't escape him. It's quite disconcerting. At least my dad will be here soon and I won't have to deal with Logan until tomorrow. I look up to Logan's towering figure. He looks down at me and winks, then takes a seat next to me as the secretary instructs.

"What are you in for?" he asks.

I get a sudden rush hearing his voice. I've never heard someone with such a deep voice. With the exception of some country music singers, of course.

I contemplate not answering him, but know he will more than likely pester me if I don't. After a few moments I finally say, "I beat up my gym class in dodge ball."

Logan grins and seems to contemplate my bad-assery.

"What did you do?" I ask him. If I had to tell, so does

he. Though, once I've asked, I'm not sure I want to know the answer. What if he really beat someone up and they are now at the hospital. What if he brought a weapon to school and used it? A shiver runs up my spine imagining what he could have gotten in trouble for. Of course, if it was something heinous, I'm sure he would have been arrested.

Logan shrugs his shoulders and says, "Apparently we aren't allowed to have lighters in school"

Serves him right. "I told you."

"So you did."

We sit in silence for a great while. Neither of us knowing what to or wanting to say anything. I feel Logan move his body, about to speak, when my dad walks into the office.

I can feel my face light up and I enthusiastically say, "Dad."

"Hi, sweetheart," my dad says back then goes to talk to the principal.

Logan chuckles beside me.

"What?" I snap.

"Nothing," he says, trying to hide his smirk.

I glare at him then raise my eyebrows, daring him to challenge me.

"You get in trouble so you can see your dad. How sweet."

I never thought Logan would pick up on that. Other than Xander and Tucker, who know me better than anyone, the rest of the school hasn't caught on.

"How perceptive of you," I say.

Logan just shrugs his shoulders and tilts his head. I look away but I can still feel his eyes on me.

My dad walks out of the principal's office and says, "Ready to go, kid?"

"Yup," I say, trailing behind him.

Once we are in the hallway I ask, "So how much trouble am I in?"

"For playing dodge ball a little too roughly? None. You better watch it though, if your mom hears about this you will be in trouble."

I smile at him and for a moment forget that he hasn't been to see me in a month, forget that he doesn't call, forget that he has turned into a crappy dad. Instead I remember how it used to be. His comment about my mom reminds me of when Nash and I would get in trouble when we were little and my dad would cover for us, or just not tell my mom. I remember how he used to play with Nash and I in the back yard; football, tennis, basketball, cops and robbers, Simon says, red rover. When Nash died, everything changed. It was like my dad no longer wanted to be a dad, even though he still had a kid.

"We could go get ice cream if you want. Or play pool down at the bar.," I suggest, hoping he will take the bait.

My dad consults his watch, looks at me, looks back at his watch, then says, "Alright. We can stop at Tracy's and grab some ice cream."

It's a small victory but I will take it. I smile at my dad and follow him out to his car. On our drive to Tracy's I try to talk to him about work, his life, school, my friends taking me to the zoo. And while he does talk back, everything he says is short, clipped, strained, like he has to make an effort to talk to his own daughter. After not much success, I keep quiet, and collapse in on myself. My twin, my perfect match, is gone, and my parents won't even make an effort to help me through it or try to make it better.

When we get to Tracy's, we order our ice cream, but when I head for my family's favorite booth, my dad chooses another. He has forgotten, or he doesn't care. We sit in near silence while we eat, my dad practically shoveling the ice cream into his mouth.

There is something I want to ask him, and if I don't ask him now, I'm afraid I will lose my nerve, so I set my bowl on the table, stare at my dad, and say, "So, Dad, the Fall Ball is coming up and I need a dress and I was wondering if you would want to take me dress shopping." There I've said it, it's out there, and he can react how he reacts.

"Um. I don't know sweetheart. I've been really busy with work lately. Can't your mom take you? I'm sure she'd be better at it than I am."

I can feel my face fall, and I know my dad sees it because he says, "Pick a day and I will make it work."

I smile at him. And though I am happy he will take me, I know he doesn't want to, and my smile is forced. I am no longer interested in my ice cream, but like my smile, I force it down and put on a brave face. I don't know why I do, it's not like my dad is hiding his uneasiness.

We leave Tracy's and my dad heads out of town to my new abode. I stare out the window and watch the endless corn fields lull my mind into nothingness. It takes much of my will power not to cry. Suddenly, leaving school doesn't sound so appealing.

When my dad pulls up in front of my house, he lets the car idol and says, "Listen, I really need to get to work now. Are you going to be okay by yourself?"

Like I'm not always by myself? I want to scream at him. But I hold my tongue and say, "Yeah. I'll be fine. See you later."

My dad doesn't say see you later back, he just says, "Bye," and drives off.

I walk to the front door, but instead of opening it, I collapse onto the front step, curl into a ball, and cry.

Six

"What is with you and this Logan guy?" Xander asks as soon as he meets me at my locker before second period.

"What are you talking about?" I ask, clearly confused. "By the way, it's nice to see you too. Happy birthday, yesterday, I might add. How does it feel to be seventeen? And how sick are you, anyway, if you were dying yesterday but you're here today?" I raise my eyebrows at him and give him the you're-not-fooling-anyone look.

"So I didn't want to come to school yesterday, give me a break. And look who's talking skipper. Don't think you can change the subject that easily."

"What about me and Logan?"

"All morning I have heard that you two got in an altercation of some kind yesterday in the library and that you were both thrown out of school for it."

"An altercation?" I ask him, digging through my locker for my Accounting book.

"Yeah. There are many versions, but my favorite is that you punched him in the face because he called you a bitch."

"Hey, I heard that too," Tucker says from behind us. "But I really hope you didn't mar that pretty face of his."

"Did you really punch him? Or do I need to talk to him and give him the what for?" Xander asks.

I finally turn to him. I am about to protest his gallant gesture, but stop when I notice that he doesn't so much look like Xander anymore. Sure he is still Xander, really he looks exactly the same. His golden hair is still lion mane golden. His golden flecked eyes still shine in the same light. His rock concert t-shirt still fits in the same way. But then, he looks completely different too. He looks more regal, stronger, more defined.

"What's different about you?" The question shoots out of my mouth without me giving it permission.

Xander gets this weird look on his face like I've offended him, or he's not sure how to react.

"What are you talking about?" Tucker asks. "He looks exactly the same as he did two days ago."

"I haven't changed," Xander states, though he says is quietly, almost cautiously.

But even though Tucker can't see it, and Xander says it isn't there, I swear Xander has changed. Even if I can't put my finger on what it is exactly that has changed, I know he is different. I decide to let the subject drop. If it's not that important, it's not something to fret about.

"But anyway," I say. What a beautiful transition. I don't particularly want to discuss my run in with Logan. I don't want to relive the memory or the way the smell of the lighter made me feel or the way Logan made me feel. But I must soldier on, as it were. "I didn't punch Logan. We didn't have an argument or altercation. And I really didn't think there was anyone in the library. Besides, I got in trouble so I could see my dad, you know that. And Logan had to leave, well, I'm not one hundred percent sure he did leave, I left before him, because he brought a lighter to school. However, he did taunt me with it and I got upset, but that was the farthest our dispute went. No need to let the rumors spread, and no need to defend my honor."

"Haha. What honor?" Tucker says, trying to lighten the mood. I am thankful for it, but for show, I narrow my eyes at him and walk to class.

***

The day passes mostly uneventful. Logan does his share of observing me in History and Homeroom, but otherwise leaves me alone. Maybe yesterday he got his fill of getting a rise out of me. I only have one class left. I can handle this. Even if it means working next to Logan for fifty-four minutes.

Xander, Tucker, and I walk into class and take our places at our stations. Shortly after I feel a strong presence beside me.

"Hello, love," Logan says.

"I told you not to call me that," I tell him, not turning to him

"And I told you it stays," Logan says. I know he is grinning without having to look at him.

I sigh and return to gathering my supplies. Today we, I, will be making a breakfast scramble. Eggs, cheese, hash browns, ham. Nothing fancy, but so delicious. I begin working, melting butter in the pan to cook the potatoes in, adding the potatoes. I look up at Tucker and Xander every so often to see them enjoying themselves. During one peering glance at them I feel Logan stiffen next to me. I stop what I am doing and turn to him. He is staring away from me, intently, almost angrily. I follow his gaze and am surprised by who he is staring at. Xander. What? This can't be. I again follow Logan's gaze, which leads straight to Xander. Logan stares, unflinchingly. It makes me more uncomfortable than anything he has done before. More so than when he scared off Ashley and Justin without saying anything.

"What is your problem?" I ask him.

Logan snaps to attention at my question. He looks fierce. "Who is that?" he asks.

"That's Xander," I tell him, speaking slowly. "He's my best friend." I'm not really sure if I should add that part. "You've seen him with me. Why? What is your sudden fascination with him?"

"He's what?" Logan barks at me, finally turning his gaze on me. "How can he be your best friend?"

"What?" I can't believe he is asking this. How can he question my judgment on best friends when he doesn't even know me? I am beyond confused.

I am even more confused when Logan asks, "When did he turn?"

"When did he what?"

"His birthday," Logan snaps, looking back to Xander.

"Yesterday," I say. "What is with you?"

"You can't be friends with him. You must stay away from him," Logan says this matter-of-factly. Like it's the most obvious thing in the world.

"Excuse me? Where do you get off telling me who I can and can't be friends with? You don't even know me." Now I'm just upset. I haven't even had a full conversation with him and he's telling me what to do.

"He's dangerous, Casslyn," Logan says, looking at me desperately. He clenches his jaw and muscles stab at his flesh.

I'm not sure if I'm more thrown by him telling me Xander is dangerous, Xander who I've known since I was two, who wouldn't hurt a fly, or the fact that he called me Casslyn, or by the way he is looking at me.

"I . . . I don't . . ." I start, but I don't know what to say. I look back and forth from Logan and Xander. I know I should just leave it be, forget what Logan just told me, laugh it off even. But there is something in the way Logan looks, a sincerity, that won't allow me to forget it. If anything, though, Logan's frigid posture, his fierce gaze, and his radiating anger, make me more afraid of him than ever. There's also something in his intense fire blue eyes that has my heart pounding in my chest. I wish class was over so I could talk to Xander about it.

What has me puzzled though is what Logan said about Xander's birthday. About him turning. I swore I saw a difference in Xander this morning, but when no one else noticed, I wrote it off as nothing, just my imagination, and I haven't noticed it the rest of the day. But now that Logan has said something, I look at Xander and see the same difference I saw this morning. Is Logan right about Xander having changed after his birthday, or am I seeing a difference simply because Logan said something about it?

Through the edge of my pondering, I smell burning. I am instantly thrust back six months ago, my body pinned under the motorcycle, my flesh burning, my lungs pleading for air. I feel like hurling. But it is only the potatoes in the pan. I am still in Home economics and I am fine.

***

"Okay," Xander says. "Explain this again."

Xander, Tucker, and I are in the library, where Logan and I had our little encounter, Xander looking almost as fierce as Logan did only minutes ago. Right after class I told

Xander and Tucker I needed to talk to them. I'd repeated, three times, my conversation with Logan, but Xander, again, wanted me to tell him. We have been discussing it in hushed yells.

"I told you," I sigh when I say this, "Logan went stiff when he saw you. Then he asked when you turned, and I had no idea what he was talking about, but then he said your birthday. Then he told me to stay away from you because you are dangerous."

This time, instead of making me repeat myself, Xander just stares at me, open mouthed. Surprisingly, Tucker has been silent this whole time, not lending his two cents. The longer Xander goes without saying something the more worried I get.

Finally, I can't stand it any longer. I slam my hands, palms down, on the table that stands between Xander and I and say, "Is there something different about you Xander? I told you this morning I noticed something different."

Xander turns an angry gaze on me. "Are you seriously asking me this? You're taking the side of a guy, who not only you think is scary but who you've known for three days? I'm supposed to be your best friend. Shouldn't you have my back?"

"I'm not taking anyone's side. And if I was, I'd take yours. You know that. How could you question my loyalty?"

"Stop it! Both of you," Tucker finally speaks. "Just stop it. Like you said Cass, Logan is probably just trying to get a rise out of you. He's probably just trying to turn you against your best friend. Don't ask me why. You're right. He's just some crazy, sadistic guy, who's trying to mess with our minds. Are we really going to let him?"

I loosen my face, not realizing that I had it pulled together. I look from Tucker to Xander. He does the same.

"I'm sorry," I tell him.

"There's nothing to be sorry about," Xander says, but there is no sincerity in his voice. I've hurt his feelings and he's not about to forget it so easily.

We move around the table and embrace each other. Maybe I was wrong, maybe he will forgive me. Xander places his hand on the back of my head and holds me tight. I relax and fall into his arms. I don't fit perfectly, like I did in Nash's arms, but then Nash and I were the same person, so of course I fit. But I feel good in Xander's arms. Then I feel Tucker wrap his arms around the both of us. It is a nice moment. I can't believe I let Logan get me worked up. He must be some good actor to have me believe he was worried about Xander being dangerous. I feel so absurd I laugh out loud at myself.

Xander and Tucker pull away from me and look at me as if I have lost my mind. If Nash was still here he would surely tell me I need to get my head checked. Maybe I do. But then again, if Nash was still here, I am quite positive I would have never let Logan bother me. He wouldn't even be my partner in Home Ec., Nash would. Tucker and Xander laugh with me.

I laugh harder at the thought that our argument was diffused so quickly. Nash and I never did have an argument our sixteen years together. Tucker, Xander, and I hadn't either. But when Nash died, things changed. I changed.

Seven

A week passes much the same. Logan continues to be creepy towards me and on edge over Xander. Xander is on edge over what Logan said about him and what I think of him. Tucker worriedly watches over all of us. And I am continually caught in the middle. Of course, Logan likes to play it cool, which only irritates us more. And we let him.

Logan stands down the hall from Xander, Tucker, and I, surrounded by a gaggle of girls. He barely says a word or even looks at them, and yet the girls are laughing at him. Every so often, I catch Logan's eye. He knows I'm watching him and he wants me to continue. I try my hardest not to look at him, not to wonder what the girls are laughing at, but try as I might, I can't help but glance his way.

Tucker, Xander, and I stuff our books in our lockers and exchange them for our next class books. Xander does not have Ancient World History with Tucker and I so we must part ways, but we can walk together for a little ways. We have to pass by Logan and his group and I can't decide whether that is fortunate or unfortunate.

As we get closer, I see one of the girls lay a hand on Logan's arm. She looks up at him and blinks, trying to flirt with him, but it looks like she's having a seizure. She asks, "So where do you live, Logan?"

His answer stops me dead in my tracks. "Do you know that old Melbourne Place? I live there. I'm in the process of fixing it up."

My head snaps up at Logan. He is already looking at me, an evil grin on his face. He winks and the blood drains from my face. Logan lives in the house that is nearest to mine. *This is not good this is not good this is not good.* My breathing quickens. I realize that all of Logan's entourage is staring at me. Logan just looks at me mockingly. Tucker and Xander have to forcefully drag me away. Xander even walks with us into the history room.

"You heard that. You both heard that," I say, my words rushed and worried. "It's just a coincidence that he lives in the house closest to mine, right? I mean, he's not stalking me is he? He's not, right?" I can feel my eyes are wide and crazed. What if Logan is stalking me? What if he really wants to hurt me?

Suddenly I can't breathe. I try hard to suck in air but

nothing comes. Then I feel a sharp slap to my face.

"Casslyn, snap out of it," Tucker says. "You are fine. I'm sure it is just a coincidence that Logan lives right next to you. I mean, how many available houses are there in this town?"

"You think?" I ask, my breathing trying to come back to normal. It is difficult, but after many seconds, I can breathe and see clearly.

"Yes. I do."

"But did you see that when he said that's where he lives he winked at me? Did you see that? He winked at me."

"How would he even know where you live?" Xander says. "Maybe he was just blinking and you thought you saw him wink."

"He *winked*," I say, sure I know what I saw. "And why are you taking his side?"

"Are we really getting into sides again?" Tucker says exasperatedly.

"Ugh," Xander and I sigh.

"I'm telling you," I assure them, as much as myself. "There is something wrong here. There is something going on. There has to be a reason he is so interested in me. A reason why he tried turning me against you. A reason why he lives so close to me."

Xander sits me in a desk and crouches in front of me, looking intently at me. "You will be fine. There is no way Tucker and I are going to let anything happen to you. Do you trust me?"

I nod my head in response. I feel insecure. I feel weak. I am weak. How could I be so weak? I try to act all macho. I try to put on this front like I'm not hurt, not scared, not a hallow shell. But I am weak and easily manipulated. It's all because I lost Nash. One can't possibly lose half of their self and stay the same. I don't know why I thought I could.

We are quiet for a short time before Tucker gasps and gets this insane gleeful look on his face. "I have a brilliant idea," he says. He pauses then says, "Okay, so maybe it isn't that brilliant, but it's an idea nonetheless. It could help."

When Tucker doesn't tell us his idea, Xander and I look at him expectantly.

"Oh, haha," Tucker laughs at himself. "Okay. So, don't kill me when I tell you this. But . . . What if you were nice to him?" Before Xander or I can get a no in or start any kind of argument, Tucker continues, "Like, super friendly. All over him like those girls. If you show him that you are boring, and there is nothing exciting about you, and that he can't get a rise out of you, then he will get bored and move on."

There was an argument on the tip of my tongue, but it dissolved. I have nothing. I can't find any problem with his logic.

Xander, however, is enraged. "No way. There is no way we are sending her into the lion's den. She should be staying as far away from Logan as possible. One of us can even trade her partners in Home Ec. And by one of us I mean you, Tucker."

Tucker gets a small grin on his face. I know he would

not disagree with this plan, but his plan is good too.

I know this is going to upset Xander, and I'm not too thrilled about it myself, but maybe Tucker is right. Maybe if I am overly friendly with Logan he will get bored and leave me alone. "I think I should try Tucker's plan."

Xander closes his eyes, tightly, like if he closes them hard enough it will stave off anything that will upset him. He reopens his eyes and grimly says, "How long could it really take?"

The three of us burst out into hysterical laughter as the rest of my class, Logan included, file into the room. Xander leaves as Logan takes his seat beside mine.

"Hello, love," Logan says to me.

I want so bad to cringe, tell him not to call me that, and look away, but we are going with Tucker's plan, not Xander's, so I turn to Logan, place a polite smile on my face and say, "Hello."

He stares at me with his fierce blue eyes. Actually looking into them, this closely, it looks like his eyes are made of dancing blue flames. They are intriguing yet disturbing. I feel like I should look away, yet I can't.

"You could take the jeans off," Logan says, catching me off guard.

"Excuse me?" I snap.

"You're wearing a dress. You don't need the jeans."

"Right," I say slowly. *Be nice, Casslyn. Be nice.* "So. How do you like it in Cedars so far?"

Logan grins at me and says, "Oh. I'm enjoying myself."

I can only imagine why he is enjoying himself so much. It couldn't possibly have anything to do with me. No. I'm sure he likes the scenery, the small town atmosphere. No. He isn't enjoying himself because of me.

I want to say something snarky in rebuttal, but again have to remind myself to be nice. If I want him to leave me alone, I have to be nice.

"I'm glad," I say.

I force a smile to spread across my face as Mrs. Glass walks in the room and takes her place in front of the marker board.

***

It is exceedingly harder to be nice than I would have thought. And that was just one period.

I sit in my desk waiting for my class to file in and for Geometry to begin. Tucker and Xander were late getting out of Rec Sports and told me to go on without them. As I read over yesterday's notes, hoping to glean some sort of understanding from them, hands slam down on my desk. I swallow a large lump in my throat. Logan couldn't possibly be mad at me for being nice to him, could he? I take a deep breath, close my eyes, and tilt my head up. I wait a second before opening my eyes.

I breathe out the breath I'd been holding. Logan isn't here to kill me. Only, the person staring down at me with a deep set scowl on his face doesn't give me any comfort.

"Tell your boyfriend to stay away from Ashley, unless he wants trouble."

"What are you talking about?" I ask, complete confused. Last time I checked, I didn't have a boyfriend.

"You know exactly what I'm talking about. That new River's kid. He's been all over Ashley today. Tell him to keep his giant paws off."

"I don't like Logan. I don't even know him for that matter. And I'm not about to tell him anything in regards to you or Ashley. She's not even your girlfriend. Now get your hands off my desk," I say, leaning back in my desk and crossing my arms.

Justin leans closer to me and says, "You listen to me."

"Is there a problem here?" Mr. Street asks walking into the room.

Justin looks to Mr. Street, says, "No, we were just discussing homework for another class," then turns back to me with a glare that shoots daggers.

"Right," Mr. Stree says. "Well this is my class now and I don't believe you are in it, Justin. So why don't you leave?"

A few of my classmates begin to trickle in. Xander and Tucker finally walk in. When they see the close proximity of Justin and I and the looks shooting between us, they sprout worried looks on their faces.

"No problem," Justin says and walks out of the room, slamming shoulders with Tucker and Xander.

They take their seats on either side of me and Xander says, "What was that about?"

I sigh, not wanting to get into it. It's odd, I used to want to share everything with the two of them, and my brother, not that anything exciting ever happened to me, but it's different now. I feel like keeping things inside, keeping things from them. But as soon as I think it, I feel guilty. They are my best friends. They are only looking out for me, trying to do what is best for me.

I clench my jaw and say, "Our bestie, Justin, just came by to tell me to tell my boyfriend, Logan, to stay away from Ashley." I tack on a superfluous smile and tilt my head.

Tucker's mouth drops open but he corrects himself, laughs under his breath, and says, "It never ends with you and Logan does it? Wait a second, Justin isn't even Ashley's boyfriend. Isn't she dating some college guy?"

"That's what I thought. I don't know if he's keeping her warm for that guy or what," I say.

"I am sick of that guy tormenting you and pushing you around. I'm going to do something about it," Xander says, bringing the conversation back around to Logan.

"No, Xander," I say. "This wasn't really Logan's fault."

"So you get yelled at and threatened so he can talk to a girl? I don't think so."

"Justin didn't threaten me."

"So just because he didn't threaten you makes him yelling at you alright?" Xander says back.

"Is there a problem here?" Mr. Street says for the second time in ten minutes.

"No sir," Xander, Tucker, and I say at the same time.

I turn back to my best friends and say, "Can we *please* stop fighting?"

"Hallelujah," Tucker says to which Xander and I turn wicked glares on him. "I'm just saying. What has happened to us? Are we going to let Logan destroy our friendship? We've been friends for too long to let that happen."

"No," Xander and I say begrudgingly.

"Okay then," Tucker says and nods his head, satisfied that he made us comply. "Now, we are going to stick with my plan. Casslyn is going to continue to be nice. But I think you are right about not telling Logan what Justin said, Casslyn. We don't want Logan to think you are jealous and then get even more interested in you."

I purse my lips and nod. Xander looks pissed but does the same. I realize Xander must feel that he needed to take up the role as my protector when Nash died, but he's taking the job a bit too seriously, and it's starting to annoy. If I even needed protecting, I would want my brother to have the job. Of course, I can't have what I want. Especially when I no longer have a brother.

Eight

Nothing could bother me today. Not fighting with Xander over Logan. Not Logan being a pain in the rear or creepy as hell. Not Tucker being worried about Xander and me fighting. Not my mother being extremely distant. And just today, for the afternoon, I'm not going to let Nash's death bother me. Because I get to spend the entire afternoon with my dad.

I was so excited that, of course, the day dragged on. But finally the end is nigh. I just have to get through Home Ec., which shouldn't be too hard. Being nice to Logan has gotten easier. And I'm in such a good mood about seeing my dad, I'm sure the hour is going to fly by.

For the first time since he arrived, Logan is already seated at our cooking station.

"Hello, love," he says as I walk up behind him.

I still hate the nickname, but the being nice strategy is actually working, and I'm not about to mess it up. So I simply say, "Hi, Logan."

"What are we cooking today?" he asks.

"I don't know," I say, my mind wandering off to the afternoon ahead of me. "Why don't you pick."

"How about spaghetti?"

"Yeah, sure."

I sit and think about what my dad and I will talk about. If we will just pick up where we left off. If maybe our relationship will be better now. If he will act like my dad again and not just my legal guardian. And while I sit and contemplate, Logan, again, does something for the first time. He begins cooking. And I let him. Really, it serves him right. He has done nothing in the weeks he has been here. It is his time to do something. And I don't plan on helping him.

But I watch him. Logan is lean but so, so muscular. His muscles poke through his tight t-shirt, and I am overwhelmed by an urge to touch them. I mentally chastise myself and try to think about my afternoon with my dad. And it works. For a little while. Until my eyes are drawn back to Logan. His black hair lies roguishly on his head. It looks messy, but on purpose. It's too perfectly messy not to be on purpose.

He turns back to me and grins his wicked grin. "See something you like?" he asks, raising his eyebrows suggestively.

I resist the urge to roll my eyes. I stay seated and wait for him to turn back to cooking. When he does, my blush is full on, no holds barred. If he wasn't so sarcastic or so full of himself, he may be more attractive. Of course, that's just what I need, Logan to be more attractive.

I look to Logan's progress and see him cutting up tomatoes and throwing them in a pan. Then he adds a tub of tomato paste and some oregano, thyme, and cilantro to it.

"You do know there is a jar of tomato sauce in the cupboard, right?" I say to his back.

Without turning back to me he says, "Now, now, now. You opted out of cooking today." Then he turns to me, using the full power of his fire blue eyes on me and I shut up. "You just sit pretty and watch me work." He pivots on his heel to return to cooking then changes his mind, turns back to me and says, "You should try leaving your hair down. It would frame your face nicely."

"Excuse me?" I say, trying to ignore the fact that he inadvertently called me pretty and suggested I would look good with my hair down, but he is already back to cooking.

"By the way," Logan says, with his back turned to me. I can hear the smirk on his face, "You'll love the sauce."

My resolve is to hate the sauce. I hope it burns and that he over cooks the noodles. I don't care about the bad grade we will receive. I just want to see him fail. But much to my chagrin, the spaghetti is amazing. The sauce is the best I've ever tasted and the noodles are cooked to perfection. If I wasn't afraid of getting my pride wounded, I would say he is a better cook than I am.

***

As I wait for my dad with Xander and Tucker by Xander's car, I nervously twirl Nash's bracelet around my wrist. Oddly, it comforts me.

What if my dad doesn't come? What if he blows me off?

"He'll be here," Xander says, as if he can read my thoughts.

"Casslyn, he's your dad. He loves you. He's just going through a tough time," Tucker says.

"And I'm not?" I ask incredulously.

"Look how well you're handling it," Tucker says with that don't-give-me-any-lip look on his face.

"He's the adult," I say.

"He'll be here," Xander says, a bit to lighten the mood and also to change the subject.

I sigh heavily and lower my head. Knots twist in my stomach as butterflies flutter. I shouldn't be nervous to see my dad and yet I am. I feel like crying and laughing like an idiot at the same time. I don't know why I would believe that my dad would show up now, when he hasn't for the past six months.

I've all but given up hope when I hear Tucker say, "He's here."

My head snaps up. My heart leaps when I see him pull around the corner. He's really here.

"Call if you need us," Xander says, as I walk to my dad's car and they get into Xander's.

"Hi, Daddy," I say, with a big smile on my face, as I get into his car. My heart is racing and I can feel my face is flushed. I find it almost hard to breathe.

"Hi, sweetheart," he says, and pulls away from my school. "Would you like to eat first or go dress shopping first?"

"Dress shopping first. I don't want to be bloated trying on dresses."

"Sounds like a plan," he says and heads towards the shopping center of town.

Cedars is a small town, but just big enough that we have a wedding/prom/homecoming/tux rental shop, a Subway, McDonalds, Pizza Hut, a Caseys, two bars, one coffee shop, four churches, a hospital, one school, and a few other shops and stores. But, it is also small enough where you know everyone in town, down to their birthdays, middle names, and pet's names. You hear the local gossip before the said event is even over. And you know that new kids like Logan are bad news after their first day in school.

"So what's new with school?" my dad asks.

"Not much," I say. "Same old."

"The word around town is that there is a new kid in school."

I raise an eyebrow, tilt my head, and give my dad the why-are-you-asking-you-never-listen-to-town-gossip look. "Yes," I say slowly.

"Do you have any classes with him?"

"Three," I again say slowly, wanting to bring back the look.

"The word is he's bad news. I think you should stay away from him."

"What?" I ask, wondering where this is coming from.

My dad has never talked to me about boys before, let alone warned me away from them. And I'm pretty sure he has been sticking pretty closely to work and home lately so I have no idea where his 'the word' is coming from. And then it dawns on me.

"Xander talked to you didn't he?" I accuse him, getting huffy at the both of them.

"Now, Casslyn, don't get upset, he's just looking out for you."

"I think I can look out for myself. I've had to for the past seven months." It is a low blow but he deserves it.

My dad takes a deep breath, his jaw clenched. He exhales, his grip on the wheel still tight. "I wish you wouldn't bring that up." My dad says through his teeth.

I want to yell at him. I want to berate him for abandoning me after my twin dies. But I'm afraid it will only drive him away. So instead, I say, "Fine," as he pulls into the dress shop's parking lot.

The sign reads Missa Sue's Everything Boutique.

My dad looks up at the sign, sighs, and says, "You're really making me do this aren't you?"

"Yes, sir," I say with a genuine smile.

"You owe me child," he says, shaking his head and grinning with one side of his mouth. "You've only got an hour in there. Then supper. I have to be at the plant in three hours."

My cheer falls, but three hours with my dad is better than none. "Okay," I say and charge forward into the boutique.

The inside of the store is a mix of ancient antiques and modern technology. The carpet on the floor is an old, flower pattern with small holes in places. The racks are overcrowded and way too close together. The dressing rooms are small, but whole little rooms, not stalls. The florescent lights are too bright and tend to wash out your skin when you stand under them trying on dresses.

I move through the racks looking for something that might fancy my picky taste. I'm not a fan of sequins, bows, ties, pink, yellow, short dresses, and the list goes on. My dad follows spaciously and slowly behind me.

I pull out dresses I think I will like and throw them over my arm, occasionally asking my dad what he thinks. "Looks good, sweetheart," or "That's pretty," he answers, pretty much disinterested. One of the boutique's workers takes the dresses from me and puts them in a dressing room for me. The dance is still a month away but almost every girl at school already has their dress and not many people get married in October, so I have the boutique to myself.

When I am mostly satisfied with my selection, I walk back to my dressing room. With all of the dresses I picked I have room only to stand inside. I strip down to my strapless bra and panties and start to try on the first dress. It's a light blue strapless princess dress. It's cute, but I'm not sure it's the one. I open the door and walk out of the fitting room to show my dad. He's sitting in a chair about ten feet from the front of the dressing room. He is looking at his phone but tilts his head up at me when I walk towards him.

He smiles and says, "That's very pretty, honey." He says it as if it's one of those things dads say and he feels like he has to say it, not as if he means it. It's like he doesn't know how to be my dad anymore.

I struggle to smile and say, "Thanks, Dad. I just don't know that it's the one. I'm going to try on the next one."

"Whatever you want, sweetheart."

I return to the fitting room, unzip the dress, strip it off and throw it on the floor.

I thrust the next one on, an emerald green halter top dress with a floral pattern down one side from the top to the bottom.

My dad calls from outside and says, "Casslyn, what do you think of coming to get your car. Or do you want me to sell it?"

My body stops, my fingers stiff around the zipper half-way up my back. My mouth goes dry and feels like sand paper. I try to swallow past a lump in my throat. I don't want to drive my car. I may never want to drive that car. For so many reasons. It's the last thing I have of Nash and I want it to stay in perfect condition. If we would have taken my car for a drive instead of Nash's bike he would still be alive.

I'm afraid of driving my car and wrecking it. I don't want to drive my car. But there is no chance in Hell I want someone else to have or drive my car. "Casslyn? Did you hear me?" my dad asks.

"Yeah," I bark, my throat thick. "Sorry. I'll come get it sometime. I've just been busy."

"That's fine, sweetheart."

I finish zipping up my dress and step out of the fitting room. This afternoon was supposed to be fun. I was supposed to reunite with my dad, make him fall in love with his daughter again. But now, he's more concerned with making me stay away from hot guys, getting my car off his driveway, and talking on his phone. Again, when I step out, he is looking down at his phone. But this time, when he looks back up, there is a genuine smile on his face.

"That's beautiful, honey."

I smile at him and say, "Thank you." I do love this dress. The color is especially beautiful. But there is a couple more I want to try on before I make my decision. "I have a couple more I want to try on."

"Go ahead" he says.

I return to the dressing room and try on an orange dress. As soon as I have it on and look in the mirror, I know the color is wrong with my skin type, but I want to show my dad anyway. As I put my hand on the door knob, I hear my dad talking. He must be on his phone. I try to listen to what he is saying, but I cannot hear him from behind the door.

I open the door and walk through. My dad says, "Yes,

sir," and hangs up the phone. I know he's leaving me without him having to tell me.

"Who was that?" I try to sound curious, not furious.

"That was my boss. Listen, sweetheart, I need to go into work. Now. I'll leave my credit card number with the sales lady. Are you going to be able to get home okay?"

So much for my entire afternoon with my dad. He doesn't even care. And I don't know why I keep trying. I want so badly to be mad at my dad but I miss him so much that I can't.

"Yeah," I say. "I'll just call Xander and Tucker to pick me up."

"Okay, honey," he says walking up to me and kissing me on the forehead. "See you later."

He doesn't say he's sorry. He probably isn't.

My bottom lip quivers. I bite it to make it stop but I bite too hard and taste blood. Tears threaten to spill over my eyes. I close them to stave off the tears but they spill over anyway. I return to the dressing room to try on the dress I really want. I put it on, zip it up, and turn to the mirror. It's as beautiful as I imagined and my dad didn't get to see it. A deep purple satin, floor length, straight dress that hugs me in all the right places and flows in all the right places. It fits me perfectly, makes my skin look like it's glowing, my hair looks like it's surrounded by a halo.

My breathing becomes quicker. I clench my jaw to stop myself from sobbing. My vision gets blurry and dark. I brace myself against the wall and sink down to the floor, curling into a ball.

How could my life be falling apart like this? My brother is gone. My best friend, my confidante, my equal, is gone. My dad wants nothing to do with me. I've barely seen my mom in weeks, let alone months.

I can't handle all this. I can't live like this. I can't feel so much pain anymore. I can't do it. And I don't want to any longer.

My nose burns. Tears fall freely down my cheeks. My ears are ringing and I can barely see to the door of the fitting room. I slowly release and slip into unconsciousness.

Nine

For as long as I could remember, my dad and I were inseparable. Even when we were in the same place, I had to be near my dad. We shared many of the same tastes in movies, music, TV shows, food, and so forth. My dad and I were always closer, whereas my brother and my mom were closer. I could never make my mom proud like Nash could. But I could make my dad proud by doing mostly nothing. After Nash, my dad was my favorite person in my family. He understood me. He believed in me.

Now, I am falling through the sky. I am falling and can't see the ground. My neck and the back of my knees tingle, sizzle even. I feel weightless and I revel in it. But falling through the air frightens me.

I open my eyes to see a large figure looming over me and I am still falling. But I learn that my arms and knees tingle because that is where Logan holds me. I am in Logan's arms. Why am I in Logan's arms? My head is foggy, but the last I remember, I was in the dress shop with my dad. No, he had left me. But Logan certainly wasn't there. And I don't remember leaving. Doing my best not to panic I try and roll out of Logan's arms, but he is quick and strong and doesn't let go until I am placed on something soft.

I look down and realize Logan has placed me on my bed. *My bed.* Okay, I realize Logan obviously knew where I lived from the whole winking at me when he told those girls where he lived thing, but how did he get into my house. I always lock it, and last time I checked, I didn't give him a key, and we don't have a hidden spare. Unless he stole the key from my purse. And for that matter, I don't know where my purse is.

When I am free from Logan's arms, I scoot myself as far from him as I can without falling off the bed, which is a struggle because I am still wearing the dress from the dress boutique.

This is not good. This is not good. Logan kidnapped me, while I was unconscious, and now I am alone with him in my house. *This is not good.*

Logan steps forward. I jerk back and say, "Stay away from me."

"I'm not going to hurt you," Logan says like the idea is so absurd.

My heart races and hammers against my chest. It is quite uncomfortable. The back of my neck and knees still tingle. Logan scares me. I have no idea what he wants from me, or why he would bring me to my house when his house is only a mile down the road. How did he know where I was? What does he plan to do with me? Questions race through my head. I can barely keep up with them. Scarier questions replace others. From the day Logan walked into class, I thought he was creepy, and I somewhat joked about him doing something to me, living so closely to me, but I don't think I ever thought he really would do something to me.

"What do you want from me?" I ask, my voice shaking.

"Nothing. I brought you home," he says this with his hands up, as if he is trying to reassure and calm a wounded animal.

"How did you find me?"

Logan moves towards me again and when I again jerk back, he sits in my chair across from my bed. His massive figure makes the chair look like it was made for a child. "I was in the coffee shop across the street from the boutique. I saw you and your dad go in, then he came out and you didn't. I waited for a long time and you never came out. I went into the boutique to talk to you and didn't see you anywhere inside. When I asked the sales lady where you were she said she didn't know, that she thought you left with your dad. I got worried so I looked in the dressing rooms and there you were, passed out on the floor."

"So you thought you should take me out of there and

bring me home?" I ask, not even wanting to think about him telling me he was worried. Stalkers worry about their victims right? Is Logan a stalker, or were his actions admirable, chivalrous even? "This dress isn't even paid for. They will think I stole it."

"The dress is paid for," he says with his stupid half grin.

My mouth falls open. No way did he pay for my dress. Why did he pay for my dress? Why did he bring me home when he could have left me there? Why was he watching me in the first place?

Before I can ask him why he paid for my dress, Logan says, "I didn't say I paid for it. I said, it's paid for."

This puzzles me. Everything about Logan puzzles me. He exudes this hard, cynical exterior, but could he really be not too bad of a guy? No. Logan is bad. He is as bad as they come. And why would he even bother with me when Ashley was hanging off of him. I am confused and I feel lightheaded. I don't want Logan in my house. And I certainly don't want to be alone with him.

Again, before I can say anything to Logan, like ask him to leave, he says, "Look. I didn't mean to scare you. I'm not here to hurt you. I was just trying to help you."

My brows furrow, trying to figure out what Logan is all about. In school he acts like a smug jerk, but now he is trying to help me. Is the school Logan the real Logan, or is this Logan the real Logan? I can't tell. But I'm almost intrigued to find out.

"Well. Thanks. I guess," I say, still on the edge of my

bed, and still a little freaked out. But my heart rate has slowed.

"You're welcome," Logan says softly. "If you don't mind me asking, why did your dad leave, and what made you pass out?"

He had to go there didn't he? "I don't want to talk about it," I say, a little too curtly.

"Okay. Well, you are fine now. Maybe I should go," Logan says, and gets out of the chair.

For some unknown reason I say, "Wait."

Logan turns to me with a gleam in his eye. Great. Maybe he does have an anterior motive and was just waiting for me to stop him from leaving, knowing I would. Wow. I really need help.

I look down at myself, embarrassed, my cheeks flushing. That is when I realize I am still wearing the dress that somehow got paid for, and feel stupid and inconspicuous.

"Um. Give me a sec," I say, getting off the bed and ushering Logan out of my room.

When I have closed the door behind him, I scramble for decent clothes to change into. I find that my room is a mess which only mortifies me further. Complete disaster, like a tornado went through. Luckily I haven't unpacked ninety percent of my things. Unfortunately, that makes my room look uncomfortable, unlived in. Whatever. I don't even know why I am obsessing over this, but having Logan in my room, my personal space, is unnerving. I finally find a decently clean pair of jeans and a cute black sweater, slip out of the dress, put on the new clothes, and open my door. Logan is standing with his back to me, looking down the stairway.

"Okay," I say, but instead of taking him back into my bedroom, I lead Logan down the stairs to the living room. He sits on the couch and looks up at me. There is no way I'm going to sit on that couch with him. I take a seat in the recliner across the room. I pull my legs up and tuck them under me. Then I think better of it. If I need to run, having my feet tucked under me will only be a hindrance. So instead, I pull my knees up to my chest and wrap my arms around them. This is comfortable, allows easy access if I do in fact need to run away, and I feel in some way protected. Guarded.

Logan is quiet. I suspect he is waiting for me to speak first. I don't blame him after I yelled at him for bringing up my dad. But I don't want to be the first one to speak. I've never actually had a conversation with Logan. The most we get out of each other is a *hi, hey, shut up,* or *I know I look good.* Other than creeping me out, I have no idea what type of person Logan is. Maybe it is time to find out.

"So what brought you to Cedars?" I ask slowly.

Logan smirks, for some unseen reason he finds my question funny. I don't think it is all that funny. He's already off to a bad foot.

Logan places his hand around his jaw and pulls down, mulling over the questions. I really didn't think it would be all that difficult. "Let's just say I came because of a job."

"Oh, you work? Where?"

"Let's just call it a security job."

"*Okay*," I say, resting my chin on my knees. I am really getting sick of the *let's* he keeps using.

We sit in silence for a time, neither one of us knowing what to say or what to talk about. I don't know why I told him to wait. The silence is awkward. Logan has only been in town for a few weeks. I know nothing about him, and he knows nothing about me. There is a way we can change that, but I'm not sure I want to. Logan frightens me. He has given me no reason to open up to him, and about every reason not to. But the way he is looking at me now, his eyes fierce and tender, curious and patient. My eyes narrow, my brows pulling together. I try to deduce what he is all about, but I get nowhere by just looking at him.

"So you live in the old Melbourne place," I begin. When he just nods I continue, "I hear that place is haunted and completely unlivable."

"I've had it fixed up. Renovated."

"You?" I ask. "Don't you live with your parents?"

"No," Logan says, obviously not wanting to share more.

I don't know that I blame him. I don't want to talk about my dad, mom, or Nash, even with people I know. Xander, Tucker, and I barely talk about Nash and my parents. I'm not sure they understand, and I'm sure I hurt their feelings, but they try and they don't complain. I really take my friends for granted. But then again, it would seem Xander likes to undermine me, telling my dad about Logan. Which reminds me, I need to call Xander and chew him out once Logan leaves.

Silence falls again. But I don't feel the awkwardness this time. I'm not sure what I feel. I am not comfortable with Logan. I don't know that I ever will be. But for some reason, I feel there is some unspoken understanding between us. I don't know what that understanding is, but at this moment I don't mind. I lay my head on my knees. My stomach rumbles and I hope that Logan doesn't hear it. My dad bailed before I could even pick out a dress. I haven't eaten since lunch and school lunch always leaves one wanting. I ignore my stomach-I will find something when Logan leaves-and rest curled up in the recliner. Even though Logan is sitting across the living room from me, I focus on my breathing, and zone out. A little over six months ago my life was normal, great even, and now it is a shit storm raging, devastating anything in its path.

When I come back to myself and my surroundings, there is a plate on the side table with a sandwich, apple slices, and baby carrots. It's not the bacon cheeseburger and fries I was promised, but it will do. I look up to Logan, the only possible culprit to the food on the table, whose face shows no change. Logan's thoughtfulness touches me deep. I would have never expected it from the school Logan I thought I knew.

"My dad had to go to work, that's why he left early. That's why you found me in the dressing room," I blurt out before I know what's happening.

"You passed out because your dad had to go to work?" Logan asks, curious more than chastising, like he thinks it's stupid but is also intrigued by the thought.

I don't answer him. It's so much more complicated than I could express into words to make him understand. Sure, he would understand that my family is grieving because of the loss of my brother. And sure he would understand that divorce is hard on the parents as well as the kids. But he wouldn't understand my particular situation because he knows nothing about the relationship I had with my dad and what it has now turned into.

But Logan doesn't push me to answer him. He doesn't even seem to expect it. Instead, he lets the question slide and asks, "Do you pass out a lot?"

This question throws me, but I answer, "No. Not normally." He looks pleased by my answer. I don't mention the fact that I was so overcome by sorrow that I couldn't stay conscious. My heart still aches, but oddly enough, it dulls with Logan here. I almost feel stupid for having freaked out when I woke up in his arms. But I also feel stupid for being so at ease with a basic stranger alone in my house.

Almost as if he read my mind, Logan says, "Eat. I should get going."

My heart leaps unexpectedly. Possibly at the thought of him leaving. Possibly because I will, again, be alone. "Okay," I whisper.

When he stands up, so do I. "Will you be okay?" he asks, walking towards me, and again my heart leaps.

"Yeah, thanks," I say as he is now directly in front of me.

My breathing becomes fast and heavy. I can't believe I

let Logan affect me like this. Worse yet, he leans in so close to me that I can feel his warm breath on my ear. I stop breathing completely. "If you ever need anything," Logan says and slips something in the front of my jeans pocket with two of his fingers. They linger longer than I think is necessary and I grow dizzy from the contact and lack of oxygen. I feel the warmth of his fingers through the layer of denim and feel like passing out all over again. My heart rate picks up until I feel my heart will burst from my chest. When he pulls his fingers from my pocket my knees buckle. He catches me under the arms sending a whole new wave of fire through my body. Who knew a simple touch could ignite something so alive in me.

He's creepy. I remind myself. *He scares you. Possibly dangerous.* But none of that does anything to deter me from the way he makes me feel at this very moment.

The humming my body does now only reignites the feeling on the back of my neck and knees from when he held me.

He leans close again and I close my eyes, savoring his closeness. "I'm not all bad, Casslyn. See you in school," he says. When I open my eyes, he is gone.

***

"Are you insane?" I yell into the phone.

"Not since I last checked," Xander says, sounding confused but slightly amused.

"You might want to check again, jerk."

Xander chuckles under his breath and says, "I'm not sure what I did, so please enlighten me."

"How dare you talk to my dad about Logan. Our relationship is shitty enough as it is. The last thing I need is you putting it in his head that I'm in danger. Or stupid. Or falling for a creeper."

"You're not are you?" he asks almost stricken.

"Xander!" I yell.

"Alright. I'm sorry. I shouldn't have talked to him. . . . No. I'm glad I did. I don't think you are taking Logan's fight factor as seriously as you should. Logan is dangerous. He scares me and he's focused on you. I'm afraid he's going to hurt you, or worse."

"Xander," I say exasperatedly, "I appreciate your concern, but I can take care of myself. And in the rare occasion that I can't that's what I have you and Tucker for."

Xander is quiet for a time and I can only hear his breathing through the phone. Finally, he concedes and says, "Alright. Other than my snafu, how was your time with your dad?"

I sigh into the phone and say, "I don't really want to discuss it right now. We can talk about it tomorrow in school. That way I won't have to tell you now and Tucker tomorrow."

"Fine by me. Are you okay though?"

"Uh. Yeah. I guess. I'll see you tomorrow."

Ten

Being in school today is just not worth it. School is never worth it. But today is another level of bad. Luckily today is Friday and I can spend the weekend wallowing. I have come to the realization or conclusion or assumption that I should give up on my dad. It hurts too much to try and fail at getting his attention. I sadly feel the need to let my dad go. I feel like a sinking ship or a drowning rat when it comes to my failing relationship with him. Perhaps I have clung on so strongly because he was one of my best friends. Perhaps because if I can keep my relationship with my dad afloat, I can fix the rest of my family. Perhaps because if I have nothing to cling to I will simply fall apart. But maybe it is time I fall apart in order to pick myself back up.

I breathe in and out very slowly. It helps to stave off the tunnel vision that threatens to take me over. I look over to Logan for a distraction. He hasn't looked at me or even acknowledged my presence today. Odd. Unusual. Not like Logan. He still doesn't look at me, though I'm sure he can feel my stare. Maybe he thinks I'm pathetic for passing out over my dad going to work. Maybe he thinks I'm weak and no longer wishes to associate himself with me. Whatever it is, I miss his gaze, his taunting, his arrogance, and mannerisms. This is exactly what I, we, Tucker, Xander, and I wanted. To be rid of the overwhelming danger and creep factor that Logan is, and for some reason, I am remiss.

I turn back to the front of the room and try not to think about how far I have fallen. The bell rings and Tucker and I make our way to the hallway. So far, Tucker and Xander have not asked me about last night. But I know they won't wait forever, and I can't avoid it forever.

Tucker and I meet Xander at our lockers, placing our books from the previous class inside and head down the stairs to the gym. I am in the middle of the two of them and can feel their steady gaze. They want to know about my time with my dad but they don't want to ask.

"Just ask."

"How was your afternoon with your dad?" Tucker asks in such an upbeat tone he must know it went badly.

I recant to them my very short afternoon with my dad. I tell them the plans we had; the dresses, the bacon cheeseburger, and the rebuilding of our relationship. And I tell them the failures of our afternoon; the three dresses I tried on before my dad bailed, the bacon cheeseburger I did not get to eat, and the wipeout of my hope for my dad to once again love me. What I don't tell them; is that I passed out from misery, that the one person the three of us fear found me unconscious, brought me home, made food for me, and acted like a normal human being and not a creepy stalker, and that I have lost faith in love and life.

"So how did you get home?" Tucker asks, completely befuddled and a bit worried.

"Why didn't you call one of us?" Xander asks, completely upset.

"I didn't want to bother either of you," I lie. "I just went to the library and waited for my mom's shift to get over."

"Bother us?" Xander sounds exasperated. "Jesus Casslyn, just call one of us."

"What Xander is trying to say, in his own way," Tucker says, "is that we are always here for you and you don't need to worry about bothering us."

"Thanks guys. But it's okay. I need to take care of myself sometimes. And my mom and I haven't spent that much time together lately so it was good for us," I say which is totally a lie. The good for us part, not the we need it part. Because my mom and I really need to spend time together. I fell asleep before my mom got home last night, and I didn't see her before I left for school this morning.

I feel a sense of self hate for my relationship with my

mom. For as hard as I try to hold on to my relationship with my dad, I let go of it with my mom. Nash was always my mom's favorite and I feel, as horrible of a daughter as I am, that she would rather that he had lived and I had not. Like my dad, my mom is distant, but instead of holding on for dear life, I let her slip away. And as much as it hurts, I can't help but feel as if my parents wish they lost both of their children and not just one. I can blame them, I can blame myself, but the blame truly lies with all of us. But then, I can't help but feel just in the way I act because I am in fact the child, the one who can act childish, and they are the adults, the parents, who are supposed to hold everything together.

I lose every match of pickle ball Xander, Tucker, and I play in Rec Sports. They take it easy on me, realizing I have a lot on my mind. It does many things to make me feel bad, though. Tucker and Xander are the best, most supportive, understanding friends I could possibly ask for and I don't do enough to show them my appreciation.

When my best friends and I walk through the hallways towards dinner, Tucker sucks in a deep breath that frightens both Xander and I. "I have a brilliant idea," he says.

"Oh, like your brilliant idea for Casslyn to be nice to Lex Luther?" Xander says.

"Better," Tucker says and looks so proud of himself. "The two of you are going to come over tonight for a night of good old times. Movies, pizza, popcorn, friendship, and just good plain fun."

Surprising both of them, I am the first to say, "Heck

yes." A night alone with Tucker and Xander is the perfect way for me to show them how much they mean to me and how much I truly appreciate them. Away from the hassle of school, away from thinking about Logan, away from the sorrow from losing my brother, and away from the struggle to hold my family intact. *I can do this*, I tell myself. I can spend one night not thinking about my life's shit and focus on my best friends who do their best to get me through everything. I have to do this.

"Oh yay. It's the gay one, the straight one, and the broken one," I hear from behind us. Great. Exactly what I needed, Ashley and her posse. "Gunna have a sleep over huh? I bet that's one awkward threesome."

Running away only makes the taunting worse. Staying and fighting back may give her more to work with, but sometimes I can get in a few good jabs that make her think twice.

I turn around and say, "Like how awkward it was the first time you and Justin had sex and he learned you stuff your bra?"

"And you learned he has a mini dick," Xander says. "So you dumped him for someone with a bigger dick."

Ashley and Justin's mouths drop open. I smile smugly and cross my arms. I'm not sure why they continue to try to humiliate us. Xander, Tucker, and I tend to get in more digs then they do. Of course, Ashley and I have a past that will not let her stop.

"How's your dad, Casslyn?" Ashley asks. "Did he leave your mom because he found out how boring and bad in the sack she is?"

"Yeah, Ashley, bring up her dad, like that isn't over-played," Tucker says.

"Just like your love life?" Justin says. "Oh wait, I mean lack thereof."

"Ouch. You hit a nerve," Tucker says sarcastically. One of the great things about Tucker is that is so comfortable in his own skin. He knows who he is and is proud of it.

"They couldn't hit the broad side of a pig's butt if they were kissing it," Xander says.

"Says the one who has never kissed anyone," Ashley says.

"Yes because kissing the entire high school male population and some of the female population is so much better," I say.

"Oh, why don't you just go join your brother," Ashley says.

Before I can cry or cut a bitch, a large shadow falls over me. Two guesses as to who it could be; Logan or Logan. I turn around to face him, glad for the distraction. But Logan looks pissed and I'm not about to speak to him.

"Logan," Ashley says cheerfully. "How are you? I was just talking to Casslyn."

"I heard what you *said*, Ashley," Logan says through his teeth. That shut Ashley up.

I didn't tell Logan about my brother last night. I didn't plan on ever telling him. But that doesn't mean he hasn't heard about it here at school or around town. In a town as small as Cedars, news travels fast and continues to travel until there is something newer and bigger to talk about.

"Well I . . . she . . .," Ashley stammers.

"She what? The two of you were having a back and forth, which you started, and she insulted you, so you decided to tell her you wish she was dead, like her twin brother," Logan is fuming mad.

Again, I am scared of him. Even when he is defending me, he frightens me. Ashley cowers where she stands. Justin stands behind her. Their posse leaves dust in their wake. I could laugh if I wasn't afraid of Logan blowing up, or if I wasn't still hurt by what Ashley said.

"Care to apologize?" Logan asks.

Ashley's expression changes now from scared to mad. She huffs, stomps her foot, turns on her heel, and walks to the gym, which serves as our lunch room. Tucker, Xander, and I stay put, not knowing exactly what to do. Logan turns to us, looks at me, nods his head, and walks away. One of my brows lifts up unconsciously. What was that? I turn to my best friends in turn. They wear the same expression I wear. With one exception, Xander looks confused and pissed. I'm not sure why he would be angry. Whether it be Ashley's comment about our sleepover, Ashley's comment about Nash, or Logan standing up for me when he couldn't get the job done.

"So, we're not going to let this bother us," I say, shocking my friends again.

"Right," they both say as once.

"Let's get this day over with," I say.

We walk through the lunch line, into the gym, where Ashley and Justin are subdued and proceed to *get the day over with*.

The next time I see Logan is the last class period of the day, sitting at our cooking station. I tell Xander and Tucker I will meet them after class and walk over to stand by Logan.

He looks down at me with all his severity and says, "How are you?"

I'm not sure if he is referring to last night, three hours ago, or how I am in general, so I simply say, "I'm fine." I think about saying, "Thanks for asking," but I don't think Logan and I have that sort of relationship and it feels awkward just thinking about saying it.

"Welcome class," Mrs. Sherman says. "Before we begin today, I want to tell you about your project for the end of the semester. You and your partner will be creating a meal to be prepared the last week of the semester for the entire class. I expect each pair will come up with your meal, inform me of what you will be making next week so no one doubles up, then spend the rest of the semester preparing your meal, on your own time. Now, get to work."

I look up at Logan wondering what he thinks about this. He raises an eyebrow and shrugs, like he couldn't care less. The trouble is, I'm not sure how I feel about this. Logan and I would have to spend a few nights together, practicing making our meal, together, at my house, because I will most definitely not allow myself to be alone with him at his house. Let me reiterate, Logan and I will be together. More than likely alone. Xander is not going to like this. Tucker will be jealous because he still has a crush on Logan. Me, however, I'm not entirely turned off by the idea. Logan is gorgeous, a good cook, he has stood up for me twice with Ashley, and brought me home when I passed out. But then again, he's moody, he is sarcastic, he thinks way too highly of himself, he stares at me way too much, and he scares the living daylights out of me. This should be interesting.

"What would you like to cook today?" Logan asks.

"Um, chicken alfredo," I say offhandedly.

Logan chuckles beside me.

"What?" I ask, wondering what he could possibly find funny about what I said.

"You must really like Italian food," he says.

"Like a baby likes milk."

Logan grins and prepares the ingredients and pots and pans for the alfredo. I join him in the preparation and making of the pasta. I salt the pasta water while he cuts up breasts of chicken and tosses them in the hot pan. I do this in part because Mrs. Sherman will expect Logan and I to work together for the final project, and I do it in part because I want to know what it will be like to work side by side with Logan. Surprisingly enough, we make a pretty good team.

Eleven

On the best friend docket for tonight: pizza, popcorn, cheesy movies, and overall best friend catching up. Not on the best friend docket for tonight: Xander warning me away from Logan for like the zillionth time, me dismissing the warning, and Tucker trying to bring us all back together.

"Xander, you are acting paranoid. Logan hasn't been creepy in like a week. Can we please just forget about him for one night?"

"Casslyn, I'm not being paranoid. I don't like this guy. I don't trust him. He's dangerous, I know it. You need to stay away from him."

"Xander, stop it! I don't want to do this anymore. Just stop, please," I say, sighing heavily, throwing myself on

Tucker's couch.

Xander closes his eyes, breathes in and out through his nose, and says, "Sorry. I'm just a little over protective."

"You don't need to protect me," I say, softening to his sentiment. Since Nash died, Xander has been way over protective. He was never even protective before, well a little bit, but not at all like he is now. I realize that losing one best friend and almost losing another in one night is a bit traumatic, but instead of taking Tucker's plan of action and make the most of still having a best friend, Xander went the opposite direction and decided to become my personal body guard and act crazy protective. As much as I appreciate it, it gets a little stifling.

"I'm sorry," Xander says. He sighs and plops down in a recliner as if he is exhausted.

I follow Xander into the recliner and lay on top of him. He wraps his arms around me, rests his chin on top of my head, and says, "I'm sorry, Cass, I just hate to see you in danger."

"What makes you think I am in danger?" I ask him.

"Because I . . .," Xander begins, but then there is a shift in his eyes, and he says, "It's just a feeling. And I can't shake it. Every time I see you with him, the way he looks at you, like you are a possession or something, I hate it. He's no good. Will you please just do me the favor of looking out for yourself, if you won't let me?"

"Yes," I say, because there is nothing else I know of to say.

"Okay," Tucker says to break the tension. "Let's get this party started."

As soon as he says this, the doorbell rings signaling the arrival of the pizza. Finally. I give Xander a reassuring hug, hop up, walk to the TV, and pop *The Goonies* into the DVD player while Tucker pays for the pizza.

After the first awkward half hour of *The Goonies* my best friends and I have gotten back to our rhythm. Tucker makes jokes about how he'd like to set some booty traps, Xander tries to explain the logistics of treasure hunting, and I just bask in the happiness of being with my two best friends, and for once in seven months I don't think about my crippling fear of being alone in this world and I don't think about the process of breathing, I just do.

In the middle of our second movie and our first tub of ice cream, we laugh until tears stream down our faces, our stomachs hurt, and we are about to pee ourselves. As fun as it is, I can feel the stares of Xander and Tucker. I know they worry about me, and I appreciate it, but I wonder if we will ever really get back to the way we were. The easy way we talked. The way we never once fought. The way we never had to try. But I don't bring it up. I don't let them know that I know they wait for the ticking time bomb that is me to go off. I don't let them know that I feel on the verge of exploding every second of every day. I especially don't let Xander know that when I'm with Logan I can actually breathe without reminding myself to.

By the end of the third movie, we are exhausted, out of

food, and acting so ridiculous we need to separate. I rode with Xander and Tucker from school to Tucker's house, but now Xander is too tired to drive me all the way out to my house, and even though Tucker has offered to let me stay, I just need to be back at my own house, in my own bed. Even if it isn't really my home.

"Okay, here's the plan," Xander says. Tucker is already almost passed out on the couch. Xander looks at me and says, "You will drive me to my house, then you will take my car and drive to your house. You can bring my car back to me when you come to school Monday."

"I can't," I say. I can feel my breaths become slower. I haven't driven but about twice since the accident. I only drive when it is absolutely necessary and I have a panic attack every time. I drive about ten miles an hour, look for oncoming cars or oncoming anything of any kind, and otherwise stop breathing until I have reached my destination. I get a head pounding, ear throbbing, neck aching, vision blurring migraine every time. I repeat myself, "I can't."

Xander places both of his hands firmly on my arms, looks me dead in the eye, and says, "Yes. You. Can. I promise you. Drive me to my house, and if you can't handle more than that, you will stay at my house and we will worry about it next time."

My vision blurs just thinking about driving down the road with blinding headlights bearing down on me. Xander slaps me, bringing me back to reality. I shake my head trying to focus.

"I won't make you do anything you don't want to. But I promise you can do this."

I furrow my brows at him, showing him I don't approve of his tactics, but concede and say goodbye to Tucker, who we have to pry off the couch. When Xander and I walk out the front door, rain is coming down in a sheet. This only adds to my fear. I take a deep breath and don't let the rain mess with my resolve. Xander hands me the keys and I get into the driver's side. I turn the key and the engine roars to life. A lump catches in my throat. My best friend is much taller than I am and I have to adjust the seat and mirrors. I take a long time to check the rear view and side mirrors, messing with the radio and the heat, and anything else that might stall our departure. But eventually Xander clears his throat and I run out of things to adjust.

I slowly, but surely, back out of Tucker's driveway, put the car in drive, and head towards Xander's house. The wipers run furiously, barely able to keep up with the pouring rain. I eventually make it to Xander's front door and by that time, the rain has slowed to a steady mist. I can only imagine how muddy the gravel road is going to be. A wave of nausea rushes over me. Xander must see it because he says, "You can stay here tonight. You can have my bed. I'll take the couch."

I think about taking him up on it. It would be easier, safer. But then I think about the faith that he has in me. How he promised me that I could do it. I can't let him down. And I can't let myself down.

"It's okay. Like you said, I can do this," I try to say it as bravely as I can, but my voice quivers. I know Xander can hear it, but he chooses to ignore it, and I'm thankful for it.

"Alright then," he says. "I'll see you Monday."

"Bye Xander. And thanks for the use of your car."

"No problem," he says, gets out of his car, and walks to his house.

As soon as he has escaped into the safety of his house, my panic sets in. I am assaulted by images of that truck's headlights bearing down on us, blinding us. I haven't even started driving yet and I can't do this. It's not too late, I can take Xander up on his offer to stay with him for the night. But no, I can't. I need to do this for myself, for my best friends, and even for my brother.

I pull away from Xander's curb with a pounding headache. My vision blurs on the outside, but I focus and push it away. I need to be clear and level headed in order to get to my house. I move through town easily, successfully. It gives me confidence that I really can make it to my house just fine. I move out of town and finally make it to the gravel road. It is wet, but not yet muddy. I can so do this. Ten miles, that's all I have left till I am safe and sound in my bed. My head has stopped throbbing, my vision is clear, and my breathing is normal. Maybe I made too big of a deal out of this.

I glance down at the trip meter as I drive just to know how far I have left. In no time at all, I find myself in front of Logan's house. The house is dark but for one light on the first floor. I wonder what he could be doing at this hour. I wonder if he thinks about me. I wonder if he actually likes me, or if he just likes to pester me. I really need to stop thinking about it. I need to stop thinking about him. Xander hates him. My dad doesn't want me to be anywhere near him. My mom couldn't care less, but I'm sure if she met Logan she would feel the same way. And Tucker has the hots for him and would probably hate me if I went after Logan.

I shake my head feeling ridiculous and turn back to the road. Out of nowhere, headlights shine directly in front of me. *This has to be a dream*, I think. A nightmare is more like it. Just like that night seven months ago. That's what this is, just a horrible flashback of that night. I just need to wake myself up, get back to reality. Again I shake my head to clear it, but after, the headlights are still there, and getting closer. I tap the breaks to slow down but the road is slick and I end up sliding. I try to get the car under control and get off to the side so the other vehicle can go past me. I can't see anything because the other vehicle has its brights on, and I end up driving on the shoulder of the gravel. The other car won't turn its brights off, and won't get over. I try the brakes again but this results in more sliding and finally the other vehicle is on top of me. I swerve so I don't hit it and fly off the road. As soon as I go into the ditch, the impact makes me black out and when I come to, I feel like I am upside down, because the car is rolling over. When the car stops, I black out again.

I am hung upside down and held there by the seatbelt. My head throbs worse than ever. There is so much pressure pushing against my skull. My ears ring badly. I can't see anything and I'm not sure if that's because it is dark or if I really can't see. Something wet and sticky runs all over my face. Every part of my body hurts. I feel tired, drained. I want to just go to sleep.

From somewhere far away I can hear someone calling my name. Or at least that's what it sounds like. I wish they would just be quiet so that I can fall asleep. But they get closer and yell louder. I try to tell them to be quiet, but my words do not leave my throat. The door of the car opens and someone calls my name. I fall in and out of consciousness. I'm out longer than I'm in. When I come back to, the back of my neck and my knees tingle. The sensation feels familiar but I can't place it. That doesn't matter right now. I'm just tired and need to sleep. The person who was yelling at me earlier is so close it sounds like they are yelling directly in my ear. It hurts my pounding head, stabs my ear drums. I try to pull away but I can't seem to be able to move. Then I fall back into darkness.

When I am aware again, I hear that voice again, so familiar, yet different than I remember. I'm used to snark, sarcasm, but all I hear now is fear and desperation, "No. You can't be dead. Wake up, Casslyn."

His voice sends shivers through my body, or is it the loss of blood. I'm not sure. But it's a deep, rich voice that I love. "Logan?" I ask.

I hear a sigh of relief and he says, "Stay with me, love." And as much as I'd love to listen to him talk to me, I can't keep my eyes open, can't keep my brain open. It closes and darkness envelopes me.

Twelve

I wake up to a fog and a steady beeping. My head hurts and I can't think straight. I don't want to open my eyes. It feels good just to lie here complacent. I don't even know why I hurt. I don't know why I keep hearing the beeping noise. I know it's not my alarm clock. And why would my alarm clock be going off on a Saturday?

I open my eyes to a bright light above me. Then I remember, I was run off the road last night, landed in a ditch, and possibly died. Why else would I be facing a blinding white light? Why would heaven be so annoying though? If I have to spend eternity here, I hope this beeping will go away.

But then the light isn't so blinding and I discover where the beeping is coming from, a heart monitor. I am in a hospital room, hooked up to various wires and machines. My room is just like any other hospital room I have ever been in or seen in movies or TV shows. The wall that faces to the outside is not really a wall but a large window. The wall behind me has a row of plug-ins. A rather large florescent light is above me. There is a reclining chair next to my bed. The wall opposite me is adorned with a small, old looking TV. The sound is off but it currently plays an old episode of Friends where Rachel is having her baby and Joey pretends to be a doctor. There is a small dresser that probably holds extra sheets, blankets, and pillows. Then there is a miniscule bathroom tucked away in the corner nearest the door.

This brings back so many horrible memories. My parents telling me that Nash and I were in an accident and that he didn't make it. Me not being able to attend his funeral because I was unable to leave the hospital. Me learning that my parents now hated each other and were going to get a divorce. Me almost dying and almost wishing I did so I didn't have to live without my brother.

I lie in the stiff hospital bed with tears running down the sides of my face. I close my eyes and they stream harder. Then I hear someone come into my room. I open my eyes to see my mom standing at the foot of my bed. I don't think I've seen her all week.

"Oh, Casslyn, you're awake," my mom says, worry and relief in her voice.

My mom and I don't look alike. She has thick mousy brown hair that she keeps tied up in a bun. She is short but thin, very petite. If I ever see her out of her scrubs, she wears slacks and button down shirts. Nothing like my outrageous fashion sense. She has brown eyes with no life behind them. I love my mom, but she is boring. Too safe.

"How long was I out?" I ask, my voice hoarse. My throat is dry and my tongue feels like sand paper.

"Thirty-two hours. You fractured your left wrist, the air bag cut up your face pretty good, and the glass from the windshield cut your leg so you have a few stitches. But other than that you are just fine. Are you okay, honey? Do you need anything? Water? Pain meds?"

So it's Sunday, not Saturday. Yay. I have to go back to school tomorrow. "Um, I'm okay right now. Well, I could use a glass of water," I say. I can't believe I was asleep for so long. And no wonder my wrist and face hurt. I look down and see a brace around my wrist. I think I can even feel the stitches above my right knee.

My mom fills a Styrofoam cup with water and holds it to my mouth so I can drink from it. The cold water burns on the way down. I swallow it down, trying not to choke on it. I rest my head back on the pillow, feeling the feathers poke my ears. The water reaches my stomach and I feel like I might throw up.

When I grasp my stomach my mom says, "When you were upside down in the car, the airbag deflated and the steering wheel pressed into your stomach. Your abs, stomach, and intestines are deeply bruised but nothing is damaged, so you will be fine."

"Awesome. I love feeling like I got ran over by a steam roller."

"It could have been so much worse. Casslyn, what happened?" my mom asks, a stricken look on her face.

I recant to my mom the events of last night-well Friday night, which was technically yesterday morning, I think-to the best of my knowledge. There are gaps, and the pain makes the memories fuzzy. I see headlights and flying gravel. I feel glass slicing my skin and strong hands pulling me from Xander's mustang. But whose hands they were, I don't remember. I hear a voice in my head. It's far away and I can't place it, but I know it has to be the voice of the person who saved me.

I can't believe it. I had to be saved, again. The person on the road that night ran me off of it. There was no trying to get over, no accidental driving on my side of the road. I mean, they may have forgotten to turn off their brights, but the rest I swear was on purpose. How could it not be? But I leave all this out when I tell my mom about the accident. She might think I suffered a blow to the head that did major damage. Telling her might result in her thinking about our accident so many months ago and about the truck that ran us off the road. It might make her think about Dad leaving and their divorce. She might tell me it was just an accident and that there was no other vehicle. I'm afraid of what she might think or say and therefore I say nothing. I keep it to myself and pray that there really was no other vehicle, that it was an accident, and that it will never happen again.

Maybe I'm just crazy. Why would anyone want to run me off a road? Why would anyone try to kill me? Were they trying to kill me? Maybe I have lost my mind. I have to have lost my mind. I close my eyes, trying to clear my head.

"I'm so sorry, honey. I'm so sorry you were alone," my mom says.

"It's not your fault, mom. I was just coming home from Tucker's. There's nothing you could have done."

My mom gives me this pained look, then turns away from me. I can't see the look on her face. It wasn't her fault. There really was nothing she could have done about it. Or could she? If she was home, if she talked to me more often, if she checked in, she would know when I was supposed to be home, she would know that when I didn't get home on time, there may have been something wrong. But then, I could have checked in, I could have let her know when I was supposed to be home. No. I am not the parent. I am not the responsible adult. I'm the kid, I'm supposed to do irresponsible things like staying out late, not checking in.

I'm so tired right now. I'm in so much pain. "I could really use a nap. I feel drained."

"I have rounds to do anyway. I'll come back in an hour or two and check on you."

I nod, smile weakly at her, and rest my head on the pillow. I'm out before I hear the door close behind her.

I open my eyes and I'm back in my old room. Nash is sprawled out on my bed flipping through a magazine. I smile from ear to ear when he looks up at me. My heart constricts and for a second I can't breathe. This isn't a memory. I would know if it was. This is something entirely different. This is my brain and my heart making up for lost time. This is me missing my brother so much that I need to meet him in my dreams. If that is the case, I might as well spend my life sleeping.

"What do you want dork?" Nash asks me. "Are you just going to stand there in the doorway or are you going to join me? I'm reading this riveting article on the breakup of Selena Gomez and Justin Bieber. Apparently she is happy as a clam and he is so distraught that he is acting out and smoking joints. Go figure."

I laugh at him. It really doesn't matter what he says, I would laugh anyway. I plop myself onto the bed next to him. I punch him in the arm then steal the magazine from him. Flipping a couple pages, I land on an article about not fighting with your significant other through texts.

"I'm totally going to do that just in spite of this article," Nash says.

"Haha. Go for it. First you need a girlfriend," I joke, poking him in the side.

"Yeah, that may be a necessity. But you have room to joke. You've got *all* the guys lining up for you."

"Shows how much you know," I say. "That is by choice. I am gorgeous, I could have any guy I want." There is no truth in that, but it may be nice if there was.

"Sure, you keep telling yourself that. But you want to know the truth?" Nash asks, a sly grin on his face and mischief in his voice.

I turn to him and cock one of my eyebrows. "Maybe?" I say as more of a question than an answer.

"I don't let the boys line up for you. There is no one in our school good enough for you," Nash says this as a joke, but I can tell that he is dead serious. For a moment I've forgotten that this is a dream, that none of it is real, and wonder if that really is why I've never had a boyfriend, if Nash really has warded off all potential suitors. Even so, it's not like I haven't done the same on his behalf. I've never actually stopped a girl from asking Nash out, or told anyone that they couldn't, but I've sent out a vibe and they knew what was what.

"Over protective much?" I ask jokingly, but he gives me this look that says he isn't joking. And all of a sudden everything comes crashing down on me. The seven months I've spent without him. The soul crushing heartache I feel every second of every day. The hole I feel deep inside of me that can never be filled. My brother was my very best friend in the entire world and I lost him. "I miss you, Nash."

He smiles at me with knowing eyes, touches me on the temple and says, "I'm right here, Cassie." Then he touches me above my chest and says, "And right here. Don't miss me, twin. I'm always with you. I will never leave you."

I am crying now. Nash wipes the tears from my cheeks. "Listen. It's going to get hard before it gets easy, but I promise you everything is going to be okay." He smiles at me and I feel like I'm losing him all over again.

"Nash, what are you-," I begin to say, but I am cut off by a knocking at the door.

I turn to see who it is and find myself back in my hospital room. A strong fist grasps my stomach and yanks. I have to hold my breath to keep from crying out or throwing up. I try my hardest to reign in my emotions and face who is coming into my room. Xander and Tucker walk through with balloons and flowers and stuffed animals. They smile, but I can see the looks in their eyes, the look that says, this-is-the-last-time-I-come-to-the-hospital-thinking-one-of-my-best-friends-has-nearly-died. I return their smile but it is lacking.

"Sorry about your car," I tell Xander

He lets out this panicked laugh and says, "Don't worry about it. I've got insurance."

An awkward silence falls that I can't stand. "So, school tomorrow, should be interesting."

Tucker and Xander look at me like I've shot someone. It occurs to me that not only was my family affected by the accident several months ago, but so were my best friends. I may have lost my twin, my best friend in the whole world, but so did they. And now, they are in the hospital after almost losing the other one. How could I have been so blind? The looks on their faces now send a shooting pain through my stomach. They look defeated, sad, scared, guarded. They remind me of Sam Gamgee. The way he knows that Gollum has corrupted Frodo and there is nothing he can do about it. But still he stays by Frodo's side because Frodo is Sam's best friend, no matter what Frodo puts him through, no matter the cost. What will my best friends have to pay? What more will I put them through? What more can I put myself through?

"Don't give me that look, I'm fine," I tell them, though I feel as though I've been ran over by the Knight Bus.

Xander's eyebrows pull together. He looks at me with so much sorrow and he says, "You're not fine. Your mom told us the car rolled three times and that you were hanging upside down for who knows how long until that guy came by you."

"What guy?" I ask. The memory from last night is still foggy and I'm not clear on the details of how I got out of the car or to the hospital. That voice comes back to me, calling my name, but I still can't place it. It rumbles deep inside me.

"Nobody knows. Your mom checked with everyone she could to find out who brought you in, but the ladies at the front desk said he carried you in, yelled for a doctor, and left when they took you away. The attendees didn't even get a good look at him, he was hooded and didn't let anyone get a good look at him," Tucker explains.

Nothing he says gives me a clue as to who my mysterious masked hero could be. I close my eyes and try to focus on last night, get an image in my mind. I strain to hear his voice, *Casslyn! You can't be dead.* It's so close. So deep and rich and beautiful. *Stay with me, love.* Then I have it. And I can't help but smile. A rush of pure emotion fills me and I tingle all over the place. Logan saved my life. More than likely, I wouldn't be here if it wasn't for him. And he sounded so concerned, so panicked. *You can't be dead.* Like he would have lost everything if he lost me.

"What are you smiling at?" Tucker asks.

I open my eyes to see my best friends staring at me intently, watching my every move. I'm not sure if it's because I'm doped up, or if I suffered a mind altering head injury, but I must have lost my marbles. Did I really have myself believing that Logan would have lost everything if he lost me? Wow. Maybe I need a CT scan.

"Nothing," I tell them. "Just feeling lucky. Anyway, I have to pee."

"Really?" Tucker and Xander ask at the same time, their faces scrunched up.

"Yes," I tell them. "Which one of you is going to help me?"

"Xander is," Tucker says, at the same time Xander says, "Tucker will."

"Just give me the damn robe and I'll do it myself," I laugh at them.

Xander brings the hospital issued robe to me, helps me put both my arms through it and then stands back so I can climb out of the bed. I pull the blanket off my legs and see my bandaged right knee. A dot of blood has seeped through the gauze. I swing my legs over the side of the bed and stand up, only to fall right back onto the bed. My head wobbles a bit making me feel like a bobblehead. I focus and try to stand up again. I feel unsteady and am about to fall back onto the bed when a strong hand grabs hold of my elbow. I look over to see Xander looking down at me intently. Then he smiles and he and Tucker start laughing at me.

"Don't laugh at me you knot heads," I tell them. I don't like them making fun of me in my current situation, but I'm glad to see they are no longer shaken, no longer marred by my accident.

Xander helps me walk to the bathroom then says, "This is as far as I go."

"Yeah, yeah," I tell him, playfully shoving him away from me.

My friends end up staying for a few hours. We turn to the Spanish channel and laugh as we try to figure out what they are saying. Tucker finds a Chinese checkers set, a game we haven't played in years, and we try to remember how to play, but we end up making our own rules. We have fun, and try to forget about my accident, which goes decently well. But when I steal glances at Xander or when he thinks I can't tell that he's looking at me, he has this look on his face that I can't describe. It's so sad, so worried. Protective? And yet almost hopeless. I've never seen him look this way before. I don't know why he looks like this. I feel terrible for wrecking his car, but I don't think that is the reason for this look. I'm fine and he knows this, so it couldn't possibly be for fearing for my life any longer. He hasn't said anything about it, much to my thankfulness, but maybe Xander thinks that Logan had something to do with my accident and is trying to figure out how he can get rid of him. I don't know. Maybe I'm putting too much into it and there's nothing behind his look other than him being glad I'm okay.

When Tucker and Xander leave, they both hug me. Xander gives me a quick kiss on the forehead, something he's never done. They both look back at me before they walk out the door, as if this may be the last time they see me and they want to remember me. I smile at them, trying to reassure them. They smile back and walk out the door.

"Hello, boys," I hear my mom say from out in the hall.

"Hello, Mrs. Evans," They both say to her.

They must be caught in an awkward silence because I don't hear any of them say anything, then my mom is walking through the door.

"How are you feeling?" she asks me.

"I'm still sore. And tired," I tell her.

"Okay well, you can go to sleep for the night. I will make sure none of the nurses bother you."

I really don't want to stay in the hospital any longer than I have to so I ask, "Can I go home?"

My mom frowns like she doesn't think this is a good idea. Her eyebrows knit together and her mouth, which is set in a firm line, moves from side to side. Finally she says, "I have to work, Casslyn. I can take you home, but I won't be able to stay with you. You don't want to just stay here for the night?"

"I'd really rather go home. Sleep in my own bed. I feel uncomfortable here."

My mom takes a breath, sighs, then nods her head once and says, "Okay. Let me go check you out."

"Thanks, mom," I tell her before she leaves.

She smiles at me, a smile that reminds me of my childhood, of happier times, then it slips away as she walks out the door.

Thirteen

On our way home, I try my best to pay attention to the route I took last night. To see where and how everything went wrong. The road has dried and I can see the tracks Xander's car made the other night. When we pass Logan's house I get a rush of feelings. I wonder what he is doing, if he is thinking of me, if he wonders how I am doing. But then I get back to the task at hand. I ask my mom to slow down, telling her the ride is making me sick. She tells me we are almost home but slows down anyway. I pay close attention to the swerving of my tracks and try to find the other vehicle's tracks, but there is nothing. No tracks but my own. That can't be right. I know there was another vehicle. I didn't make it up. I know that I was run off the road.

I close my eyes and concentrate, finally able to remember the details from the other night. I was looking to Logan's house and when I turned back to the road, there were headlights barreling down on me. Headlights, where before there were none. The driver of the other vehicle swerves onto my side of the road. But it's not because of the wet road, they did it intentionally. I open my eyes and try to forget about someone trying to kill me, about almost dying.

My mom and I walk into the front door of our house and it is like stepping into an alternate world. Someone else's world. Like I'm a visitor, an outsider. I can watch, but I can't participate.

Every step hurts. The slightest movement sends needles of pain shooting to every nerve ending in my body.

"I'm going to go up to bed and sleep," I tell my mom.

"Okay, sweetheart. I'll put your pain pills and a glass of water on the counter. Make sure you take them in two hours. If you need anything at all, make sure you call me. Or your dad. Or Xander or Tucker. But if you need anything at all, call someone. Don't hesitate."

"Did you tell dad?" I ask mom.

My mom's eyes dart around the room, landing on many things but me. Finally, she says, "Yes I did. He's working, but he thought he should be able to stop by sometime tonight."

I am crestfallen. I could have died and my dad would rather stay at work than come see me. I shouldn't be surprised. This is what my life has come to. "Okay."

"Listen, I need to get back to work. Are you sure you're going to be okay by yourself?"

"I'll be fine. Anyway, when I wake up from my nap I'll call Xander and Tucker to come over. Don't worry about me, mom."

"I'm your mom, it's my job to worry," she says, but she smiles and walks towards the door.

I wait for her to leave then head slowly up to my bedroom. The stairs hurt more than walking straight. When I step up it feels as if the stitches will rip out of my skin. It takes me minutes to climb the sixteen stairs and when I finally make it up them, I have to take a break before heading to my room. As I walk closer to my room a deep sensation rushes through me. I tingle in the places Logan touched me. I walk through my bedroom door to find Logan sitting in the chair by my bed. Surprised does not begin to explain the way I feel upon seeing him. I am startled but too tired to react. I smile but it only reaches half of my face because it scares me to wonder how he got into my house. I contemplate running screaming from him, or throwing myself into his arms for saving my life, but settle for walking over to my bed and carefully placing my damaged body onto my bed.

"Should I even ask how you got into my house?" I ask.

Logan looks at me with a pained look when he sees the brace on my wrist. But the look is quickly replaced by a stone cold look of hatred, which again is quickly replaced indifference.

"Nope," he says.

I rest my head on my headboard and close my eyes. I can feel him stare at me, but instead of it being creepy, it's soothing. I place my arms over my stomach. The fingers of my injured hand search out the bracelet surounding my other wrist and rub circles into the cool metal of the pendant.

"Why are you here?" I ask, though I want to kick myself for it. I'm no longer afraid or creeped out by Logan. Xander and Tucker don't know it, and won't understand, but Logan saved my life, he couldn't possibly be a bad guy. And there is a growing part of me that wants him here.

My mattress shifts and when I open my eyes, Logan sits on the edge of my bed. He leans in close, staring deep into my eyes and says, "I wanted to make sure you're okay."

My heart stutters and my stomach does a flip. "Really?"

He nods and leans back. "How are you feeling?" Logan's tenderness takes me by surprise. How can he be so intensely frightening one moment then soft and tender the next? How can he scare so many people, but make me feel so strongly for him?

"Okay," I tell him. "I ache pretty much everywhere, but I think I'm going to make it. No thanks to you."

He looks away from me and returns to my chair. I miss his closeness as soon as it's gone. I can't explain what he makes me feel, but whenever he is close to me, or whenever he touches me, my skin tingles and every nerve ending in my body is alive and on fire. It feels amazing. I wonder if he feels it too. I hope he does. I wonder if he feels anything for me. I hope he does.

"How did you find me?" I ask him.

He looks as if he doesn't want to answer me, but says, "I heard the crash, came outside to see what it was, then took you to the hospital." He doesn't say any more than that.

I didn't realize my pulse picked up but I am able to calm down and say, "Sorry I'm such a damsel in distress. I'll work on that."

Logan's eyes narrow and he cocks his head as if he is confused. "What?"

"Well you've saved me four times now. Twice with Ashley. When I passed out in the dress shop. And then the other night."

He just stares at me. He doesn't say you're welcome. He doesn't say it was no problem, that he was glad to do it. He doesn't say anything. His silence makes me nervous and leads me to say, "I just wanted to say thank you."

Logan is still quiet and I think he's not going to say anything, but then he says, "You're welcome."

I can't help but smile. I never thought I'd want or even need a knight in shining armor but maybe I do, and maybe it's not such a bad thing.

"But like I said, I'll try to no longer be a damsel in distress."

I thought this would make Logan laugh, maybe smile at the least, but it makes him angry. He stands up abruptly and looks sternly down at me. "Don't say that," he says.

"What's wrong?" I ask, almost frightened of him. I

shrink into my bed as he looms over me. So much for feeling comfortable, or even safe, in his presence.

"You're not a damsel in distress. And I'm nobody's fantasy. I'm not about to be yours," he roars and storms out of my room.

"I was just trying to thank you," I say in his wake.

I'm more exhausted than I was when I arrived home. Logan fills me with life, but he can also take a lot out of me. All I want to do it fall fast asleep, but what Logan said haunts me. I didn't ask him to be my fantasy. I don't expect him to be. So why does he think that's what I want? And if it is what I want, why does it bother him so much? My mind is consumed with troubling thoughts. Thoughts of Logan. Thoughts of my accident the other night. Thoughts of my brother and my best friends and my parents. They all run together until finally exhaustion overtakes me and I am able to fall asleep.

When I wake up, the house is dark. I am in more pain than when I got home. I get out of bed, hobble to the kitchen and down my pain pills. My phone sits next to the medicine bottle and a flashing light indicates a missed call. It's from my dad, and there is a message. I dial my voicemail and listen, "Hey sweetie, it's Dad. I'm so sorry to hear about your accident, but I'm happy to hear that you are okay. I'm sorry, but I can't make it tonight, I have to pull a double shift. I promise I will make it up to you. Get some rest kiddo. Bye."

My mom instructed me to take my pills with food. Walking to the fridge, I open it and rummage through it till I find ingredients for a sandwich. Once it's made I grab my cell phone and head for the living room. I turn the TV on and flip through channels till I find something to fancy my interest. I land on an episode of *Supernatural*, one where Sam and Dean go back to the past and have to take down a phoenix in human form.

I doze off on the couch. Images flash through my mind. Nash. Blinding headlights. Fire. Xander. Tucker. Logan. The images flash faster and faster, then slow down until there is only one. Logan and I are back in my bedroom, right when I came home from the hospital.

"Should I ask how you got into my house?" I ask him, getting the familiar rush of emotions and desire.

"Nope," Logan says, a cocky grin on his face.

I just smile and walk over to my bed. Luckily, dream world is more forgiving than the real world and I have no pain. But the accident still happened, and Logan's tenderness is still there. "Why are you here?"

"I wanted to make sure you are okay," Logan says, sitting next to me on my bed. He leans close and smiles.

"Really?" I ask, my heart rate spiking.

Logan nods but this time he doesn't lean back. "How are you feeling?"

"I'm okay now. No thanks to you."

"Is that so?" Logan asks, one side of his mouth lifting up, his tone playful.

My toes curl and it takes all of me not to giggle. "Yes," I say, breathlessly.

"And how is it you reward those who save you?" he asks, leaning in even closer.

My breathing stops and I close my eyes waiting for the explosion of electricity I know I will feel when our lips touch. But just when we are about to make contact, we are interrupted by a shrill ringing.

My eyes snap open. My breathing is ragged, thanks to the anticipation of kissing Logan. Stupid dream. The TV is off and it is now light outside. No way did I sleep all the way through the night. The clock on the wall says it is now four in the afternoon. The ringing sounds again. I turn my head to see my phone lit up, a call coming in from Tucker.

"Hello?" I say into the phone.

Tucker, in his ever chipper voice says, "Hey! How are you feeling? We missed you in school today."

Right. It's Monday. And I missed school. I can't believe mom let me get away with missing a day of school. I've never missed a day of school in my life, well if I don't count the month I missed after my first accident.

I move my body and am sore everywhere. My muscles ache, leaning forward on my bruised stomach stirs the sandwich I ate last night, my head hurts, and my knee could use a new bandage. I'm really glad I didn't go to school today. If moving inches causes me this much pain, I can't imagine what three floors and many rambunctious students would do to me.

"As good as can be expected I should think," I tell him.

"Good, good," Tucker says, but he sounds distracted.

"Uh-huh. Why don't you tell me what you really want to tell me?"

"You noticed that huh?"

"Tucker, you're about as subtle as dynamite."

Tucker laughs but it's not genuine. "Well. Don't get mad. I really shouldn't be telling you this."

"Spit it out, Tucker."

"Okay, okay. You missed school today. And Logan missed school today. Xander has it in his head that Logan ran you off the road the other night and he missed school today to cover it up, or spy on you some more."

Of course that is what Xander would think. Though I find it odd that Logan would have missed school. Maybe I really pissed him off last night. But why would that make him miss school? I don't know what has gotten into Xander lately. He has never been this protective before, or this suspicious of anyone. Sure, I thought Logan was a little sketchy when he first came to school, but now I know he's not a bad guy. I wish Xander would give him a chance. Maybe if Xander gave Logan a chance, got to know him, then we could all be friends. Yeah right.

"Tucker, I can assure you Logan had nothing to do with running me off the road. And anyway, how does Xander know I was run off the road? I never told you guys that."

"It's Xander. You know where his mind goes lately. But wait, you were run off the road, I thought you just slid in the mud."

"I didn't want to worry you guys. But I swear, Logan

didn't run me off the road."

"How do you know that? And didn't want to worry us? We're your best friends, it's our job to worry. Being run off the road is a little more serious than sliding in the mud. Not to mention it's something we need to know about. You can't keep something like this a secret from us."

"Look, I'm sorry. Next time something like this happens, I will let you know. And I know because he saved me. Logan pulled me out of the car and raced me to the hospital. I wouldn't be here if it weren't for him. Logan really is a good guy."

"Holy crap that is so romantic. And I agree with you. I have always thought he was a good guy. But try convincing Xander of that."

"Ugh," I sigh loudly into the phone.

"Yeah," Tucker says.

My phone beeps. I pull it away from my ear to see I have an incoming call.

"You'll never guess who is calling me," I say to Tucker.

"Good luck," Tucker says.

Pressing the call button, I say, "Hi, Xander."

"How are you feeling?" he asks. I want to be upset with him but there is pure concern in his voice and it makes it difficult.

My anger reverts and I tell him, "I'm fine. Still sore but I'll live."

"I should have made you stay. I can't believe I let you leave."

"Xander, I told you before, it wasn't your fault. You could have never known that would have happened."

"I swear it was that Logan. He has been watching you too closely since he got here. And you were run off the road right by his house." I'm surprised it took him this long to bring it up.

"I really don't want to get into this, Xander. You know I don't share your opinion so I wish you wouldn't bring it up." I feel that Xander should know that Logan saved my life, that he may finally give Logan a chance, but I'm tight lipped and say nothing.

"I'm just trying to protect you and keep you safe, is that such a bad thing?" Xander asks, but before I can say anything the line goes dead.

Great. Now Xander is pissed off at me. I'm the one who almost died in a car accident, but still I'm the one who has to appease my best friends, keep the peace. Why can't I catch a break?

I take more pain pills and fall back into a deep slumber.

Fourteen

Over a week passes without so much as a glance from Logan. Xander looks at me but won't talk to me. Luckily I still have Tucker in my corner. If I didn't, I wouldn't have anyone to talk to. Although it's not like Tucker approves of our fighting, so he's not the most accommodating when it comes to conversing.

Everything has changed. Ashley, who was bitchy before, has stepped her torture up to a whole new level. Logan, who besides the fact that he won't talk to me or even look at me, looks exhausted. His usually bronze skin is now pale and there are dark circles under his eyes. Xander, who also won't talk to me, has gained this look about him that if I didn't know him better, I would call malice. And worst of all, he has started spending time with Ashley. Not to mention the fact that when she feels particularly spiteful, neither Logan nor Xander have my back. I didn't think I needed either of them so much, but now that I don't have them, I feel two holes in my heart.

Tucker has remained loyal to me, but it is hard for me to ask him to choose between his two best friends. But then again, Xander is being stupid. I have every right to keep Tucker to myself. So why do I feel so bad about it?

My life is going to Hell in a hand basket. What's new? At least it's an artfully crafted hand basket. I'm sure Satan is amused.

This is what fills my mind as I sit at my work station waiting for the suckfest that Home Ec. has become. It is hard to come up with a final project when your partner won't talk to you. Of course, there wouldn't be an issue if Nash was my partner, which he was supposed to be, but he isn't here and life must go on. If only he was here.

I feel Logan's presence in the room before he sits down beside me. Great. All I need right now is an hour of silence.

And that is exactly what I think I'm going to get when I hear, "Hi, Casslyn."

My breath catches in my throat. My brows pull together sharply, my head snaps in his direction. How could two words affect me so deeply? His eyes bore into mine and I melt.

I open my mouth to say hi back, to tell him to kiss me, to say anything at all, then think better of it. He can't go over a week without speaking to me then say hi to me and expect me to crawl into his gloriously large, sculpted arms, even though that is exactly what I want to do. And then there's the fact that a longing for him to kiss me passed through my head. The guy saves my life and suddenly I'm in love with him?

I am so pathetic.

I turn away from Logan and stare intently at my hands.

"Casslyn?" His voice is so deep and smooth it takes all of my willpower to keep from looking at his gorgeous face. I am in so much trouble.

I glance up at my two best friends, hoping for some semblance of . . . something. I don't know what I'm hoping for, but I certainly don't find it. Tucker is grinning like an idiot. And Xander. Well, Xander gives me a look that speaks volumes as to where our friendship stands, volumes that are far too loud. I'll be lucky if Xander ever speaks to me again. This whole mess makes me wonder if even talking to Logan is worth it. I need my best friends more than I need a boy. But the way Logan makes me feel. The way my body reacts whenever he is near, when he enters a room. The way my heart races when his fingers touch my skin. The way I lose my breath just to better hear him speak. The way I don't think about anything, don't worry about anything when he has my attention. Maybe I need him more than I thought.

"How is your day going?" he asks.

And that is the crack that bursts the dam. I turn to him with fury in my eyes. I may need him, but right now I am pissed. "Are you serious?" I want to yell but I'm in a class full of my peers that would love nothing more than to have one more thing to make fun of me for. My tone is clear in my whisper. "You save my life without taking credit for it. You come to my house just to make sure I'm okay, then freak out for some reason I can't even fathom. Then you don't talk to me for over a week, and now you want to have a stupid chat about absolutely nothing. I don't think so."

Logan closes his eyes and rolls his shoulders back like he did that day in my room. It must be his way of relieving stress, or calming himself, or possibly getting himself in check so he doesn't say something he doesn't want to. Who knows. I don't care right now. I wish he would just blow up at me. This guarded, controlled Logan is getting us nowhere.

"I'm sorry," he says.

I lay on the snark as I say, "Oh? Whatever for?"

Logan looks deep into my eyes and says, "Everything."

Well, damn.

My shoulders slump. Defeated. Fuck. I can't hold on to my anger. Why can't I hold onto my anger? Be angry Casslyn. *Be angry.* One look. That's all it takes for him to make me forget everything I've felt this week. Logan's neglect. Xander's anger. Ashley's contempt, torture, whatever you want to call it. One look and I know my feelings for him have turned from Logan-is-hot to Logan-makes-me-feel-special. Ugh.

I look away from Logan's fiery blue eyes. One more second and I might lose all of my resolve. I've already said too much. I reach for the bracelet around my wrist and play with the cord, trying to distract myself.

"Casslyn," Logan whispers directly into my ear. He is way too close. His breath is hot on my skin. Way too close. "Look at me, Casslyn."

I turn so slowly it might as well take me an hour. When I finally face him he is barely an inch from me. My chest is heavy and won't cooperate when I try to make it do its job. I nearly yank the bracelet from my wrist I'm so startled by Logan's proximity. One side of his mouth pulls up and his eyes blaze. He is sexy as Hell.

"I'm sorry," he says. "Let me make it up to you."

My brows arch up and I say, "How?"

"Hang out with me tonight. We can grab a bit to eat, go . . . somewhere. I guess I don't really know what this town has for hang out spots."

"We could go to the bowling alley. They have food, an arcade, bowling."

The other side of his mouth lifts up and he says, "I'll pick you up later."

Despite myself, I smile. My heart pounds in my chest. Races. There is pressure in my head, tunnel vision. I'm dizzy but so euphoric. I have a date with Logan. I haven't been this happy since Nash was alive. Would it be crazy of me to think that Logan could erase my pain? He is doing a good job of it so far.

"Now," he says, "What are we going to cook for our final project?"

I smile, thinking that fifteen minutes ago this was one of the too many things weighing on me. "I was thinking we could make chicken and shrimp alfredo."

Logan chuckles and says, "What is with you and pasta?"

"I think I was an Italian in another life."

Logan's eyebrows knit together. He has worry written on his face. It was supposed to be a joke. Again, he rolls his shoulders back but then smiles and says, "Maybe."

***

Tucker and I walk towards our lockers after the bell rings. He still has the idiot grin on his face. "Tell me what happened. Don't leave out a single detail."

"He asked me out. Tonight."

As quickly as words can fall out of a person's mouth, Tucker says, "OMG, that is amazing. I am so jealous. He is so hot. Where are you going? What are you doing?"

"Slow down, Tucker. Listen, please don't tell Xander." Just saying so dampens my mood, but I refuse to let Xander ruin my night with Logan. If Xander won't come to his senses, then forget him. If he wants to let a sixteen-year friendship go down the drain, then so be it.

"No problem. You're already not talking, I wouldn't want to add to it," Tucker says, a drop in his voice. I know he feels the strain on our relationship and I wish he didn't have to.

"Thanks."

"No problem. So, no offense, because, well . . . I love

you. But as your best friend I feel it is allowed for me to ask how you got the hottest guy in school to ask you out."

"Ha," I laugh out loud. "I honestly don't know, but thanks for the self-esteem booster."

He smiles and wrinkles his face in an I'm-so-funny look. "What am I here for if not to keep you grounded?"

"Because I have such a big head," I say and give him the same look.

"Hey, when you date the hottest guy *ever* it is bound to happen."

"Ha ha ha," Tucker and I turn to the direction of snide, sinister laughter coming from, who else, Ashley. "Like you could get a date with the hottest guy ever, let alone the ugliest guy. Pray tell, who is this oh so lucky guy?"

My eyes shift from Ashley to her posse surrounding her. My heart falls when I see Xander behind her. He drops his gaze when he sees me looking at him. I can't even fathom what is going on in his head. I don't understand why he hates me purely because I refuse to hate Logan. I don't understand why he could throw away everything we have been through for something so stupid.

I sidestep and try to skirt around Ashley, but she pulls the same move and blocks my way. "Well Ugly Duckling, who is the lucky guy?"

That dumb bitch just called me the Ugly Duckling, jokes on her. "You're calling me the Ugly Duckling?"

"Yeah. You got a problem with that?"

"Other that the fact that it is I 'have' a problem with that, it's not much of an insult. I'm a swan, bitch."

Ashley's mouth drops open, struck dumbfounded. She is so confused and I love it. Plus, it doesn't hurt that Xander snorts laughter.

"Yeah, once you figure that out you can get back to me," I say and walk away.

"Did you see the look on her face?" Tucker says. "Priceless. Her retaliation is going to suck though."

"I'll deal with that once it comes. Tonight is my night and I am going to enjoy myself."

Tucker smirks and says, "Sure you are. I'm sure you're going to enjoy a little Logan action too."

I smile but say nothing more. We walk out of the school, my anticipation growing stronger.

"Have fun tonight," Tucker says, hugs me, and walks towards his car.

I head toward the bus and am about to get on when I hear, "Can I give you a ride home?" Xander. Great.

Fifteen

"I think I'll take the bus," I say, my eyebrows wrinkled.

I turn away from him and step onto the bus, but he says, "Please, Cass. I just want to talk."

Despite my anger towards him, Xander is my best friend. And despite him turning his back on me, I can't do the same to him.

"Fine," I say, walking to his car, as far ahead of him as I can.

He catches up with me and opens my door for me. Good for him. I get in the car and cross my arms, waiting for him to get in the driver's side. His new car suits this new Xander. Hard and rigid. Uncaring.

Xander starts the car and pulls out of the school parking

lot. An awkward silence falls over us. Nothing has ever been awkward or forced between the two of us. It just goes to show how far we have fallen. I stare straight ahead waiting for the ten miles to pass and this train wreck of a car ride to be over. I feel Xander's gaze on me. I don't feel like giving him the satisfaction of looking back at him.

Until now, I'd never felt a ten-mile drive pass so slowly. Xander tries to talk to me after a while, asking me things like, "How is your week going?" and "What's new?" but I have no answers for him. If he still acted like my best friend he wouldn't need to ask me those questions, he would already know the answers.

When we drive past Logan's house Xander's eyes stay firmly in front of us. But between there and my house, he slows the car and peers into the field where his car landed. Because of the late rain, the farmer who owns the field hasn't gotten to harvest. There is a mowed path of corn stalks where Xander's car rolled. The memory of that night hits me and I have to look away.

Xander notices my unease and says, "Are you okay," knowing full well that I am not. "This is the place isn't it?"

I nod but do not speak. I know my voice will give out if I do.

"Did you ever find out who it was that saved you?"

I think about telling him that it was Logan. It might settle Xander's hatred for him. We could be friends again. But I know Xander. I know that when he puts his mind to something, nothing can change it. I shake my head, again saying nothing.

Xander pulls through the lane to my house and cuts the engine. I get out of the car without saying thank you or even looking at him. I know he will follow. He may be a different Xander now, but he is still a gentleman. I unlock my front door, walk through, and leave it open for him to follow me.

I throw my bag on the couch and move to the kitchen for a Mountain Dew. Xander quietly follows me. Patience has never been one of his strong suits but he is the one who wanted to talk so he can wait. I think about going back into the living room and taking a seat, but think better of it, the way Xander and I have been *talking* lately is a bit more suited to the kitchen.

I take a long pull of my Mountain Dew, only slightly wishing it was alcohol, and turn to Xander. The look on his face displays more emotions than I would have thought were plaguing him; anger, sadness, fear, joy, relief.

His shoulders slump and he says, "God I've missed you."

"Whose fault is that, Xander?" my voice is raised, I can't help it. I am not wrong and he needs to know it.

"Mine. I know," he yells too. I knew we couldn't just talk.

"Then what the Hell is wrong with you? You hate Logan for no reason what so ever. You pick fights with me over Logan for no reason. You stop talking to me for no reason. You start spending time with Ashley, *of all people*. And for what reason? Why, Xander?"

His chest heaves up and down. He stares at me then turns away. Instead of answering any of my questions or commenting on any of my criticisms, he says, "I know about your date with *him*."

"What of it? How is it any of your business or concern?" I ask him, sick of his nonstop harping on the Logan topic. Frankly, I'm tired of it all.

"He's dangerous, Casslyn. Why can't you see that? What is it going to take?" he crosses the room and takes my arms in his hands. His grip is rough like if he holds me tight enough, even if he shakes me, I may come to my senses.

"Let go of me," I say firmly.

"Casslyn, please, don't be with him."

"Why not?"

Without thinking Xander says, "Because I love you." He pauses, realizing what he has just admitted and says, "Because I'm in love with you."

I don't know what to say. How does one react to their best friend telling them they're in love with them? My head pounds and I can't catch my breath. I walk around to the other side of the island. I need to put some space between Xander and I.

I begin to speak, needing to say something, but not knowing what to say. "I . . . I . . . I . . . you . . . I . . . I don't know what to say."

"I know this is a lot and I'm sorry to just throw it on you. I don't know what else to say but that I'm sorry."

"How long? How long have you felt this way?"

"About forever. Since we were kids. Nash figured it out. I still can't believe he didn't say anything to you. I was afraid to say anything because I didn't want to ruin our friendship. I wanted to so bad, but every time I tried I got so nervous and afraid you would turn me down I panicked and couldn't do it. And the longer I went without telling you the harder it got to try to bring it up. Then you and Nash got in the accident and I thought I lost you. . . I couldn't deal. I went ballistic. When my mom told me, I tore apart my whole room and half of our house. When I saw you in that hospital bed, so broken, I . . ." he lowers his head and stops speaking.

"Why didn't you tell me?" I ask, knowing he's already told me, but I still don't know what to say.

"Because you lost your brother. What was I supposed to say? 'I'm sorry Nash died but I love you and I want you to be with me.' How selfish is that?"

"I don't know what to say," I say for I swear the twelfth time.

Xander shrugs, raises his eyebrows, smiles a half smile, and says, "You could tell me how you feel."

How I feel. How do I feel? I've never thought about Xander in that way. Obviously he's had a lot of time to think about this and suddenly he tells me he loves me and I'm just supposed to know exactly how I feel right away? I don't know how I feel. I need time to think. My heart feels heavy. My vision is blurry. I have a panicky, caged in, ick going through me.

I look at Xander, who has this puppy dog face. Pure hope

in his eyes. The seconds tick by. I know, with every second, as I'm sure Xander is catching on, that I can't give him the answer he is looking for. I do love him. As a best friend. As a confidant. As a person I can tell my deepest secrets to. As a quarter of the foursome that keeps me together. But do I love him the way he loves me? Do I have romantic feelings for him? I search my soul, thinking of all the times we've spent together, everything we have shared. Xander has been a part of my everything for my whole life and I do love him. But not in the way he loves me. Sure, he's good looking. Yes, he treats me better than anyone. Without a doubt, he looks after me. But I'm not attracted to him. I don't imagine us kissing or in the throes of passion.

"I'm sorry. I do love you. You know that. Just not the same way. I'm so sorry, Xander." My heart hurts. I can't imagine how he feels.

His face falls. His heart is breaking and it is all my fault. I know rejection and he wears it well. I reach for him but he flinches away from me as if I have shocked him. So much for getting my best friend back.

Xander blinks rapidly, trying to keep tears at bay. He bites his lip then says, "I should go."

He walks up to me, looks me deep in the eyes, and breaks my heart. He places a hand on either side of my face, leans down, and plants a kiss on my forehead. I close my eyes and tears roll down my cheeks. "Just be careful, okay. You're important to me."

"I'm so sorry, Xander," I say.

"I know," he says, and walks away from me and out of my house.

I collapse onto the kitchen floor. I try to breathe deep to calm myself but all I get are short, chopped breaths. I've never had a panic attack before but I feel on the verge of one. *I will not cry. I will not cry.* I tell myself this over and over. It doesn't work well, but it works.

My phone rings from my bag in the living room. I actually crawl from the kitchen into the living room. Something I haven't done since I could walk. I pull my phone from the side pocket of my bag and look at the caller id. My mother. I can't talk to her right now. She'd hear my strained voice, ask if I was okay, and that would be the end of it. She wouldn't leave work for me. She wouldn't buy me ice cream and sit on the couch with me watching sad movies and crying. No, she wouldn't, because Nash was her favorite and he is no longer here. And how am I supposed to compete with my dead brother?

I lie on the floor of my living room, clutching my cell to my chest. It's times like these I need my brother most. He would know what to say, or what not to say. He would hug me, or punch me in the arm and tell me to get over myself. I can't breathe without my brother. I need him more than I've needed anyone. And he's not here. Why couldn't I have been the one to die in that accident?

I lie on the floor and hum to myself. Music soothes me. It keeps me sane in times like this. When emotions threaten to pull me under. The humming gets a little louder. A melody forms. Words overlap until my eyes are closed and I'm lulling myself into a sense of calm singing *She Will Be Loved* by Maroon Five.

My phone rings in my hand. I don't want to answer it, figuring it's my mother again, but open my eyes and look at it anyway. Tucker. He I can talk to.

"Are you okay?" he asks before I can say hello.

"He loves me."

"I know, sweetie."

"And you didn't tell me?"

"It wasn't my place. You're my best friends. You two put me in the middle enough, I wasn't putting myself there."

"What am I going to do, Tucker?" I ask, pulling myself into a seated position.

"I don't know, Cassie. This one's hard."

"Tell me about it."

"For the time being, I suggest you get ready for your date tonight."

"Right. I've got to go," I tell him. I stand up and head for the stairs.

"Smile, Cassie. It's going to be okay," Tucker says. I almost cry. That is exactly what Nash would have said.

I pull myself together enough to get in the shower.

Sixteen

I get out of the shower in a daze. Xander is in love with me. How could I have missed this? How could my brother and my best friend have known and I didn't? Could I have known and disregarded it? No. I did not know. I would have done something about it. Maybe I would have loved him back if I had known. Maybe. But would I have? Yes, I love Xander. But as a best friend. As a confidant. As so many things. But romantic love? Again I try to delve deep into the recesses of my heart, try to find some spark, some gut wrenching feeling that I know I love Xander. But as hard as I search, there is nothing. No fire. No desperate need to take him in my arms, his mouth to mine.

There is a feeling in me that wants to want him. But

nothing like the deep seeded need and want that I have for Logan. A single touch from Logan sets my skin ablaze. The longing looks he gives me stop my breath. Tonight I have a date with him. Something I have wanted since the day he walked into my English class. Even if I didn't know it at the time. I'm not going to let anything spoil this night for me. I will worry about it tomorrow. I will break down tomorrow.

Rampantly, I rummage through my closet. I have many clothes and yet nothing seems good enough. He has seen all of my looks. The baggy, the tight, the short, the long, the mismatched, the put together. Nothing I have will wow him, surprise him, excite him. That is, until I reach into the far corner of my closet and find a dress I have all but forgotten. A grey t-shirt dress with lime green stripes, long sleeves, a mini skirt, and a lime green belt. It is almost too perfect. It fits me almost too well. Accentuating what curves I have. I pair the dress with knee high lace up combat boots. The perfect combination of formal and edge.

I descend the stairs anticipating the look on Logan's face when he sees me. When I get to the living room, I do not expect to find Logan resting against the back of my couch, but that is what I find. My heart flutters at the sight of him. He is wearing fitted dark blue jeans, a tight black v-neck t-shirt, and a grey vest. I never would have thought a vest could be so sexy. My breath hitches in my throat and from across the room I can hear his do the same. He is caught off guard and I am proud of myself for it.

But then he catches himself and is very serious. "There

was someone here," he says.

"Yeah," I say. "It was Xander."

"He upset you." It is not a question.

How could he possibly know Xander was here or that he had upset me? "I don't want to talk about it."

Before I know what is happening, Logan is mere inches from me, cupping my face in his hands. "Did he hurt you? Are you okay?" the quiver in his voice suggests panic, but he has a hard look in his eyes.

"I'm fine. I promise." I say pulling from his grasp and spinning around in place so that he might inspect me. His concern warms my heart. I don't think I will ever get used to his hot and cold demeanor. "See? Just fine."

I see a hint of a smile play at Logan's lips and again my heart flutters.

He holds out a hand to me and says, "Shall we go?"

"Yes."

Logan opens my front door and leads me outside. I step off the porch and am assaulted by a start of the nightmares that have plagued me for the past several months. An exact replica of the motorcycle Nash got for our birthday. My breathing stops and so does time. I am blinded by headlights swerving in our direction. There is no way the driver of the truck tried to get out of the way. Then I am crushed by the bike and my skin is alight with flames. My body is on fire but I do not feel the heat. Why can't I feel it? The bike weighs on me and I cannot breathe.

"Casslyn," Nash calls out.

But that is not his voice.

"Casslyn," he calls out again.

"Nash," I try to scream but it catches in my throat. "Nash!"

"Casslyn." This time the voice is closer, right next to me.

I look over with dead, blank eyes, at Logan.

"Casslyn?" his voice again displays panic. "What is it?"

I just stare, not able to actually see him and say, "I'm not riding on that," and walk back into my house.

As soon as the door is closed behind me I sink to the floor and begin to weep. Not tears falling down my cheeks, something Logan might find cute, but hard sobs that wrack my whole body. Because weeping is different than crying. It takes your whole body to weep.

I don't hear the door open but suddenly I smell the fresh scent of rain and know that Logan is in the room. My skin sings where he touches me. He picks me up and we begin moving. Then he sets me down.

"Casslyn, speak to me," his voice is controlled, hiding his panic.

I ignore him, continuing to sob. But Logan is patient with me, running his hands down my back and over my arms, waiting for me to explain myself.

When I have finally gained an ounce of control over my body and speech, I say, "My brother died on one of those bikes. I almost died that night, trapped under the bike. When I saw yours, it all came rushing back to me."

Logan is silent for a long time then finally says. "My God, Casslyn, I am so sorry. I had no idea." There is deep sincerity in his voice. For a moment I thought this might all be a cruel joke played by my classmates. Use the new kid to make the crazy chick have a break down. But unless Logan is the world's greatest actor, he really didn't know.

I have no words for him. I don't feel alive right now. I don't want to be alive right now. Not without Nash. But then Logan strokes my arm again, and sparks fly through my body. At least it wants to live.

"I know this sounds crazy," Logan begins, "but would you still like to spend the evening with me?"

I look up at him, into eyes of blue fire, and can't help but want to spend as much time with him as I possibly can. Somehow, in some unfathomable way, Logan brings peace to my life. He makes me want to live. When I am around him, I can actually breathe again. I swallow hard and say, "Yes."

"We could stay here if you'd like," he suggests.

I would like nothing more than to spend the evening with him, alone, in my house. I would be safe. It would be easy. But I would not be living my life. "No," I say. "Let's go out, like we planned."

"Really?" Logan asks, surprise written on his face.

"Really," I say, with resolve.

"Give me fifteen minutes and I can have a new vehicle."

"We could take my car," I offer, the thought coming out of nowhere.

Logan lifts an eyebrow, mulling it over.

"Well, it's at my dad's but I have the keys and he did tell me he wanted me to come get it." There is no way in Hell I am about to drive that car, but if Logan drives it, then we could still get it and kill two birds with one stone.

Logan continues to think it over, then says, "No, no. I will get your car tomorrow. But tonight just let me fix this one thing."

I nod, consenting to his plan. He leaves and within fifteen minutes he is back, with an H3 of all things, and we are headed into town.

The H3 is decked out in more safety gadgets than on any vehicle I have ever seen.

"What's with the armored car? Are you excepting to wreck it?" I ask him, joking.

"You were almost-you almost died, I thought you needed something safe," he says.

"You were going to take me on a motorcycle."

"You would have been holding on to me. It would have been perfectly safe."

"That makes no sense," I tell him, then drop the subject and instead ask,"How long have you had this thing?"

"Not long," he says with a shrug of his shoulder, almost as if he is ending the conversation.

We ride most of the way in silence. It is not an uncomfortable silence. But a pensive silence. I can't begin to fathom what Logan is thinking about, but he stares out at the road, concentrating hard. Once in a while he glances at me, but it is brief, and never a full look. My mind shifts from how he reacted to my freak out, the accident that I now am convinced was no accident, or that second accident that I now don't think was an accident, Xander telling me he loves me, Tucker saying he and Nash knew all along, my parents love, or lack thereof, Xander spending time with Ashley and her bitch troupe, his sudden transformation, and his crazy reaction to Logan. No wonder I have a headache.

I mindlessly give Logan directions to the bowling alley. But when we get there I scold myself. Tonight is about Logan and me. I need to focus on him, and get him to focus on me.

Logan stops the car, gets out, and walks over to my side. When he opens the door I swing my legs out for him to ogle. The mini skirt makes them look longer than they actually are. I get my way, noticing him stare at me. But then he catches himself and helps me the rest of the way out of the car.

"Thanks," I say, looking up at him with my eyes only, my head tilted down. Way girly.

Logan stares at me intently. Just that has me breathing heavily. I smile involuntarily. Could there actually be a chance that the hottest guy in school is interested in me?

We walk into the bowling alley and take a table between the lanes and the bar. I smile again because, while the bowling alley may not be the most romantic place for a first date, it feels right. Logan gets us rental shoes, then we order food. Again, bar food may not be the most romantic, but I love it, so no complaints from me.

I strip from my combat boots and exchange them for the bowling shoes. Logan does the same with his boots.

"Am I about to be put to shame?" he asks me.

"Excuse me?"

"I've never bowled before. And I'm not very good at losing."

My mouth drops open in shock. "You've never bowled before? How can this be? How have you never bowled in your entire life. Whatever. Don't worry, there's nothing to it. Also, I've never even gotten a score of one hundred so you have nothing to worry about."

"So, you'll show me how to do it?"

I wink at Logan and say, "You're in good hands."

I take my time finding the perfect ball. I prefer a certain color and weight so it takes a bit to find the right one. But when I do, I sashay to the lane we are using, turn back to Logan and say, "Watch closely." A one sided grin lights up his face, paired with that devilish grin I have come to love. He raises his eyebrows and his gaze moves downward. "Don't stare at my ass," I say playfully.

Logan laughs and then contorts his face so that he looks like the perfect student; attentive and astute. I turn back around, smiling, and march toward the lane, swing the ball back, forward, then let it go. It rolls down the lane, curves so far I think it may go in the gutter, then curves back to the middle of the lane then hits the first pin. Somehow, every one of the pins falls down in a strike. I stand there, flabbergasted, not able to believe I got a strike on the first throw. I throw my arms up, shriek, and do a little happy dance. Then realize I am not alone, stop, completely embarrassed, and turn around to see Logan laughing at my spectacle.

Placing my face in my hands, I say, "I can't believe I just did that, I am so embarrassed."

Logan chuckles again then says, "Don't be. It was cute. So are your red cheeks."

"Shut up."

Logan picks a ball at random then steps up to the lane, and bowls. He knocks down four pins and walks back to the table. I bowl again, knock down eight pins, and walk back to the table.

"Let's make it interesting," Logan says.

One of my eyebrows spikes up in curiosity. "*Okay.*"

"Truth or dare bowling. If I beat you I get to pick a truth or dare for you, if you win the same thing."

"Fair enough," I say. This could be interesting. "Your turn."

He gets up and knocks down four pins.

"Okay," I say, wondering whether I want to give him a truth or a dare. It might be safer to start off with a truth. "Truth. Where do you come from?"

Logan's eyebrows furrow in thought. "All over the place. I've never stayed in one place for very long. I've been to Maine, New York, Tennessee, Montana. I've even been to England, Rome, Australia, Canada. Then most recently I was in Hawaii and California."

"Wow. That must be awesome. I would love to travel

like that. It also explains the tan."

"Traveling is fun, yeah, but you never stay in one place for long enough. The connections you make never last, so what is the point of making connections?"

I never thought of it like that. I would love to travel, but I would always want a home to come back to. There is a wistful look in Logan's eyes, and I almost feel bad for him. But I would never want someone to feel bad for me, so I know Logan would be the same way.

"You're up," Logan says, breaking me from my reverie.

"Right."

This time I knock down seven pins and Logan gets a strike. Great.

"Truth," Logan says. "What is your relationship with Xander? And what is with his name?"

"Hey. That's two," I say, but Logan is not deterred.

"He's my best friend," I say. I'm not about to tell Logan how Xander feels about me. "We've been friends since kindergarten. And Xander is short for Alexander. But that is his dad's name so he goes by Xander."

While we talk, our food comes. I scarf down my fries and start on my burger. Who knew I was a stress eater. I'll have to watch that. Logan laughs at my eating.

"What?"

"Not a single girl I have ever been on a date with has eaten more than a salad and water. And here you are eating a burger, fries, and chugging Mountain Dew." Embarrassment colors my face. I suddenly feel like a pig. But Logan says,

"No. I like it."

"I don't think they have salads on the menu here. But I can understand those other girls. It must be rough walking around as good looking as you are."

"Have you looked in a mirror lately?" Logan asks.

"What?" I ask, not sure if I actually heard him say what I think he said.

"Nothing," Logan says. "You're up."

Logan wins again and picks another truth. "Why are there a bunch of packed boxes in your room?"

"I don't like living in the middle of nowhere. I don't like living so far out of town, so far away from my dad. Not that he cares. But I figure if I leave them unpacked, my mom will change her mind and we can move back into town."

Logan nods like he understands but doesn't say anything.

We apparently don't have any dares for each other, because when I win next, I choose truth. "When I came home from the hospital after my accident and you were in my house, why did you get so upset with me when I said I was sorry for being a damsel in distress?"

"You will never be a damsel. You were born to survive. You have already proven that twice now, from what I can tell, and you will keep on doing it. You will not only survive but you will thrive. Just remember that the next time you are feeling down on yourself."

I'm not sure what surprises me most, Logan's sincerity or his frankness. Logan's intensity sometimes frightens me. His flares of anger, of protectiveness, of strength, sometimes frightens me. But I have never once felt afraid for my safety and well-being. With Logan I feel a sense of security I haven't felt since Nash was still alive. What frightens me is the insecurity of knowing whether I like Logan for the comfort he brings in to my life, or if I like him for who he is. Logan is so multifaceted that I can't decode him. Ashley is easy, she is a stuck up bitch. Tucker is easy, he is my gay best friend who knows who he is and is loyal to a fault. I thought Xander was easy, but since the day Logan arrived he has grown many personalities. But despite not liking Logan, and refusing to talk to me because of it, Xander still looks out for the ones he loves and will do what he believes is the right thing. Logan is a different story. I don't know what he believes in. I don't know where his loyalties lie. I don't know what he is passionate about or what he will fight for.

Before I can get all choked up, I ask, "Whose turn is it?"

Logan grins and says, "Yours, I believe."

When our bowling match is over and our meals eaten, Logan and I move to the downstairs of the bowling alley, where there are two pool tables and four arcade games, otherwise known as the arcade.

"Same rules?" I ask Logan as he racks the balls.

"No way. This game I have a clear shot of winning."

"You've played pool but you have never bowled?"

"Yes. Are you any good at pool?"

"Sadly, no," I answer, holding in a grin. "Would you be so kind as to teach me?"

Logan shakes his head, smiles, raises an eyebrow seductively, and says, "I would love to."

I position myself over the table like I have seen all the bimbos do in the movies and say, "Like this?"

Logan chuckles and shakes his head again. Without a word, he comes up behind me, places his hands on my hips, and repositions me. The warmth of his hands sears right through my dress and burns my skin. My spine straightens then relaxes into Logan when he presses himself up against me. The wonderful scent of fresh rain washes over me and I breathe deeply. Slowly, he curves his right hand over mine around the cue. Then he uses his left hand to position mine around the top of the cue and over the table. I feel flushed and have to move my head to hide it from Logan. This causes my hair to cascade over my face. Logan inhales sharply, his body shudders. He exhales, slides my right hand back then forward, causing the cue stick to strike the white ball which rolls forward hitting the pile of balls and a striped one falls into the corner pocket.

I turn around and hug Logan excitedly. He laughs and hugs me back. Our bodies fit perfectly together. I never knew hugging someone could feel so good. Every nerve ending in my body is alive and wants to feel more. Logan releases me far too soon.

"Okay," Logan says, "the first game can just be for practice. You can get a feel for it, then the next game can be the real deal."

"No," I say, "it's okay. If I lose, I lose. No big deal."

"If you say so," Logan teases. "You're stripes, go again."

I pull the stick back and push it forward, strike the white ball and do not hit what I am aiming for. "Shoot," I say.

Logan laughs at me, claps his hands together once, and shakes his head.

"Don't laugh at me," I say and pout my bottom lip out.

"Do not make me come over there and turn that frown upside down," Logan says, his eyes growing dark.

"Who's stopping you?" I ask, winking at him.

Logan closes his eyes, exhales hard, and rolls his shoulders back and around. I've come to the realization that Logan does this when he is trying to relax or gain control over himself. I can't fathom why he would do so now. I didn't think I was stressing him out, but maybe he is trying not to like me, or let himself like me. Again, I don't know why he would do so.

Logan hits the white ball knocking two solid balls into two different pockets. He hits it again and another solid ball goes into a pocket. When he hits the white ball again, he finally misses.

"Okay, it's time to get serious," I say walking up to the table.

Logan raises an eyebrow as if to say *oh really?* but says, "How so?"

"We'll make a bet out of it. Like, if you win you get to pick what you want me to do or whatever and so on."

"Hm, this may take some thinking." Logan screws up his face in many different ways and I can't help but laugh.

"Okay, I've got it. If I win, you have to wear the same outfit to school every day for a week. And if you win?"

"Have you seen the things I wear to school on a daily basis? Wearing the same thing for a week is not even a challenge. If I win," I say, having to turn my face away from him to answer, "You have to kiss me."

He stares at me intently, and I'm afraid he will say no, that the deal is off, but he nods and motions to the table so I can play.

I step up to the table, eye the placement of the striped balls, and start shooting. They go in one by one, except for when I hit two in at once. My shots are practiced, smooth. I strike with precision and concentration. Before I go for the eight ball, I turn to Logan and wink at him, call my pocket, and send the ball sailing into it.

I turn around and rest against my pool stick with a shit eating grin on my face. "Pay up."

"I don't think so," he says, awe in his voice. "I just got played. How on earth did you learn to play like that?"

"My dad brought Nash and I down here every Sunday for pizza, grape soda, and pool. I've been playing since I was tall enough to stand over the table. That is, until Nash died, and my parents split up." The memories slam into me like a steam roller. Me and Nash on our tiptoes trying to make the tip of the stick hit the ball. Me and Nash both holding part of the stick and working together to hit the ball. Me and Nash working together to finally beat our dad. My dad playing us both in turn. Me and Nash against each other. That one was hard, until I started beating him, which was harder, so I let him win, even though I'm sure he saw right through me. I'd forgotten how much I love to play pool, and I just remembered why I now hate it. "I don't want to play anymore."

Seventeen

"Do you want to talk about it?" Logan asks slowly, like he is approaching a wild animal.

"I don't know. . . Not really. . . Maybe. . . I don't know," I stumble, feeling slightly uncomfortable. The bowling alley does not seem to be the place to have this conversation, even if I wanted to have it.

"You don't have to tell me about it. I'm not going to push you into it," Logan's brow is furrowed, as if he is appalled I would think he would be so pushy.

"No, it's okay," I say, surprising myself. I don't talk about my parents or Nash to anyone but Tucker and Xander. What if Logan betrays me and gives Ashley cannon fodder by telling her everything I've told him. No, he wouldn't do that. But then again, I don't know him all that well. I have no idea what he will or won't do. Faith. That is what leads me to say, "My parents split up eight months ago."

"What happened?"

"I don't know," I say, tears springing to my eyes. "After Nash died it was like a switch flipped and they didn't love each other anymore. Before the accident they were the happiest couple I had ever seen. Then when I woke up in the hospital, they were fighting and seemed to hate each other. I don't even think they have talked since Nash's funeral, and I wasn't even there." I close my mouth, biting down hard to keep from crying.

Logan says nothing. He gives no words of solace. He doesn't try to explain it away. He doesn't tell me I'm making a big deal of nothing. He just stands there, leaning against the pool table, staring intently at me.

"Well, anyway," I say, trying to break the dark mood, "that's my sob story. But who doesn't have one. I'm fine."

"Would you like to go get some ice cream?" Logan asks.

I laugh, catching him off guard, and agree to it. He leads me up the stairs and out of the bowling alley. When we walk outside I remember something vital, that Logan tried to avoid. I turn around and stop him in his tracks, pointing a finger into his chest. "I beat you fair and square buddy, it's time to pay up."

Logan looks confused for one, two, three seconds before realization dawns on him.

"You owe me a kiss," I say as sexy as I can.

Logan moves around me and walks away. My eyebrows furrow, confused, but I follow him, beyond curious. He takes a turn and walks into the alley between the bowling alley and the bank. When I come up behind him, he turns on me, presses me into the side of the bank, and leans in. His lips are so close to mine, his body pressed up to mine. I stop breathing all together. My heart, however, slams into my rib cage. Logan has to feel it. He breathes evenly. Stares intently at me. I can't tell if he is waiting for me to make the next move, or simply torturing me.

When I think I can no longer take his proximity, Logan leans in further, then says, "Not a chance. You cheated." He chuckles, then looks away. I'm glad to see he's not affected by this in the least.

I exhale my first breath since he pushed me against the wall and pull myself away from it. Logan looks at me with that grin that gets me every time. Then he looks down and his face darkens, turns fierce, his eyes widen, he clenches his jaw. I look down to see what could have affected him so and see that the skirt of my dress has ridden up and my legs are more exposed than they were. Luckily they are all that is exposed.

I pull the skirt down and when I look back up, Logan is inches from me, the storm brewing in his eyes, his chest rising and falling heavily. I look up at him with my eyes only, and something in Logan snaps. He uses his hand on my stomach to back me up against the wall of the bank, his body pressed hard against mine. We both breathe heavily.

He leans down, stares intently into my eyes, then leans in further and whispers into my ear, "Do you know what you do to me in that dress? In all the clothes you wear to school." He growls, then gently but firmly places his lips to mine in a kiss so passionate and explosive I see stars. He grabs me by the waist and lifts me up. Then he places one of my legs on either side of him, his hands cupping my thighs. Flames dance under my skin. I almost regret wearing such a short dress. Almost. He never once breaks the kiss. Instead, he deepens it, holding tighter to me, as if I am water, and he's gone months without a drink.

I could lose myself in Logan. I want to lose myself in him. Forget the pain I feel every time I think of my brother. Forget that my father no longer loves me and my mother has abandoned me. Forget that my best friend is in love with me and I can't reciprocate his feelings. Forget that my other best friend is caught in the middle and doesn't know how to fix it. Just forget everything. Just for a little bit.

I never knew a kiss could be so liberating. I never knew a kiss could feel so amazing. Logan teases my lips with his tongue, asking permission. I spread my lips, welcoming the touch of his tongue meeting mine. When they collide, I moan in pure ecstasy.

Logan pulls away sharply, seeming to remember where he is, who he's with. He lets go of me, steps away, and drops me. On the concrete. Directly on my ass.

I pant, not able to catch my breath. I look over at Logan who is now a good five feet away from me, doubled over, his hands on his knees. He, too, is breathing heavily. Good. I'm glad I'm not the only one affected by what just happened.

When I regain my breath, I say, "What the hell?" my voice rising on the last word.

Logan's head snaps towards me. When he sees me sitting on the pavement he rushes forward, grabs my hand, and pulls me up. Even though my tail bone throbs, I could have gotten up myself. However, it serves him right. "I'm so sorry, Casslyn. That should have never happened."

Which part? The kissing or the dropping?

As if he read my thoughts, Logan says, "That can never happen again. We *cannot* do that again." As if to emphasize his point, or clarify, or possibly just stab me in the heart, he says, "We cannot be together, like that."

"What?" I yell at him. "Then what the hell was that?"

"That was a mistake," he says without emotion.

My eyes widen and I lose my breath. Was he playing me when he kissed me? Was it part of some game or joke? No. There is no way he could have faked that kiss. No way he could have faked that passion. But where is the emotion now? "Thank you for making it so clear for me." I turn away from him, not wanting him to see me cry. Our kiss gave me such a high, how could I now be so low?

He walks closer to me. I can feel his overwhelming presence. His hands reach out to grasp my arms but he thinks better of it and pulls away. "I don't mean to hurt you."

I want to tell him he should have thought about that before the knives flew from his mouth, but I will not look weak in front of him. Instead I swallow my tears, and say, "You didn't." Unfortunately, my voice wavers. He won't believe me.

Instead of trying to fix things or make things worse, he says, "Let me take you home."

"No. I can find my own way home," I say defiantly.

"You're going to make it ten miles home? On your own?" he sounds incredulous or maybe he is mocking me.

"I've been on my own for eight months. One night's not going to kill me." I don't let him say anything to the contrary. I just walk away

Logan comes up behind me, grasps my arm, and spins me around. I glare at him and say, "Don't touch me."

"Casslyn, don't do this."

"No. You don't do this. You can't just . . . do that . . . just kiss me like that and tell me we can't do it again." I can't believe what is happening. I don't even know what is happening. One moment we were kissing and everything was perfect, and the next Logan is acting crazy and saying we can't kiss, even though he really means we can't be together. I see it written all over his face. My hands shake at my sides. My body reacts to my anger and the residual effects of our kiss and Logan's hands on my body. Plus, my tailbone still hurts. I clench my fists to keep from shaking, but it is no use, only causing my arms to shake.

Logan notices my unease and says, "Please just get in the car so I can take you home."

"No."

"Do not make me put you in there," his tone is harsh, forceful, yet gentle. He makes me so mad. When I don't answer he says, "If you get in the car we can discuss it on the drive."

I look up at him, not believing him, thinking he will get me in the car and be silent, but I find only sincerity in his fire blue eyes. Without saying a word, I walk to the car and climb in the front passenger seat. I look in the rearview mirror to see Logan roll his shoulders back. Great. I've upset him. That move is really beginning to anger me. I wish I had a move to relax myself that angered him, like his shoulder rolling angers me. I sit in the H3 for minutes before Logan gets in and when he finally sits in the driver's seat, he doesn't even look at me. He starts the Hummer and pulls away from the curb. Nothing. No looks. No words. Silence. Like I feared.

Suddenly, Xander loving me and no longer talking to me doesn't seem like such a big deal.

I'm not about to let Logan get away with it. He told me we would discuss it if I got in the vehicle. I'm in the vehicle. Time to talk.

"What was that all about?" I ask.

"The . . . *kiss*, shouldn't have happened. Tonight shouldn't have happened."

"And why not?" I ask through my teeth, trying not to yell at him.

"I can't get close to you, Casslyn. There is no future for us."

"Why the hell not?" I no longer care about not yelling.

"There is a connection between us. You know that. I can feel it. And I know you can too. There is no way you didn't feel anything when we kissed."

"You don't understand. It can't happen. There are rules."

"What's that supposed to mean? What rules?" I ask, my gaze hard on his face.

"Nothing. Nothing. Don't worry about it."

"You don't want to be with me?"

"Even if I wanted to be with you, it's not like I have a choice. We cannot be together. Just please forget about it. I'm not trying to hurt you, please believe that. We just can't."

"Then why? Why kiss me at all if nothing can come of it?"

"Because. I had to know." Logan says, dropping the conversation and pulling even further away from me.

Eighteen

I wake up feeling depressed. No. Not depressed. Depression is the lack of feeling. I feel all too much. I wake up this way most days anymore.

Every sadness in my life decides to compound on me. Ashley, Xander, my parents, Logan, Nash. Especially Nash. I am in serious need of therapy. Or a nice long hug. But as I get dressed and ready for school, I decide not to let my sadness run my life any longer. Nash is gone and there is nothing I can do about that. Logan doesn't want to be with me and I don't think I can change his mind. Xander loves me but hates me. However, that is because of Logan, and now that he is practically a non-issue, I believe I can repair our relationship, or rather friendship. And who knows, perhaps when I have gotten over Logan, if that is a possibility, I may one day discover I really do have feelings for Xander.

My car showed up in my driveway the morning after me and Logan's disastrous date, just like he promised. He could have come in and told me he stopped by, or handed me the keys, but no, he chose to ignore me. So be it. Two can play that game.

And two have been playing that game. Neither Logan, nor I, have talked to each other or even looked at each other all week. Even when we have to work together in Home Ec., we fake it when the teacher is near, then go back to ignoring each other. Tucker got all of the details of our terrible date from me, although I'm sure he will say doing so was worse than pulling teeth. But because he knows all of the details, he understands how I feel and only tries to make me feel better. Xander, on the other hand, has made it his mission to tell me he told me so. Tucker and Xander's Home Ec. classes have been strained as well. I feel bad that it is my fault, though not completely my fault. Xander has become so head strong, so spiteful lately that he is hard to be around. He made me cry on Wednesday, after telling me he was right about Logan and that I was stupid not to listen to him. Luckily, I made him feel bad, and he has toned down quite a bit.

Xander, Tucker, and I are trying to get back to some semblance of our friendship, though it is going to take a lot of work. It is especially strained with Xander and me. Now that I know his feelings for me, it is hard to ignore them, hard to know if he wants me to acknowledge them, or if he would rather I forget about them. I also don't know if he plans to act on those feelings, knowing I don't feel the same, or if he will try to forget about them himself.

It is a very confusing time for me. I try my hardest to just get through the day, as quickly as possible, with as few challenges as possible. Thankfully, I have one more class period before the weekend. Unthankfully, I have to spend that hour sitting next to Logan. He wouldn't have hurt me so deeply if my feelings for him weren't so strong. I'm afraid I am falling in love with him and he wants nothing to do with me. In the long run, I may get over him, but right now, only the death of Nash cuts deeper.

I sigh heavily when I walk into class. Logan is already at our work station. His body stiffens when I sit next to him, but he doesn't look at me, doesn't acknowledge my presence. Awesome.

When everyone is seated, Mrs. Sherman takes role then says, "Before we get started today, I'm going to give you your homework for the weekend." My class groans aloud. "Don't give me that. Now, this weekend, I want you to pair up with your partner and prepare the meal you have planned. I expect a full report on it on my desk first thing on Monday's class period. When you write your report, I want you to document the steps you took, in what order, the ingredients you used, how long it took you, your rapport with your partner, and so on. I will know by your report if you actually did it or not. If you wish to fail, don't worry about it, have fun this weekend. But if you wish to pass, meet your partner, take an hour or two out of your weekend, and cook some food. Now get to work. Today I want you to make chocolate chip cookies."

My heart races. I get to spend time alone with Logan this weekend. And there is no way for him to get out of it. I know he knows it, his death grip on our table makes that apparent.

He turns to me, but before he can say anything, I start, "Don't. Just come over to my house tonight and we can get it over with."

"I can't do it tonight. I have something . . . going on," Logan says, a stern look on his face.

I take a deep, calming breath, and instead of acting like a stupid jealous girl, wondering if he is going on a date, or what he is doing, I say, "Fine. Come over on Saturday, at one o'clock, and we will do the project. Don't worry about getting the food. I'll do that. Just come over, we'll get it done, then you can leave, you only have to spend minimal time with me."

I think he is going to yell at me, tell me he doesn't want to spend any time with me, but instead, he says, "Is that what you think? That I don't want to spend time with you?"

My heart jumps. No way did he just ask me that. What else would I think after he so daftly rejected me just under a week ago, after he has spent all week ignoring me? I want so badly to question him about it, but I fear it will only make this worse. So instead of asking him what he means, I turn away from him, and gather the ingredients needed to make cookies.

After a time, Logan leans in close and whispers, "Cass-lyn."

Just that one word, my name, unnerves me, and I can't help but look to him. I swallow hard, but don't say anything. I feel as though I have no control over myself when I am around Logan. I become a pile of mush, a bowl of Jell-O. I don't want to be like that any longer. Since Nash's death, I have let those around me control my actions, push me into what they think is best for me, what they think I should do. But no longer. I need to start taking control of my life. And that starts now.

"Don't, Logan. For whatever reason, you said we can't be together. Fine. Whatever. I will accept that as best as I can. But don't you do this. Don't make me feel like you care. I can't be friends with you, and not have more. You said we can't be more, so I'm saying we can't be friends. So don't try. We'll do the project and then forget about each other."

***

I spend all morning cleaning my house. Even though Logan has seen it in its varying degrees of disarray, I need to show him that I can take control of my life, even in the smallest form. Also, I need something to take my mind off of spending the afternoon with him.

The minutes tick by so slowly I think the world might have stopped spinning. And then he is just here, knocking on the door. At first, I don't believe it is him, because Logan has never knocked on my door before. But when I open the door, sure enough, it is him.

Still feeling sour from our *date*, I say, "So you do know how to knock, here I thought you just perpetually walked into peoples' houses without being invited."

Not appreciating my humor, Logan steps around me and into my house. "Funny."

So that's the way it's going to be.

"Your car hasn't moved," Logan says it as a statement, not a question.

It makes me mad that he thinks he knows me. That he thinks he can judge me.

"I haven't driven it in eight months. What makes you think you bringing it here is going to change that?"

Logan rolls his shoulders back then crosses his arms. He scowls then says, "Is this how it's going to be? You're just going to hate me?" Did he read my mind?

I cross my arms and scowl in turn, "Are you going to give me what I want?"

"No."

"Then yes."

Again, Logan rolls his shoulders back. I'm getting to him and it thrills me. It is only fair that I affect him when he affects me so. His eyes burn blue fire as they burn a hole through me.

"Maybe I should leave," he says.

As much as I don't want to be alone with Logan and my

feelings for him, I want him to leave even less.

"No. Stay," I say, then glare at him. "I'll play nice."

"I'm sure," he says, and walks to my kitchen. "So, how do you want to do this?"

The tension between us could be snapped like a taught rubber band.

I stand at my place by the front door and look after Logan. Today, as with most days, he is wearing dark jeans and a black t-shirt. The t-shirt is fitted, his muscles and abs showing through. I have fantasized about touching those muscles. I've had dreams of Logan taking me into those strong arms and kissing me square on the mouth, deep and passionate. But of course those will stay dreams, because as he made clear only a few nights ago, we will never be anything more than what we are, acquaintances, classmates, two people with incredible sexual tension that for some unknown reason cannot be together. I just wish that if I can't be with Logan as anything more, I wouldn't have to spend so much time with him. And yet, the thought of him no longer being in my life is unbearable. Ugh. All the feelings. They suck.

Logan clears his throat and I realize I have been caught staring. Damn.

"What?" I ask, petulant.

Logan smirks and shakes his head and turns away from me. Anger flares in me. How could he treat this so lightly?

I charge up behind him, grab his arm, and turn him towards me. "Hey, don't. This is hard for me, alright. You don't get to treat it like it's nothing."

He stares down at me. His eyes smolder. "You think it's not hard for me? God, Casslyn. This is hard for me too. What do you want me to say? That I want you? Because I do. You want me to say I want to be with you? Because I do. But you don't understand. I can't be with you. I can't. So please, could you just drop it and leave it alone?" He attempts to roll his shoulders back but the gesture is lost and the look on his face is one of defeat. I want to drop it. Want to forget about him, but I can't. There is something in me, a deep seated need and assurance, pulling me to Logan. And I know he feels it too. An idea surges through me, filling me with a glimmer of hope.

I look up at him, resolute in what I am about to say, and begin, "Could you, for one day, forget all of your bogus reasons for why we can't be together, and just be with me? Give me one day, just today, and I will try my best to abide by your wishes."

I watch him, waiting for a yes or no, or some form of rejection, but get nothing. And yet I watch. He has to give me something. Just when I expect him to huff in derision and walk away, something within him snaps, his eyes flare, and in a split second, he is crushing my body to his. Kissing me with every intensity he possesses. It's all too much and yet I can't get enough. A fire ignites under every one of Logan's finger tips and spreads through my body, creating a warmth so enveloping I fear I will freeze to death when it leaves me. Logan deepens the kiss, which I didn't think was possible. My breaths are heavy but are few and far between.

My heart races and may just beat out of my chest. But I don't care because I cannot get enough of him. My hands find his sides, under his shirt, then trail up his sides. He shudders but does not break the kiss. He picks me up, I wrap my legs around his waist, and he carries me to the couch. He sits and I straddle his lap. I could die of ecstasy and yet we still kiss, breathing each other's air, hands roaming, bodies colliding. He breaks away to trail kisses down my neck, between each one saying, "Oh, Casslyn." Goosebumps erupt on every inch of my body.

Only now, with Logan's hands and lips on me, do I realize my mistake. I told him after today I would let it go, stop pursuing him, because it is what he wants. And he will hold me to it, for whatever reason is keeping him from me. But that was before I knew I am in love with him, which is what this kiss has shown me. I am in love with Logan, and after today, I will have no chance of being with him. My heart breaks all over again. I pull away from him with a sharp intake of breath.

"Are you okay?" he asks.

"Yeah, fine," I say, leaning forward to kiss him.

"Casslyn?"

"Will you just shut up and kiss me. I get one day, damn it."

Logan pauses as if he wants to say something, or is mulling something over. But then he leans the rest of the way in and presses his lips to mine. This time, the kisses are slower, more passionate, less insistent. And it only makes me fall more in love with him.

Logan has meant so much to me in the few months that I have known him. He's been a distraction, a guide, a mirror, a friend, a protector. And now that I know he is even more than that, I can't take it.

Silent tears brim over my eyelids and slip down my face. Without breaking our kiss, Logan uses his thumbs to wipe them away. He says nothing, and I am thankful.

***

We cook and we play. We cook and we touch. We cook and we kiss. And we laugh. And we joke. And we do our best to forget that tomorrow it will all be over. Just like I try desperately to forget that Nash is dead and my parents abandoned me. Unfortunately, it always seems as though the harder I try to forget something, the more thoughts of it slam into me. But it's time to buck up. I won't let my troubles conquer me.

***

Logan stands behind me while I cut the chicken. His hands are placed on my hips, but then they venture north. His hands slide under my shirt and up my sides, making my skin sizzle. My arms jerk and I nearly throw the knife.

"Be careful," I say. "You're going to make me cut myself."

Logan's hands fly from my sides, leaving a bitter cold in their wake. He places them on either side of the cutting board on the counter and says, "Fine. Fine. I'll be good."

I return to the task at hand and cut a few more hunks of chicken off a breast. Then I feel warm lips on my neck and lose my shit. I slice the knife down but it misses my mark and slices the skin of Logan's thumb. The knife enters deep, deep enough I feel bone. I pull the knife away and stare in horror.

"I'm so so. . ." I begin to say.

Instead of bleeding like most cuts, Logan's thumb lights on fire. Actual flames. On his skin. I can feel the heat radiating from them. And if I wasn't staring straight at it, I wouldn't believe it, but as quickly as the flames ignite, they die out and the cut is completely gone, as it was never there to begin with.

My body goes rigid. From shock, or fear, or processing, I'm not sure. Logan jerks back, quickly, like he thinks maybe I didn't see. Thunder cracks, loud, outside, causing me to jump, the knife still in my hand, I look out one of the windows in the kitchen and see that it is almost completely dark from the oncoming storm. I watch a cloud engulf and roll over a hill. I'd been having so much fun with Logan I failed to notice what was happening in the outside world.

I can feel Logan's presence behind me. He waits, quietly, for me to react.

I look down to see that I still clutch the knife in my hand. I whip around and pull it on him. Logan steps back but does not otherwise react.

"What was that?" I ask, my voice shaking.

There is no way I just saw what I saw. People's hands don't just light on fire. Maybe it was a trick of the light. Or maybe I didn't actually cut him. I look at the blade in my hand, and sure enough, there is blood on the edge. I search for Logan's hand, but when he notices, he swings it behind his back.

"Casslyn, don't freak out," he says, moving toward me like I might be unstable.

"Don't come any closer," I shout.

"I'm not going to hurt you. Don't you think if I was, I would have done it already?"

"What was that?"

"Nothing. You didn't see anything."

"Damn it, Logan. Don't lie to me. I know what I saw."

Logan jumps when I yell. I jump when thunder rolls outside.

"I don't know what to say to make you believe me, or not freak out." He steps toward me and I thrust the knife at him.

"Just tell me," I say through my teeth, though I want to yell.

"I'm . . . a phoenix," he says, rolling his shoulders back but never losing eye contact with me.

My heart still pounds so hard it might burst from my chest.

A phoenix. What does that mean? What is that? A phoenix. My mind tries to process this, but I get nothing. I am too flustered. My vision is blurry and I have this terrible throbbing at the base of my skull. The harder I think, the harder it throbs. But through the beating I get one thought. *Harry Potter*. Why Harry Potter? Then it hits me. Dumbledore's bird was a phoenix.

"You're a bird?" I ask, feeling slightly stupid.

From Logan comes a burst of laughter. It is nervous and uncertain. Not funny.

"Not exactly."

Thunder rolls outside and a down pour starts. I can hear the rain pound the roof. I can't handle this. He's a bird. He's not a bird. His skin lights on fire and heals instantly. What else don't I know? Why he's taken such an interest in me? How he can always find me? How he can just get into my house? This is too much.

"I need you to leave," I say calmly.

"Casslyn, please let me explain."

"I need you to leave," I say a little more forcefully.

The way he looks at me, his eyes pleading, twist my heart, but I just can't.

"Please, I-"

"Leave," I shout, startling us both.

I feel wetness in my eyes. I close them, trying to hold the tears back. I fell in love with a guy who isn't even, what, human? How could I have been so stupid? How could I have not seen this coming? This cannot be real. Surely when I open my eyes, Logan will be laughing because I fell for his prank. But when I open them, Logan is nowhere to be found.

My breaths come faster, but chopped and difficult. The guy I love is a monster. What is happening to my life? I really didn't think it could get worse than a dead twin and deadbeat parents. But then add an estranged best friend and a nonhuman nonboyfriend.

I throw the knife on the counter then turn around and lean against it. Emotions overwhelm me. I feel a panic attack coming on. I slide down the side of the counter and collapse on the floor. The cool tile feels nice against my cheek when I lie on it. I focus on the cool of the tile and the pattering of the rain. They help, but not a lot. My breaths are short and choppy. It feels as though I have a car sitting on my chest, making it difficult to breathe. I sing to myself, trying to calm the rising panic within me. I know the words. I know the melody. I sing the song, but I can't focus on it. I can't find the calming effect singing to myself usually brings.

Eventually, my panic calms and I am able to breathe normally and think clearly.

Girls find out their boyfriends are not human all the time in books and movies and they don't always freak out. They date these guys, fall in love with them, marry them, and even have babies with them. Surely I can love Logan for who he is. He said he wasn't here to hurt me, and surely if he wanted to, he would have by now. Right?

Okay. So my thinking may be clear, but obviously it is not rational, or logical, because this is real life. There aren't even mythological creatures in real life. Are there?

I don't even know what a phoenix is other than a red bird that bursts into flames. But wasn't there something else in Harry Potter about healing tears or something? And maybe something about beautiful voices? Oh my. I am getting my facts from Harry Potter. I really have hit rock bottom. But then there is the *Supernatural* episode I saw a while back about phoenixes. Wasn't there? That phoenix was human, or at least wearing a human's skin. I can't remember what he was able to do. But I remember seeing the episode.

Maybe I should have let Logan explain himself when he wanted to. What if I've lost him by throwing him out? As far as I know, phoenixes aren't lethal in any way. No bloodsucking. No shape shifting. That I know of.

I have to find him. I have to go to his house and at least let him explain. Right?

I pick myself off the kitchen floor and walk out the front door. It is still pouring rain, but I don't care. I have to get over there and he has to explain. I deserve that much. Logan has lied to me since the day I met him. Maybe I should be thinking, *so what if I have lost him, he's lied to me this whole time.*

The rain quickly soaks me through. The mile walk to Logan's house is not a quick one. I have to trudge through the mud and standing water. But I make it. And when I knock on his front door my heart races. This house scares the crap out of me and I'll be alone with Logan, knowing his secret.

But maybe it's not a secret. Xander has told me repeatedly that Logan is dangerous. How would he know that if it was a secret? And why wouldn't Xander tell me what Logan is if he knew? Maybe Xander doesn't actually know what Logan is or that he is dangerous. Maybe he was just acting out of jealousy. Ugh. I just don't know. It's all so confusing and heart tearing.

When Logan opens the door, my vision of him is obscured by the raindrops in my eyelashes. I blink them away then look at Logan hard. He looks devastated but relieved at the same time. Guarded, but still like he would tell me anything I asked him.

I stand in his doorway, my soaking clothes and hair dripping, and say, "Start talking."

Logan sighs, all the air escaping from him. He smirks and says, "About what?"

I take a step into his house and say, "Are you kidding?"

Nineteen

I sit in a leather chair in Logan's living room. It is nothing like what I have heard or expected. The wood is not rotting. There are no bats flying overhead or mice crawling underfoot. There are no ghosts floating about, no creaking floors.

From what I can see, everything has been remodeled. New walls, floors, furniture, appliances. I don't know how everything was done while I lived a mile away. I didn't even know anyone was living in the house until I overheard Logan telling someone.

My wet clothes are soaking into the leather of the chair, but I don't care. He has a lot to answer for. I am slightly uncomfortable but I want answers more than I want to be comfortable.

Logan sits on the arm of a couch on the far side of the living room, giving me my space.

"What do you want to know?" he asks me.

"Everything," I say simply.

"I'm not going to tell you everything. That would take all night, and besides, it would be information overload."

"Fine," I say, crossing my arms. "Then tell me the basics. You're obviously not a bird, how does that work? Do you have healing tears? How did your skin light on fire?"

Logan takes a deep breath, narrows his eyes, and breathes out. "Okay. First, the bird thing is an evolution slash mythological thing that I wish not to explain right now. I promise you I will tell you, but it is a story for another time.

"Yes, I have healing tears. I don't heal everything when I cry. I have to want to heal someone. However, I can cry on demand to heal someone. With me so far?"

I nod, not sure if I *am* with him, but I want him to keep talking.

"My skin lit on fire when you cut me because I am self-healing. My body will regenerate when damaged. It lights on fire because the flames knit the skin back together. What else would you like to know?"

"How many of you are there?"

"I don't know the number. There could be hundreds. There could be thousands. Some live in groups. Some are nomads. I lived in a group. That, also, is a tale for another time."

He was right, this is a lot to take in. None of this can be possible, and yet I find myself compelled by what he is telling me and believing it.

I've never heard of a phoenix in human form before. Sure there are all sorts of books and movies and TV shows on vampires, werewolves, witches, ghosts, even zombies. But phoenixes? Nothing. Again, my mind goes to Harry Potter. My only source of info, other than Logan.

I don't know what questions I should be asking. Or what questions I shouldn't. Bella didn't really ask any questions, so that is no help. Nora kind of just went with it too. Wow, girls in fiction are seriously dumb. Their boyfriends could be ruthless killers but they don't need the details.

Logan's diet doesn't really seem like it is a factor. I have seen him eat on numerous occasions. I don't think shape shifting is an issue. Sleeping is another story, but do I really care if he sleeps or not? But then again, after my accident, he had severe dark circles under his eyes indicating he hadn't slept. So that's out.

"How does one become a phoenix? Were you born one? Or did you turn into one?"

Logan narrows his eyes at me. "You're very smart."

I glare at him, mad that he could possibly think I was stupid.

He just smirks and continues to talk, "We are born as phoenixes. No one can be turned into one. We are not bitten or infected. We do not die and then become this. Also, it is a patriarchal parentage. Meaning the dad has to be a phoenix for the child to be one."

"I know what it means," I snap.

This is a lot to take in and apparently I can't handle my shit.

"Sorry. Go on."

Logan just raises an eyebrow, indicating for me to ask another question. By now, my clothes are drying a bit, making my legs chafe and the leather of the chair uncomfortable. Also, I'm sure my hair looks like a disaster. However, I can't stop now, I have to know more, even if it means being uncomfortable for an hour or so. Then I can go home and this awful day will be over.

"Do you have any other *powers*," I cringe when I say the word, but I can't think of another word for it, "besides healing?"

"I don't know if you would consider it a power, but our bodies do not register temperature change. We don't get hot or cold. We also don't ever get sick."

I sigh and feel a sense of relief. Nothing he has listed is lethal in any way. Sure, every fictional girl has stuck by her man when he could kill her in the blink of an eye, but I find it hard to believe they would do so in real life.

Then Logan continues, "And then there are the super human abilities. Super strength, enhanced senses like sight and hearing."

Okay. That's not so bad. I was definitely expecting him to come out with something like he eats babies for breakfast, or maybe that he can time travel and he's been messing with me for years, not just months, or even that he is part of an evil race that can control people making them kill other people or themselves.

But then he says, "There's one more thing."

"Oh, God!" I say. It just slips through my mouth.

"We can light things on fire by touching them."

"Anything?" I ask cautiously.

"Anything."

Before I can let that sink in, I move on. "How long can you live? And how old are you?"

"When we turn seventeen we come of age. It's the first time we . . . burn. After that we have a seventeen-year lifespan. In this lifespan I am currently nineteen years old. Do you really want to know how old I am?"

I start to picture Logan as an old wrinkly man then staunch that thought quickly. I do not want to picture him as anything less than the way I do now.

"No. But you're saying this isn't the first time you've been nineteen?"

"Nope. Any other questions?" he asks.

"One," I say.

This is a question I have wanted to know since the day I caught him staring at me in my History class. Why he has an interest in me. How he found me in the dressing room that day. How he saved me after I was run off the road.

"Why me?"

Logan falters. I've never seen him flustered before. Never seen him fully lose control. Even when he kissed me at the bowling alley, he was able to control himself. But now that he has promised to tell me everything, answer every question I ask, I have asked one he either can't or won't answer.

"I promise that one day, when the time is right, and you are ready, I will answer that. But right now, I can't. It's not that I don't want to, but I can't. There are things happening that are bigger than you and me. And for right now, for reasons I don't even know, you cannot know why you."

"Are you saying . . . what are you saying?" I am more confused than ever. And now I am just scared. Actually scared for the first time. Even Logan sounds concerned. And he is the strongest, most capable person I have ever met.

I find that I can no longer sit still. I have to get up, have to move. I walk the perimeter of the living room, looking at everything, but not really seeing anything. But I soon become light headed and feel claustrophobic. I don't feel Logan follow me when I move between rooms, but he must. When my vision blurs to the point I can't see and the throbbing at the base of my skull makes my feet falter, he is there to catch me.

I open my eyes to see him looking down at me with concern. He doesn't say anything. And neither do I. He sets me back in the chair and I sit there for a minute before I become restless again. My clothes stick to me and make noise when I move.

"Would you like to take a shower? I can dry your clothes while you are in there."

Do I want to shower? It would give me a chance to be

alone with my thoughts. Away from Logan and his influence. Also, I have become almost unbearably uncomfortable.

"Yeah, sure."

Logan starts upstairs and I follow. Again, the house could not be further from what I expected. Newly finished and painted walls, new lights and décor. The bathroom is practically brand new. The shower is something I've only seen on TV or in movies. It has multiple shower heads with different massage and pulse settings, and a radio, and a bench seat built in, and even a TV. The sink is one of those bowls built on top of the counter and made out of jade. The lights have mood settings. The floor is stone but it must be heated because it is not cold to my bare feet.

Logan shows me where I can find fresh towels, shampoo, conditioner, and anything else I may need. Then he brings me in shorts and a t-shirt of his I can change into if my clothes aren't dry in time. Finally, he shows me how to operate everything and tells me to leave my clothes outside the door before he steps out to give me my privacy.

I feel numb. Or maybe I am in shock. Or perhaps I am suffering from information overload like he told me I would.

I undress and step into the shower, turning the water on as hot as my skin can bear and stand there. I try to shut down. To not become overwhelmed by everything that I have learned in the last few hours, but instead I feel everything. Every emotion, every confusion, every everything escapes the trap I put it in and rushes me.

After Nash died, my mom wanted to send me to a shrink

because she thought I was depressed. But no. I'm not depressed. Depression is a complete numbness. A lack of feeling. What she didn't know was that I feel all too much. I feel at all times like I can't handle what is inside of me. I always feel like I am one break away from being engulfed by my heartache.

I feel a wetness on my cheeks. I'm not sure if it is tears or the water from the shower. Perhaps it is both.

I sit on the shower floor and let the water pound a rhythm on my skin that I can focus on.

I do a mental review of the day. I discovered that I am in love with Logan. Right before that, I told him after today I would stop pursuing him. Then I find out fiction can actually become real life. I don't even know what this means for me. Do I still love him? Do I still want to be with him? Will he still hold me to leaving him alone? Does he expect me to keep his secret? Would I actually tell anyone about his secret? I don't have answers to any of these questions.

I don't even feel my body right now. I don't feel like I fit in my own skin. I just want to drift away. I just want to leave this place for a little while. Maybe see Nash again. Just escape.

So that is what I do.

Twenty

When Nash and I were seven, we had Tucker and Xander convinced that we could fly.

One winter day they came over to our house. We had a babysitter but she was on the phone with her boyfriend. We took a sled and climbed to the top of our roof. Nash and I would sit on the sled then push ourselves off the sled when it left the roof, our arms spread out like we were flying, then land in a snow bank in our yard. Tucker and Xander were so impressed. They practically worshiped us.

And that is what I envision now. Only, I am not a part of the memory now. I am not in my head as a little girl. I stand in what was then our neighbors' yard and watch us as little kids. Having fun. Not a care in the world. And no knowledge of how messed up the world really is.

"Those were good times, weren't they?"

I turn my head, and standing right next to me, is Nash.

Without thinking, I throw my arms around his neck and squeeze.

"Oh my God, I have missed you," I say, squeezing the life out of him. Or maybe the afterlife.

"You too, sister."

We pull an arm's length away from each other and just stare at the other.

When we release we go back to watching the seven-year-old versions of ourselves. It really was a simpler time back then.

"I've been watching you, you know," Nash says, squinting from the sun rays reflecting off the snow, with his arms crossed. "Your life is a mess."

"Don't judge me, Nash. You're the one who isn't there," I snap at him, turning to glare at him.

"I wasn't judging. And don't blame me. It's been eight months."

"Are you telling me you would be over it in eight months if it was me who died?"

"No. I was just hoping you would be better than you are. Though that *man* that you have been spending time with seems to be helping."

"Yeah," I say, turning back to the happy, giggling children, not wanting to discuss it and not even knowing what to say.

Nash confuses my short answer for moving on and says, "It's okay to be happy, Cass. I would hope you would want me to be happy if our roles were reversed."

"Of course I would, but it's not that. With Logan . . . it's become complicated."

I watch our former selves. This time, Xander tries to fly but ends up belly flopping in the snow, the sled landing on top of him. He cracked a rib. We got in so much trouble for that.

Nash chuckles at Xander's mishap but says to me, "Oh, you mean that your boyfriend is a mythological creature? Yeah. I have to admit, that is one plot twist I did not see coming."

"I'm glad I can entertain you."

Nash smiles but then his face grows dark. He is quiet for a long time. He shuffles his feet and I can actually hear the snow crunch under them.

"Listen," he starts. "I've been back to that night. I don't think it was an accident. And I don't think that driver was drunk. You need to be careful. You can't trust everyone you think you can. A lot has changed. People and their loyalties are different. Promise me you will be careful."

"You're being really cryptic, Nash. And you're scaring the shit out of me."

"Good. You should be scared. I'm scared for you. Promise me you will be careful."

"Fine. I promise," I say and we go back to watching our younger selves.

We are both quiet for a time. Neither one of us knowing what to say. That is, until Nash says, "So what's he like? Built like an ox? He seems scary. But he also seems like he cares about you. Man, I bet Tucker hates you." Nash has a playful grin on his face.

"Can you be serious? For one minute."

"I was serious. About five minutes ago. Besides, it's not every day I get to tease my sister about her boyfriend."

"He's not my boyfriend. I don't even know what to call him."

"Oh, I could give you a few ideas," Nash says, tipping his head back so he can laugh fully.

"Shut up," I say swinging my arm to hit his, but my hand doesn't connect. When I look down, my hand is not there. "What is happening?"

"You're waking up. This is just a dream, Cass."

"But I don't want to wake up. I don't want to leave you."

"I know. But you can't stay here forever."

"Why not?" I ask, as more of me slips away and I become less aware of my surroundings.

"Bye, Cass. I love you," Nash's voice becomes faint until I can no longer hear it.

I'm in this in between state. This fuzzy blackness.

***

When I open my eyes, I don't know where I am. And I don't remember the dream I just had. I know it was something important. It had to have been important. But what was it?

I feel a warm tingling in my body that can only mean one thing. Logan is near.

I look around the strange room I am in and find him standing in front of a large bay window staring out. He is wearing a pair of pajama bottoms that hang seductively low on his hips, and nothing else. His muscles stand out everywhere. His tan skin glistens in the rising sun. I feel a stirring in my body that is not merely the result of his presence.

Then I remember everything I found out last night.

I look around what I assume is Logan's bedroom. The walls are a dark grey color. The floor is a dark hard wood. There are very few accoutrements. A dresser, a closet, and the bed I am lying in.

The most comfortable bed I have ever laid in. My body rests in it like a cloud. The pillow holds my head so perfectly I want to lie here forever. And the sheets. The silk sheets caress my skin like the softest touch.

My skin.

My bare skin. All of my bare skin.

I am completely naked in between the sheets of Logan's bed. How I got here is a complete mystery. The last time I remember is getting into the shower.

"You passed out in the shower," Logan says, still facing the window.

"You knew I was awake?"

"I can hear your heartbeat. It picked up when you woke

up."

"Oh," I say, embarrassed. If he can hear it, then he must know how I reacted when I looked at him. I pull the sheets up so they completely cover my body.

Logan finally turns to face me. His eyes are sunken like he didn't get any sleep last night. A thin layer of stubble covers his chin. I thought he couldn't get better looking, but I was wrong. And his chest. I have the strangest urge to lick it.

Logan's eyebrows go up and I am instantly embarrassed. Then his eyebrows knit together.

"I'm sorry I lied to you. And I'm sorry you had to find out like that." His head falls and his shoulders slump. I've never seen Logan anything less than strong and stoic. It's hard to see him like his.

I sit up in the bed and say, "Is that why you said we can't be together? Because of who you are?"

Logan looks into my eyes, a look of hope, maybe. Like he can't believe I'm not disgusted by him. "You mean *what* I am?"

"I said who. Now answer my question."

"It's part of it."

"So because you are . . . *different*, we can't be together? I told you your excuses were bogus."

"I know Xander has told you that I am dangerous. He's right. I am dangerous. But besides that, being with me is dangerous. Your life would always be in danger."

"Um, if you hadn't noticed, my life is already dangerous. And I didn't need any help from you. If anything, I have been safer with you. You already saved me how many times."

"Casslyn, we still can't be together. I'm sorry, but that's not going to change."

I look down at the bed I am lying in, wanting to escape Logan's gaze. My shoulders slump causing the sheet to slide off of them. Then I realize that I still can't remember what happened last night. But of course, Logan told me what happened.

"So I passed out huh?"

Logan nods, not needing to elaborate.

"And you, what, carried me, naked, into bed?"

"I covered you with a towel."

"Still, you've seen me naked. That feels like some kind of violation."

"Did you want me to leave you there?"

"No," I say, almost pouting, but I feel a small thrill. Damn it. I really need to get my feelings in check. If Logan can hear my heart beat change it's practically the same thing as knowing my thoughts. Oh my God. He's known, since the first day I met him how I have felt about him. Now I feel violated. I swallow, a lump getting stuck in my throat.

"And you slept where?" I ask slowly.

Logan nods to a spot on the floor next to the bed where blankets and a pillow lie. Not that I would have exactly minded him sleeping next to me.

I begin to feel awkward, me naked in Logan's bed and him watching me. I feel like if I needed to escape or something I am stuck.

Logan must read my thoughts because he says, "I'll let you get dressed. Then we can talk some more. If you would like."

"Okay," I say, not sure at all what I want.

Logan leaves his bedroom and I climb out of the bed. He laid my clothes at the end of the bed. They are dried and folded. They smell fresh, making me think he washed them. My bra and underwear sit on top of the pile. Mortification doesn't even begin to explain how I feel. Logan touched, washed, then folded my delicates. *Calm down, you idiot*, I think to myself. *He saw you naked. How much worse can it get?*

I dress then run to the bathroom to compose myself enough to face Logan. My hair is a rat's nest of knots and snarls. My eyeliner from yesterday is smudged all around my eyes and runs down my cheeks. I look like a drowned rat. But the damage has already been done, Logan has officially seen me at my worst. I leave the bathroom and head downstairs. I find Logan in the kitchen scrambling eggs with ham and cheese.

"Smells good," I say.

"Sit," he says, gesturing to the island that sits in the middle of the kitchen.

His face is clean shaven and I find that I miss the stubble.

I walk across the hard wood, surprised to find that it is not chilly to the touch. Like the living room, and the rest of the house that I have seen, it is a dark stained hardwood. The fridge, stove, and the rest of the appliances look brand new.

I stare at the fridge, its stainless steel face bare. No pictures. No notes. No magnets. Nothing. I would think that even the loneliest people could find at least one picture, post card, or puppy picture to put on their fridge. Like the living room, the color scheme is black, grey, and dark brown. His drawers and cabinets black. The counter tops and walls shades of grey.

Logan slides a plate of the scrambled eggs in front of me then goes to the fridge. Soon after, chocolate milk sits in front of me. I dig in, not knowing I was so hungry. It tastes amazing. Never before have I made such delicious eggs before. I almost feel embarrassed for myself, thinking of myself as somewhat of a good cook.

Logan sits in the chair next to me and we eat in silence for a few minutes before he says, "I was thinking we could have another go at our Home Ec. project today. And maybe while we cook we can talk?"

I don't know what there is left to say. Logan answered most of my questions last night. And although he said he would answer the others another time, I don't think it is going to be today. But I don't want to leave Logan. And I don't want to go home to an empty house. Especially without Nash.

And then it hits me. I dreamt of Nash last night. I think it was a cross between a memory and a dream, but either way, I got to see him. It was almost like his ghost or angel-self entered my dream. I swear we had a real conversation. He knew about Logan being in my life. Even that Logan is a phoenix. He called it a plot twist, like my life is some romance novel or something. I don't know what he was talking about me being in danger or being careful. Xander says I'm in danger with Logan. But Logan said Xander was dangerous. Who do I trust? Could they both be wrong? Could they both be right? And what was it Nash said about not trusting people I think I can?

My life is a mess. I don't even know what is going on but I have all these different people telling me who I should and should not be spending time with. Can I not make my own choices?

"Casslyn?" I hear someone call my name.

"Casslyn?" There it is again. It sounds closer this time.

Then my body is violently jerked and I come back to reality. "Casslyn?"

"What?" I snap.

"You left me for a minute. Are you okay?"

"Fine."

"So what do you think?"

"About what?" I ask, confused.

"About finishing our homework today and talking?"

"Oh. Yeah. Yeah. I would like that. Do we need to go to the grocery store?"

"No. I have everything."

"Okay. Let's get started."

***

An hour later we sit back down to the island and are eating our delicious creation. Logan and I work well together. It was effortless. There was no questioning or running into each other. And there was certainly no cutting of skin or burning of flesh.

I was right about Logan not answering the questions he didn't answer last night. But I'm not going to push it. He said he would tell me and I just have to trust him. I just hope it doesn't blow up in my face.

While we wash and put away the dishes, Logan turns to me and says, "I want to do something this afternoon. And I want you to trust me."

"*Okay*," I say, wary of what I am getting myself into.

"Okay," Logan says, placing the last plate into the cupboard. "Let's go."

"Go? Where?"

"Your house," Logan says like it's the most obvious thing in the world.

Twenty One

"What do you think you are doing?" I ask, angry, following Logan from my house out to my Charger.

Logan hits the automatic unlock then opens the driver's side door. "Get in," he says.

I walk around the car, swing the door shut then walk back to stand in front of it, crossing my arms, and say, "No."

"You said you trusted me."

"I never said that." My nostrils flare in anger. I can't believe he is trying to make me do this. He knows what this car means to me.

"Don't act like a child."

"Shut up."

Logan raises his eyebrows at me. I can tell he is trying to

be patient with me but quickly losing that battle.

"Get in the car, Casslyn," he says, slowly, calmly.

"No," I say through my teeth, trying to keep my voice from shaking. The throbbing at the base of my skull begins and my heart thumps hard. I look up at him, with tears in my eyes. "Please don't make me do this."

Logan gazes back at me with a look that says he hates to do this but that he feels like he must. "I wouldn't do this if I thought you couldn't. But I know you can."

"I can't, Logan."

"Just get in the car. Just start there. We can go from there."

The Charger in front of me is a reminder of so many things that I would rather not be reminded of. Happier times. When my family was whole and happy and still together. When my twin and best friend was still alive. When my friends and I were close as it was possible to be.

Sad times. Losing my brother. Rehabbing from a car accident. A second car accident. Fighting with Xander and Tucker. Being at odds but also in love with Logan. My parents breaking up. My parents no longer loving each other.

It's all too much. A deep panic sets in.

"No. I can't do this," I say turning to walk back to my house.

Logan's hand snakes around my arm and spins me around. He uses his other hand to clasp my cheek and pulls me toward him, planting his lips against mine. A shudder of pleasure runs through me. But also a calming, warmth spreads deep. My arm, my cheek, and my lips tingle. Then his hands travel and more parts of my body sizzle. The panic recedes and I can breathe again.

Logan pulls away, too quickly, and says, "Better?"

"Yeah," I say. "Thanks."

"Please, Casslyn. Get in the car. I promise you can do this."

"So what if I do this? Are you going to change your mind about being together?"

"No. I'm not going to change my mind. But what are you going to get? You'll start to get your life back."

I will never get my life back. But I'm pretty sure if I don't at least get in my car, Logan is not going to drop this.

I glare at him then step around him. Then I glare at the car, daring it to bite me, then open the driver's side door. I take a deep breath, sigh heavily, and climb in. I continue to take deep breaths, trying to keep myself calm. It works for the most part.

The door to the passenger side opens and Logan sits in the seat.

"Good," he says. "Now start the car."

My head whips around and I say, "What?"

"I'm not going to coddle you anymore. Just start the damn car."

"No."

"Start the car," Logan's voice raises.

"Don't push me, Logan." I yell back.

"Start. The. Car," he says each word like a sentence.

"Ahh," I yell and turn the key in the ignition.

It roars to life and I am hit by a barrage of images of the night of my birthday. Nash starting his brand new motorcycle and revving it up. The two of us speeding away from our house and our loving parents. The blinding headlights headed straight for us.

I blink and shake my head, trying my best to remove the horrible memories. At least for right now.

I sit in the driver's seat and try to mentally prepare myself for what Logan is going to want from me next.

"Casslyn" Logan says, trying to get my attention.

When I turn to him, he takes my face in his hands and pulls me close.

I think he is going to kiss me again when he says, "Casslyn, I'm doing this to help you, not to torture you. I look at you and I see you just surviving. I want to see you live."

I look at Logan and see the true concern in his eyes. And then I know that though he says we can't be together, as a couple, or really anything more than what we are, he does care about me. And he really is trying to help me.

"As much as I appreciate you doing this. And as good as it makes me feel. I can't even imagine living, when I can barely survive.

"I know how long it has been since he died. And I know that kids' parents get divorced every day. But with Nash gone, I don't just feel like I lost my brother and my best friend. I feel like I lost half of myself. And my parents, they never fought, never acted like anything was amiss. They loved each other until that day. Our family was perfect and then something snapped and I felt like my life was over. I may just sound like a drama queen but it's the way I feel."

Logan stares at me for a long time. Then he pulls me closer to him and plants his lips on my forehead. When he pulls away a warmth spreads from my forehead to the rest of my body.

He smiles at me, a real smile, not that devilish grin he usually gives me, and we sit back. Without him having to tell me, I put the car in drive and step on the gas. The first minute is tricky. My breathing is strained and my vision threatens to blur. But eventually everything straightens out and I realize why this was the car that I've always wanted to drive. It's got power and grace and badass appeal. It even handles the muddy spots of the road well. I even handle the muddy spots well, not panicking and remembering the night I rolled Xander's mustang.

Logan and I drive around for a little over an hour then head back to my house. When I pull up the drive way, Logan becomes tense. When I park, he tells me to stay in the car, but of course I don't listen. I follow him to the front door and find Xander sitting on the front step.

"You drove your car? With *him*?" Xander sounds hurt. Like I've betrayed him somehow.

Nothing I do is right with him anymore.

"Leave her alone," Logan says.

"Stay out of this," Xander says, standing up and taking a defensive position.

I take a step between the two guys and ask Xander, "Why are you here?"

It is seconds before Xander pulls his gaze away from Logan to answer me. "You weren't answering your phone. No calls, no texts. For two days now. People got worried."

There's so many differences between Logan and Xander. They are two completely different people in almost every way, including the ways they try to take care of me. Xander doesn't push me, doesn't expect me to do anything I'm not ready for. Whereas Logan pushes me, forces me to become someone I never thought I could be. Like driving my car. Xander would never have made me do it. He would have waited till I was ready. Which I never would have been. And he would have been okay with it. They are both right in their own respect. Both looking out for me the best they know how. But like driving my car, I've found that I need to be pushed. I need to find myself beyond the parameters of my brother, parents, and best friends. Logan gives me that, Xander doesn't. That is only one of the reasons I cannot be with him.

"I must have left it in my bag or my room. I'm sorry. I didn't think about it."

"That's because you didn't think, Casslyn. I've told you and told you this guy is dangerous but you refuse to listen."

"Hey," Logan says. "Lay off."

"Why don't you just leave?" Xander says.

"Would both of you stop it? Xander you can see that I am fine. Logan, he is just being protective."

They both look at me like I am crazy.

"Look, Logan, why don't you go back to your house and let me talk to Xander. Then I can come over and we can write up our project."

"I'm not leaving you alone with this guy," they both say in unison.

I've never had two guys fight over me before. I've always thought it would be flattering, but really it is just annoying and a pain in the ass.

"Knock it off. If neither one of you can agree to what I just said, you can both leave."

"Fine," they both grumble and Logan walks off.

"Do you want to go inside? It's cold out here," Xander says.

I hadn't noticed the cold. I still don't. Maybe it is just the adrenaline.

We go into my house, make hot chocolate, and sit on the couch like we used to.

"I'm sorry I scared you," I start off, trying to ease his tension.

"Why? How could you drive your car with him?"

"It just kind of happened. I didn't plan it."

"I really wish you would stay away from him, Cass."

"I'm not saying this to be mean, Xander. I'm really not. Because you are my best friend and I never want to hurt you. But are you saying that because you are jealous of him, or because you really think I am in danger?"

Xander looks down at his feet then back up at me. "Yes.

I am jealous. You know how I feel about you. It kills me that you would rather be with him than me. But I promise you that he is dangerous. I would never lie to you."

"I understand that you are concerned, but I have never been in danger with Logan. He saved my life when I rolled your car. He took me home when I passed out at the dress shop. He-,"

"What? When did that happen? Why didn't you tell me?"

"I don't know. It never came up."

"Casslyn, why is he more important to you than I am?"

All this time I thought Xander was the one angry with me and shutting me out. But maybe we are both to blame for doing that.

"When I'm with Logan I can breathe again," I say, and though it is the truth, I feel ashamed.

"I could have given you that," Xander says. He sounds on the verge of tears.

"No. You don't understand. When I'm with you and Tucker I'm reminded of Nash and what I lost and it hurts."

"So why haven't you pushed Tucker away like you've pushed me away?"

"Because you tried to be Nash," I snap, then clasp my hands over my mouth regretting what I said instantly.

Calmly, Xander says, "I never tried to be Nash. I tried to help you through it. And I tried to love you in hopes that one day you would love me back. But I never tried to be Nash. I know I could never replace him. I'm sorry you felt like I tried."

Xander gets off the couch and moves for the door.

"Xander don't leave," I say, rushing after him. "I'm sorry. Can we just talk about this?"

I reach for him and when he pushes me away, it is with muscle he didn't have a couple months ago. I stumble back, losing my footing, and crash to the floor. The look on his face is controlled but angry. For the first time in our lives, I am afraid of him.

I back up on the floor until I am stopped by the couch. Maybe Logan is the one who is right. Maybe Xander really is dangerous.

"Don't do that, Casslyn. Don't be scared. I'm so sorry," he says, walking towards me.

I don't move. Unsure of what to do. He takes one step at a time until he is directly in front of me. He picks me up off the floor the puts his hands on my arms. Then he pulls me forward. He hugs me. And still I don't move.

"I'm so sorry," he says against my hair.

"What has happened to us?" I ask.

"I don't know, Cass. I don't know." Xander releases me then steps away. He places his hands on his head then rubs them down his face. Then he surprises me by roaring. Actually roaring like a lion or something. "God. I don't know. I want to blame it on *him*," he says, pointing in the direction of Logan's house, "but that would just make you mad and drive you further away from me. Nothing I do is right with you."

"Oh, because everything I do is? I try to be friends with

all of you but that's not right. Logan is helping me finally move on but I'm not allowed to do that because he is dangerous and he takes me away from you. I can't be mad at you but I also can't be friends with you unless I am in love with you. But yet I have to treat you the same way I treat Tucker."

"I just want you to be safe and happy. You may think you are safe with him but I promise you he is not who you think he is."

"Then tell me who he is. Why is he so dangerous? What is he going to do to me?"

"I . . . I can't tell you that. But guys like him will make you believe you are safe and they are nice guys, but they aren't."

"We are getting nowhere here."

"I will prove it to you. I will show you who he is. And then I'm going to take him down. Mark my words." Xander is more determined than I have ever seen him.

He stares at me for a long time. A time where I don't know what to say. Does he know Logan is a phoenix? How could he know Logan is a phoenix? He's going to take him down? What does that mean? Should I warn Logan? Should I protect Xander?

Before I can decide anything, Xander walks out my front door.

***

It takes me a long time to collect myself before I can head back over to Logan's. And when I am there trying to work on our project, I am barely in it.

Logan leaves me be for the most part. But after a while he says, "You know, I could just write this myself."

"What?" I ask.

"I'm just saying, I've been to high school a few times. I can finish this, if you're struggling."

"I'm not struggling," I snap. "How many times have you been to high school?"

"I thought you didn't want to know how old I am?"

I glare at him, but don't comment.

"Where's your head, Casslyn?"

"It's just something Xander said," I say, looking around Logan's kitchen, trying to find a focal point other than him. His naked fridge bothers me. I feel the need to put at least one picture or magnet or something on it.

"That he loves you?"

"How did you know that?" I ask. I look at him and he looks back at me like I'm an idiot for thinking he didn't know.

"Besides the fact that he told me? And the fact that he told me to stay away from you? It's obvious to everyone. Except you, I guess."

"I don't know what to do," I say. This is not what I meant when I said I was thinking about something Xander said. But since Logan brought it up, I want to talk about it.

"You know, I don't think I'm the best person to give you advice on this."

"I know. It's just hard. He's my best friend," I say.

Logan looks at me like he expects me to say more. When I don't, he looks worried. But I don't know what else to say without bursting open the damn within me. I want to keep Xander as my best friend, but I don't know how that is possible when he wants more.

"Do you want to talk about it?" Logan slowly asks.

"No," I say, not fully sure. "Yes." But does he want to talk about it? "No."

"Are you okay to finish the project?"

"Yes," I say, wanting to forget my troubles with Xander. But then I remember what it actually is that I was going to say regarding him. "Wait. That is not the thing I was thinking about with Xander."

"Oh?" Logan says. He actually looks relieved that I was not thinking of Xander's love for me. "Do tell."

"It's about you. He said he is going to prove to me that you are dangerous. Which I think he meant that he is going to prove that you are a phoenix. Which I already know, so no shock value there. But I don't know how he would know what you are. Do you?"

Logan's eyes jump the slightest bit, but he looks straight at me and says, "No. I don't. Maybe he is just grasping at straws. Did he say anything else?"

"Only that he is going to take you down."

"Awesome," Logan says, deadpan.

"Right," I say.

This can only end badly.

Twenty Two

I sit in my Ancient World History class twirling the bracelet Nash gave me around my wrist. Tucker sits on my left, Logan on my right. In a few hours we will be out of school for Christmas break. I've never felt happier for a vacation.

It's been weeks since Xander made his threat. Weeks since we've said a word to each other. I am unaware of how Xander will make his move. Will he make a big public spectacle? Does he only want me to know? Is he going to physically hurt Logan?

I can't help but feel like I am waiting on the edge of something huge. Even bigger than finding out about Logan being a phoenix. I feel as though all control over my life is slipping away from me. Xander is bound and determined to love me and destroy Logan. Logan is struggling to find a balance from me and be himself around me. And Tucker remains blissfully ignorant to it all.

Last week a foot of snow fell and we didn't have school for two days. Tucker tried to get the Musketeers together again, mend fences and such but I couldn't get out of my house and Xander wanted no part of it. So instead, I went to Logan's house and we spent the day eating popcorn and watching movies. My mom was stuck at the hospital, so it wasn't like she would walk in on us, but it still felt more private to be at Logan's house. Not that we needed privacy, Logan is holding me to what I said about backing away from trying to get us to be a couple. He kept a good two feet between us on the couch at all times and only touched me when absolutely necessary. He barely even looked at me unless he needed to. It wasn't perfect, but still, spending any time with him, friends or a couple, was better than not spending any time with him, or even worse, spending time alone.

As much as I am looking forward to Christmas vacation, I am not looking forward to spending Christmas without Nash. Thanksgiving was bad enough. Empty house. No family. The tears that freely flowed down my cheeks. I'm sure, like Thanksgiving, my mom has picked up extra shifts at the hospital over Christmas so she can avoid it. And I haven't talked to my dad in weeks. More than likely, we will not be spending Christmas together. Maybe, by some miracle, I could spend it with both of them, as a family, a fractured family, but a family nonetheless. But it would be nearly impossible to get my parents in the same room, let alone to play house. Unless . . . Unless I didn't tell either of them that they would be together. But am I that good of a liar? I will have to be if I want this to work. What if it actually works? I could have my parents back. My family back. My heart races just thinking about it.

Logan places his warm hand on my leg. His touch alone electrifies me but also calms me.

"Casslyn. Casslyn." Why do people always try to get my attention? "*Miss Evans.*" Oh crap. Mr. Jared.

"Yes?" I ask as innocently as possible.

"I asked whether you think the death of Caesar could have been avoided."

I turn to Tucker who taps his history book. Oh right. I'm still in class.

"No."

"Do you care to elaborate on that?"

I want to say no, but before I can, the bell rings and I am saved.

Five more classes until I am home free and able to hatch my brilliant plan. But first, I need to do a little last minute Christmas shopping. Tucker deserves an extra special gift this year, and although we are at odds right now, Xander is my best friend, and I have never not given him a gift.

Tucker, Logan, and I walk the hallway towards our lockers.

We walk by Ashley and her posse. She glares at me, but

says nothing. As of late, she has left me alone, to everyone's surprise. Xander stands by them, but talks to none of them. It almost looks as though it pains him to stand with them. He's made his bed, he must lie in it.

"What were you day dreaming about in there, Casslyn?" Tucker asks me. "You know, one day that is going to get you into trouble."

"I know," I reply. "But it was pretty good day dreaming. I had the greatest idea."

"Do tell," Tucker says.

I stop in the middle of the hallway and turn around so I am facing both Tucker and Logan. "I am going to get my parents together for Christmas. Not *back* together, just together. We could be a family for Christmas."

"How do you plan on doing that?" Tucker asks, at the same time Logan says, "I don't think that is such a good idea."

"I don't know," I tell Tucker then look to Logan and ask, "Why not?"

"Yeah, why not?" Tucker asks but doesn't wait for an answer and continues, "I'm her best friend, let me advise her."

Logan crosses his arms and raises an eyebrow at the both of us.

"You should totally do it. Oh Casslyn, you could get your parents back together and spend more time with your dad."

"I know. I miss him so much. My mom, too. She works

all the time. It's like I live alone. If I got them together on Christmas they would have to at least talk, right?"

"You would think," Tucker says. "I really hope it works out for you, sweetie. Let me know how it goes. Also, I am having Christmas for you, me, and Xander at my place the day after. No offense Logan. It is a mandatory best friend event. Neither one of you is allowed to get out of it."

"I appreciate the effort, Tucker, but I don't think it's going to work."

"Oh, it's going to work," Tucker assures me.

"Okay. I really hope so."

Tucker looks at me with this look that says, I'm-going-to-get-the-gang-back-together-if-it-kills-me. "It's going to work."

***

"Are you done *yet*?" Logan asks from behind me.

"You offered to chauffer me. That means you either plant your butt until I am done or don't complain."

"But this is taking forever," Logan says, legging even farther behind as I walk the length of the mall looking for the right store.

"You are such a whiner. Who knew, Logan turns into a big baby when forced to go shopping."

"Very funny," he says, a nonplussed look on his face.

"I only have a few more stops and then we can leave."

"Well, we can eat first," Logan says.

I grin, amused by him. When I first met Logan, he scared the crap out of me with all his intimidating glory. Then he surprised me with his soft side, his concern for me. And now I find out he whines when made to do something he doesn't want to. Other than Xander, he may be the most complex male I have ever met.

"Whatever you want," I say, smiling at him.

I spend the rest of the day putting up the Christmas tree and decorating it. With the assistance of Logan of course. In between doing that, cleaning the house, and wrapping the presents, I try calling my dad. Every time I call, the phone rings and rings and rings and finally goes to voicemail. My genius plan won't work if my dad won't answer his phone.

The fifth time I call him, he picks up. "Hey, sweetheart. Sorry I've missed your calls. It's been crazy busy here today."

"It's okay, dad," I say, though I can't help but feel I'm getting the brush off.

"So what's up?"

"I wanted to know if you would come to my house for Christmas."

"I don't know, sweetheart. You're mom and I-,"

"Mom won't be there," I tell him quickly. Lying through my teeth has never been my strong suit. "She's working at the hospital. If you don't come over, I'll be alone."

Maybe the guilt of a lonely kid will be enough to get him to come.

My dad sighs on the other end of the phone and then

is quiet for a while. "Alright kid, Christmas Day, you, me, presents, and apple cider."

My heart plummets into my stomach. He actually said yes. "Thank you, Dad," I say on the verge of tears.

"You're welcome. I'll see you then. But I need to get back to work."

"Yeah, no problem. See you then."

My chest is weighed down by relief and longing and so much more that I can barely catch my breath. From behind me, Logan places his hands on my shoulders and works to calm me.

"This could actually work," I say to him, or to myself, maybe both.

Logan turns me around so I am facing him.

"What if it doesn't? I don't want you to get your hopes up and then it all blows up in your face."

"It's a risk I have to take," I say but fall into his chest, the pressure too much.

Twenty Three

I spend the next few days frantically trying to make my house perfect for my parents' *reunion*, if that's what you can call it. I actually convinced my mom that not working on Christmas was for the best. It took a lot of work and a huge guilt trip, but it worked. They will both be here on Christmas. With me. How could this possibly go wrong?

I mop the floors, vacuum, wash every dish in the house, pick up every scrap of anything lying around the house, light candles so the rooms smell nice, and even go as far as dusting the walls. This has to go well.

Besides being so nervous I have to pee every two minutes, I feel like I have to throw up. However nauseous I am, I could not be more excited. I get to spend an entire day with my parents. It will be just like the good old days. When the four of us sat around in our pajamas all day playing board games and drinking hot chocolate. Then we'd light a fire and open presents to the sound of the crackling wood. Our parents would get Nash and I all different presents so we would feel like individuals, but one present that was the same so our twin bond would stay intact. I miss my family more than I thought possible. We were stronger together. Happier together. Better together. Being apart from them has killed my spirit. Being without my brother has nearly killed me.

But today is the day I get it all back. Well, not all. Unless a miracle occurs, I will never get Nash back.

I put some finishing touches on the house while mom showers. Pull out the board games. Line up the hot chocolate. Make sure there are no creases in my pjs.

My mom walks down the stairs in clothes that are not her pjs. A small wave of devastation rushes through me.

"Where are your pajamas, mom?" I ask her. "It's tradition."

"I thought we could start a new tradition this year sweetie," she says, laying a hand on my shoulder then walks to the kitchen.

This could work. Maybe new traditions are what we need to get past whatever it is that separated them and start over. Maybe it doesn't have to be the way it was. New isn't always bad.

"What kind of tradition were you thinking?"

My mom glances around the house, looking for inspiration maybe, or grasping at straws, then turns to me and says, "I don't know, sweetheart, we will figure something out."

I deflate. She is not into today already. Is not prepared to try. How could it possibly get better when my dad gets here?

But I see it in her eyes. The sadness. The loss. The emptiness. I know it well, because I feel it every day. Every day without Nash is like the longest day of my life. It never ends and it never gets better.

I walk up to my mom, say, "I love you," then wrap my arms around her.

Her arms wrap around me, but the hug is lacking. Her arms are weak, the embrace brittle. As much as my mom loved me, and I know she did, Nash was always her favorite, and I will never be able to replace him. No matter how hard I try. I guess all we can do is work on our relationship.

We pull away from each other when we hear a knock at the door. My dad is here.

"Were you expecting anyone?" my mom asks, but doesn't give me a chance to answer before she opens the door. "Aaron?"

"Marion," my dad says, a sigh ending her name.

"Casslyn?" they both ask together.

"Merry Christmas," I say, a guilty smile on my face.

After a *long* and uncomfortable silence, my mom asks, "Would you like to come in?"

"Maybe I should leave," my dad says.

"No," I nearly scream. "You can't leave. Please don't leave," I beg.

"Casslyn, you lied to us," my mom says.

"I'm sorry," my dad says, "I shouldn't have come."

"It's alright," my mom answers.

"Mom, Dad," I look at them, tears building in my eyes. "Please, please, just give me one day. It's Christmas. *Please.*"

"I suppose one day won't kill us," my dad says.

"Surely," my mom says. "Come in."

I rush my dad and hug him so fiercely he stumbles. "I'm staying kid, you don't need to strangle me."

"Sorry," I say, backing away. "Would you like to see the house?"

"Sure," he says.

My mom retreats to the kitchen, busying herself with anything she can get her hands on. I'm sure she is nervous. I know I am. I haven't been in the same room as my parents since the day I woke up in the hospital after our accident.

I show my dad around the house, making note of the Christmas tree I decorated, of course I leave Logan out of it. Then I show him the upstairs. He makes note of the un-packed boxes in my room. Again, I leave out the part that I don't want to live here, that I want to live with him. It would only start a fight and I don't want that today. The house tour is short, it's a small house, and we return to my mother.

Again, there is an awkward silence, until I suggest we play a board game.

Mad Gab is a bust, I swear you need more than three people to make that game fun. Also, I all but have the cards memorized making it no fun for the rest of the players. Clue is also not that much fun with only three people. We settle on Monopoly. I pick the car, my mom picks the thimble, my dad picks the hat, and we place the dog on the board in memory of Nash.

My mom plays the banker and deals out the money. My dad fidgets the whole time like he's nervous or anxious. His fidgeting makes me nervous. We begin to play, each of us rolling the dice three times, before my dad stands up.

I saw it coming, but it still hits hard.

"I can't do this," he says. "I'm sorry kid. I have to go."

He walks toward the door. I get up and trail after him.

"Dad, wait. Please don't leave."

He turns around and looks down at me. "I'm sorry, Casslyn. It's just not going to work. You can't fix it, although I appreciate you trying."

He hugs me then walks out the door.

I want to cry. I want to run up to my room, curl up in a ball on my bed, and weep till I have no tears left. But I don't. No tears come. Only disappointment. Logan saw this coming. I should have too.

"What were you thinking, young lady?" my mom asks from behind me. She is angry, which makes me angry.

"What was I thinking? Maybe that I could have my family back."

"You had no right to bring him here. And to lie to me about it."

"I had no right?" I say, calm, but fuming mad. "He's my dad. You're my parents. I had every right to want you to get back together."

"We are your parents, and that means we make those decisions."

"Oh, don't give me that shit," I yell. "You cannot act like my mom now when you have neglected me for the past nine months."

"Neglected you?" my mom asks, walking away with a wave of her hand.

"Don't walk away from me," I scream, following after her. I grab her arm and fling her around. "That's what you do. You walk away. You don't face anything. You barely even talked to Dad. Why couldn't you have at least tried?"

"It's not the same anymore. Okay? Your brother is gone and so is your dad, so just drop it."

"No! I'm not going to drop it. I get it. Nash is gone. You miss him. I lost him too. But I'm still here. Why have you forgotten about me?"

"I'm sorry you feel that way, honey," my mom says and walks toward me with her arms outstretched.

"Don't," I say. I've had enough. My dad was right, there is no fixing it. What's done is done and I need to stop trying to make it all better. "It's too late."

"Why then?" my mom yells. "Why make a big deal about it if you don't care?"

"I don't care? I've cared for nine months. But it's over. I can't make you care, so why should I? Nash was your favorite. I know that. I just thought there was a small part of you that loved me."

"I do love you. Don't you dare say that I don't."

"Well, you're shit at showing it," I say, walking away from her, and ending the conversation. If I had any hope of repairing my relationship with my mom, it just went down the tube. But right now I'm too tired of trying to care.

I can't stay at my house with my mom, though I'm sure she'll just go to the hospital, so I grab my keys and head for my car. Though it is not cold outside and it is only a mile to Logan's house, I don't feel like walking. He opens the door before I have a chance to knock.

"How good is your hearing?" I ask before he can say anything.

"If you're asking if I can hear what goes on in your house, no, I cannot."

"Okay," I say and march past him into his house.

"I gather it didn't go well," he says trailing after me.

I plop my butt into his leather recliner and say, "Right you are, sir." In all my fury and hurry to leave my house I forgot that I'm wearing pajamas. At this point I don't care. It's not like he hasn't seen me in worse.

"Are you okay?"

"No."

"Do you want to talk about it?"

"No."

"*Okay*," he says sitting on the couch.

"Do you want your present?" I ask him.

He looks at me, surprise written all over his face, "You got me a present?"

"Yes," I say, smiling. "It's okay if you didn't get me anything. I didn't expect you to."

His eyes narrow and he smirks at me, "I got you something."

Now it is my turn to be surprised. But I recover quickly and smile at him. I pull my camera from my back pocket and move towards Logan.

"You got me a used camera?" he asks.

"No, smart ass. This is only part of your present. Well, this is more of a present for me. I'm tired of the front of your fridge being bare. I am going to take pictures and you are going to put them on it."

"*Okay*," he says again.

"Stop that," I say, playfully slapping his arm. "Wait, will you show up in a picture?"

Logan bursts out laughing, but when he sees I am serious he stops and stares at me.

"Yes, I will show up in pictures. I'm exactly like everyone else."

"Except that you're not."

"*Right*."

I sit down a few inches away from Logan. I'm not sure how close he will allow me to get. He hasn't been touchy-feely lately. But then he wraps his arm around me and scoots me closer to him, so there is no space at all between us. He keeps his arm around me, only he brings it up to my shoulder. He takes the camera out of my hand, leans his head closer to mine, smiles, and snaps a picture.

Logan looks at the picture on the camera screen then shows me, saying, "Like it?"

I nod my head, unable to speak I like it so much.

"Good. I'll go get your present and take more pictures while you open it."

Logan leaves the living room in the direction of the stairs. I sit on the couch stunned. Logan is almost acting like, dare I say it, a boyfriend. And it's almost freaking me out. I run outside to get his present while he is upstairs.

We meet back on the couch and hand over our presents. Mine is small and rectangular and looks suspiciously like a jewelry box. I'm nervous and shaky before I can even open it.

"You first," I say.

Logan tears open the wrapping paper, looks over his present, and laughs deeps and true. I knew he would like it. He unfolds the apron and pulls it over his head. "Kiss the cook, huh?"

I raise an eyebrow at him but do nothing else. I don't want to start a fight when I know he won't kiss me.

Logan, on the other hand, must want to start a fight because with blinding speed, his face is maybe an inch from mine. He is no longer laughing, but staring deep into my eyes. My breath catches in my throat and I must remind myself to breathe.

"So, you going to?" he asks, resting a knee on the couch, getting closer to me.

I lean back and try to swallow, but it gets caught somewhere in the process. I blink rapidly, thinking maybe if I do it enough, I will open my eyes and he will not be in front of me and this will be some daydream. But when I stop blinking them, he is closer to me, if it were even possible.

"You haven't cooked anything," I manage to say and then feel stupid for it.

He chuckles, a laugh coming from deep in this throat. His voice alone still turns me on, but him being this close to me is doing insanely mean things to my womanhood.

"I can if you want me to," he says, his eyes smoldering, burning holes into me.

I sigh one of those hiccup-pleasure sighs that are so embarrassing and want to slap myself on the forehead. Logan has this flirting thing down and I look like an idiot.

"You can what?" I ask breathlessly. He really does funny things to my brain.

He laughs again then leans in close and blows on my ear and says, "Would you like me to try on my apron, and only my apron?"

If I sighed embarrassingly before, it is nothing compared to what comes out of me now. I close my eyes tight, trying to get a grip on myself. What is Logan trying to do to me? Seduce me? Kill me maybe? Whatever it is, it is so not going along with his no-touching-no-kissing-no-coupling policy.

I get enough of a grip on myself and reality to say, "Don't do this to me, Logan," though it hurts like Hell to say.

He rests his head on my shoulder, sighs heavily, the pulls away. "Open your present," he says.

I let out a deep breath I'd been holding and look for the box. I'd almost forgotten about it. I open the wrapping slowly and carefully wanting to savor the moment. It's definitely a jewelry box. I open the box but do not find jewelry of any kind. Instead I find a folded piece of paper. I take it out, unfold it, and read.

To Casslyn
My gift to you is a kiss. No arguments. No tricks. No holding back. And no regret.
Merry Christmas
Logan

I swallow hard and read the note again three times. When I look up at him, his swift fingers are there to wipe away a fallen tear that I didn't know was there.

"Why are you crying? I thought this would make you happy."

I smile at him through my stupid tears and says, "It does. I promise you it does."

Logan wipes away another tear before he asks, "So what's the problem? Is it because of what I am?"

"No. Of course not. And if you believe that then I have no business being here."

"I'm sorry. I shouldn't have said that. But why then?"

"I am just adhering to our agreement."

"But this is my gift. To forgo it just once."

"Yes and I thank you. A thousand times. But if you give

me one kiss I will only want a hundred more and we both know you won't let that happen. And for that reason I cannot cash this in. At least not now."

I can't believe that is my gift. It may well be the best gift ever. And yet I can't appreciate it. And what hurts too much is that Logan was so willing to give it to me. That's what he was doing after I gave him his gift. The leaning in. The whispering in my ear. He was giving me a gift he knew I wanted. One that would cost him. And yet he cared about me enough to give it to me. What a world we live in.

I lay against the back of the couch, sighing deeply. Logan leans back and places his warm arm around my shoulders. I rest my head in the crook of his arm and we sit in silence.

Some point later I wake up in the same place. My skin tingles where Logan touches me. I don't think I will ever get tired of the feeling. I lay back into Logan and revel in just being here with him. I feel more relaxed, more comfortable, happier than I have felt since before Nash died. And that has a lot to do with Logan.

Logan stirs next to me, waking up. He smiles down at me and says, "Do you want to stay the night? You can have my room. I'll take the couch. I don't want you to have to be alone on Christmas."

"I would love to. But I think I'm going to go home anyway. Thank you. For everything."

Logan's eyebrows pull together so I say, "I promise you I will be okay. I think being alone may do me some good. I think I'm afraid of being alone. I've been part of a set since I was born and not having that other person constantly with me is harder for me than anything I have ever done. But I think I need to learn to be alone."

Again Logan's brows do worrying things so I assure him, "If I need you I promise I will call you right away."

"Okay," he relents.

I smile at him, scrunch my nose, and say, "You take care of me, Logan."

He shrugs like its nothing and says, "I try. Now go before I change my mind."

"Bye, Logan. Merry Christmas."

Twenty Four

"Merry Christmas!" Tucker yells at me when he opens the door.

My eyes grow wide and I smile at him. I'm not sure I've ever seen him this excited.

"Come in, come in," he says, ushering me in the door. "How was your Christmas? How did it go with your parents? Are they back together? Tell me everything."

"It didn't exactly go as planned," I say.

His shoulders fall, clearly he is disappointed. He has no idea.

"I'm sorry, Cass," Tucker says, putting his hand on my arm for comfort.

"Don't worry about it. I'm over it."

"Are you?"

"No. But what am I supposed to do about it?"

Tucker opens his mouth to say something, but closes it without saying anything. This is the first time I've ever seen him speechless. If the subject weren't so wretched, it would be quite amusing. He recovers quickly and takes the boxes from my arms. He escorts me into the living room, places the boxes by the tree and leads me to the kitchen where his mom is placing cookies on a tray.

"Hi, Mrs. Fleming. Thanks for having me."

"Merry Christmas, Casslyn. No problem. We always love having you over. You know that. We hope you can make it for New Year's Eve." Tucker's mom is a saint. Very unlike my own mom. When Tucker decided to come out to his parents, his mom accepted him without pause, not so much his dad. She threatened to divorce him if he couldn't accept his son for who he is. The three of them have never been happier. Something that could have torn them apart has only made them closer. Unlike my family, who not only was torn apart but took the opportunity and ran with it.

"Thanks," I say, "I'll see what I can do."

Mrs. Fleming hands us a cup of hot chocolate and a plate of cookies and sends us back to the living room.

"So what happened?" Tucker asks, not missing a beat.

We forego the furniture for sitting on the floor. It is something we have done since we were kids. The Flemings have a fire place we like to crowd around. It was easier when we were younger because we were smaller. But now there are fewer of us, so I guess it evens out.

"They were shocked they were in the same house. But they at least tried. For a little bit. That is, until my dad freaked out and left. Then my mom and I had a huge fight and I left," I say.

"And you went to Logan's," he finishes for me.

"I did."

"What happened there? Did he give you a present? Did he like your present?"

"I don't tell you everything, Tucker."

"Yes you do, now shut up and tell me what happened."

"How can I shut up and tell you what happened?"

"Casslyn, stop being difficult," Tucker says, slapping my leg.

"It was fine. Good. I don't know what you want me to say. I went there. He asked me about my parents. We didn't talk about it much. Then I gave him his gift. He liked it. He gave me a gift. I liked it. Then we fell asleep on the couch and when we woke up I went home. That about sums it up."

"Where are the juicy details? What did he get you? Did he let you kiss the cook? Does he love you yet? Do I get anything good?"

I stare at Tucker for a good while before saying, "Where is Xander? Shouldn't he be here by now?"

"He's coming. Don't think you can get out of it that easily. And don't think I'm going to let the Logan thing go. Spill."

I breathe in and sigh heavily, showing Tucker just how

irritated I am with his inquiry. "Logan's gift to me was a kiss. One that I did not take."

"What?" Tucker practically screams at me. "What were you thinking? You turned down a free kiss from the hottest guy ever? What were you thinking? I don't even know you right now."

"I couldn't. Alright. I don't know what Logan feels for me, but one kiss, how could I take it and not want more? I couldn't take it and not want more. Okay?"

"God, your life sucks," Tucker says.

I burst out laughing at his frankness.

"Thanks jerk," I say, smiling at him. He is so right he has no idea.

The doorbell rings and Tucker gets up to answer it. Shortly after he returns, trailed by Xander. I get this tugging at my heart. It's a feeling I know all too well. Xander is my best friend and I love him as such, but recent events have strained our friendship. I'm pretty sure if we were any other two people we would no longer be friends. But there is something about us that can't let go, or won't. That thing may be our true friendship, it may be my dead brother, and it may be Tucker. Who knows. And as much as I hate him right now, and even fear him, I can't imagine my life without Xander in it.

When he walks into the living room, he places his gifts by the tree and doesn't hesitate to sit next to me by the fireplace. He smiles at me and begins to say something, but I lean over and hug him. I hold on tight, as does he. It may not totally repair out relationship, but it is a start.

"I have missed you," he says into my hair.

"Me too," I say.

Maybe for today we can forget everything that has been destroying us and just be like we used to.

Tucker brings in a cup of hot chocolate for Xander and we sit together, talking about the way things used to be. We tell stories of Nash and the four of us. The stupid things we did. I tell them of the dream I had, of the four of us sledding off the roof, leaving out of course the fact that Nash told me to be careful.

We take a break to find a table full of food Tucker's mom has made us, which we stuff our faces with, then go watch our favorite Christmas movie ever, *Home Alone 2: Lost in New York*. We all laugh hysterically at the part where the tool chest comes down the stairs and smacks into them and Marv says, *That was the sound of a tool chest coming down the stairs.*

After the movie it is present time. Tucker's mom has gotten us all matching sweaters like Ron and Harry get in *Harry Potter*. Tucker got Xander a window decal to put in the rear window of his new mustang. He got me the same thing, since I am now driving my car. They are both the silhouettes of the four musketeers. The decals make us laugh and remember the good times.

Then they open their gifts from me. Tucker loves his gift cards to Aeropostale, American Eagle, the Buckle, and Hollister. That gift didn't take much thinking. Tucker loves his clothes. Xander on the other hand was more difficult. There were a thousand things I could have given him if this were a year ago, or if I didn't know he was in love with me, or if he didn't hate the guy I wanted to date. But since all of those things came into play, getting him the perfect gift was more of a challenge. Finally, I decided on a car cleaning kit, since I kind of messed up his first one, the box set of Game of Thrones, which is his new obsession, and the best picture of the two of us I could find. I photo-shopped it and put it in a black frame.

"I love it. Thank you, Casslyn."

Funnily enough, Xander got Tucker the same thing that I got him.

Tucker fakes a blush, waggles his eye lashes and says, "Guys, you shouldn't have."

"One more," Xander says, then gets up from his place by the fire and walks to the door. I'm not sure what he is do-ing, but then he returns with this large, square package. "For you, Casslyn."

I look to Xander, who has this look of pure love and joy in his eyes that I practically start crying and I haven't even opened his gift yet.

I tear into the wrapping like a crazy person and look down at my gift. In my hands is the last good memory I have. The last time I remember being truly happy. My eyes well up instantly, tears streaming down my cheeks.

"It's the picture my mom took when you and Nash came over on your birthday to show us his bike."

"I know," I say, through sobs. Xander has taken the picture his mom took of the four of us, blown it up to at least three feet by four feet, and placed it on a canvas type backing. Other than my bracelet, it may be the best thing I have ever owned. "Thank you, Xander. I don't even know how to thank you."

"You don't need to. You know that. You're my best friend."

"Oh my God, that's so beautiful," Tucker says, tears falling down his face.

Xander and I laugh at him, through our own tears.

"Group hug," Tucker says.

I reverently place the picture down and turn around to hug my two best friends. They both kiss my head then pull away.

After the gifts are opened and more food is consumed, the gathering dwindles down. Xander and I help the Flemings clean up then decide to head out. We thank Mrs. Fleming for everything, hug Tucker once more, gather our new presents, and head for the door.

I load my things in my car and am about to start it when Xander stands out of the driver's side of his car and stares at me.

"What?" I ask, not having a clue as to why he would be looking at me like this.

"I'm sorry, Casslyn," he says.

Before I can ask, "For what?" he has gotten in his car and driven off.

I get in my car and start it, a sinking feeling in my stomach. What could he possibly be sorry for? He just gave me the greatest gift ever. Then it hits me, he just gave me the greatest gift because he is about to take the other best thing in my life away. He has finally decided to strike, to take Logan away from me.

I put my car in drive and tear out of Tucker's driveway like my life depends on it.

Twenty Five

When I pull up to Logan's house, nothing looks amiss, or out of the ordinary. Just as precaution, I run up to his door and rush in without knocking.

"Logan," I shout, running from room to room, trying to find him. "Logan!"

"Logan?"

Nothing. He is not in the living room, the kitchen, the dining room, the bathroom. Xander is not here, either, which I should take as a good sign. And then I run into Logan's bedroom and find them both. They are at a standstill. Xander has a knife in his hand and is pointing it straight at Logan. He whips around when he hears me come in.

"Ah, Casslyn, I thought you might figure it out," he says.

When he looks at me his eyes are bugging out of his head like he has gone mad.

"Xander, put the knife down, we can talk about this."

"Talk? There is nothing to talk about. This guy is a danger to you and I am going to put an end to that."

"Right now the only danger here is you."

"Don't do that, Casslyn," he looks at me, pleading. "I love you. I would never hurt you. He is the one that is destroying everything."

"Xander, please," I say.

I look to Logan who is just casually standing on the other side of his bed, by the window. He looks at me and smiles. He actually smiles, like he is not affected by someone waving a knife at him. Maybe he went crazy too. Or maybe I am in some wacked out dream and just need to wake up.

"It's okay," Logan mouths to me from across the room.

Xander looks between Logan and I trying to gauge the situation. Every time he looks away from me I inch forward to get between him and Logan. Right now they have the bed between them, but that could change in an instant.

Xander looks at Logan and says, "Do you have anything to say for yourself."

Logan shakes his head, no words needed.

"Defend yourself. Beg for your life. Do something. Don't just stand there."

"What do you want from him, Xander?" I ask. "He has done nothing to you."

"He has taken you away from me," Xander says.

Logan now chooses to speak. "She was never yours."

"He didn't take me away from you. You've done that. You're the one that started this. Not trusting him. Thinking he's dangerous. You put the wedge between us. And now you're only making it worse."

"Don't say that," Xander says. "I'm trying to protect you."

"There is nothing to protect me from," I say.

"You don't know what he is," Xander yells waving the knife in front of him.

It's an odd knife. The blade has a bluish tint to it and it doesn't even look like metal.

"Xander, put the knife down and we can talk about this. No one needs to get hurt."

"That's where you're wrong," he says, "he does." That's when he lunges at Logan. He steps onto the bed, using it as leverage, as he strikes toward Logan. I step between the two of them and feel a cold, sharp pain pierce my chest inches above my heart.

I feel Logan's strong arms catch me from behind. I stare at Xander who has pure shock and horror on his face. Pain like I have never felt before snakes its way throughout my chest. I look down at the knife protruding from my chest and watch as it melts away into nothing. Then, the most horrifying thing imaginable happens. The gaping hole in my chest lights on fire. I feel the flames lick my skin, knitting the hole back together. The flames go out and my skin is whole again. I stare at my skin like I'm just seeing it for the first time. I touch it like it's the first thing I've ever felt.

I look at Xander who is on the floor in front of me. He stands and the look on his face is one of shock and confusion and worst of all, disgust. "You're one of them," he snarls at me. He turns to leave.

"Xander, wait," Logan and I say at the same time, but Xander is already out the door.

Logan helps me to a standing position then turns me around to face him. He looks scared shitless. Funny when his life is in danger he smiles but when it's my life in danger he is not so care free.

"What. Just. Happened?" I ask him.

"I don't know," Logan says, wide eyed.

"What do you mean you don't know? Shouldn't you be the expert?"

"That shouldn't have happened. You haven't come of age yet. You could have died. What the hell were you thinking? You could have died." He looks purely panicked now.

"What was I supposed to do, let him stab you?"

"I could have taken care of myself and you know that."

"I'm so sorry for trying to save your life," I say, crossing my arms.

"Stop. Just don't. I don't know what just happened. You are still sixteen right?"

"Yes."

Logan sighs, his shoulders falling and says, "I'm sorry you had to find out this way."

"You knew?" I ask, though I think I know the answer.

"You knew this whole time and you never told me? You lied to me. Everything you've ever said to me has been a lie. How could you not tell me? How could you lie to me?"

"I'm sorry, Casslyn. I couldn't tell you. I wanted to, but I couldn't. I hated lying to you," Logan says taking a step towards me.

I back away from him, feeling exactly like I felt the night I found out about him being a phoenix. Only now, it is me who is the phoenix. Holy crap. I am a phoenix. Holy crap.

"Oh my God, I'm a phoenix," I say, now light headed. I sit down on the edge of Logan's bed for support.

"Please let me explain," Logan says.

"There's nothing to explain. Wait, that's why you're here isn't it? Because I'm a phoenix."

"Please," Logan says, kneeling in front of me. "I couldn't tell you. They made me promise."

"Why didn't you tell me when I found out about you being one?"

"Because you passed out learning that I was a phoenix. I was afraid you would react worse to learning you were the same."

"We are the same. That means we can be together."

"No. We can't"

"But you said we couldn't be together because we were different. But we're not different."

"We can't, Casslyn. I could get in a lot of trouble."

"From who? Who's they? Who would possibly care if

you and I are a couple?"

Logan swallows hard, takes a deep breath, then says, "Your father."

"My dad?" I ask. And then, because apparently I've lost my mind I ask, "My dad?"

"The man that you have been living with your whole life, and that you have known as your dad . . . is not in fact your real father."

"What?" I ask, leaping off the bed. "No. You don't know what you're talking about. That's not possible."

"It is. It's the reason your parents split up after your accident. Your body was refusing the blood transfusions they were giving you. So your mom tracked down your biological father to give you blood. Your dad found out he wasn't your dad which effectively ended their marriage. I'm sorry. But it's true."

"No. No. That can't be true."

"Your father came to see you in the hospital. You don't remember? Do you remember anything from when you were in the hospital?"

"I remember being in a hell of a lot of pain. I remember being told my brother was dead. I remember my parents telling me they weren't together anymore," I yell. My anger is rising, though I'm not sure where to place it. "I think you've got a lot of explaining to do."

"I will tell you everything. I promise."

"Lie to me one more time and I'm done. One more time and I don't ever want to see you again."

"I promise I will never lie to you again."

"Good."

"Where do you want me to start?"

"I don't care. Just start talking," I say then think better of it. "Start with Xander. Why was he so adamant that you are dangerous?"

"The night of your accident, it wasn't an accident. There are a group of people, like the phoenixes, called griffins. You know in books how vampires and werewolves are enemies? Well that's what griffins and phoenixes are."

"Wait, what? You're just confusing me."

"Your real dad is a phoenix. He's actually our leader. Somehow, the griffins found out that you and Nash are phoenixes and that your dad is our leader. The night of your accident, the griffins were trying to kill the both of you. Only, you survived."

"Nash would have been a phoenix too?" I ask, tears filling my eyes. I try to blink them away and focus on Logan. But I can't. I'm a phoenix. Nash would have been one too. I could go along with Logan being a phoenix because he is such a unique person that it just fit. But finding out that I am a phoenix too is too strange. I don't even know how to feel about it. Physically I don't feel any different so how can I wrap my head around being a mythological creature? I feel like I am living in this elaborate dream and any second now I will wake up and laugh at how creative my brain is.

"Yes. You both would have been. When you had your second accident, in front of my house, that was another attempt on your life. After your first accident, and your father learned about you, he sent me here to protect you. Do you remember when you asked me why you? That's why."

"Oh," is all I can come up with. Nash was right. When he came to me in that dream and told me that he didn't think our accident was an accident. I can't believe he was right. More unbelievable is that someone tried to kill us. They did kill Nash. Two kids that never did a single bad thing against anyone. Nash was killed because of our father. A father we don't even know. I was almost killed three times now because of what I am. The books always make being a supernatural creature look exciting and fun. Not so much.

"You also asked me about how we changed from birds to humans. I can answer that if you'd like, also what we phoenixes number."

"Ok."

"Okay. Our numbers, I'm really not sure on. At times your dad has a camp of hundreds of phoenixes. Most of the time phoenixes live like normal people. It is only when the race feels threatened that we all get together. Your dad is the leader of all the phoenixes, but then he has people under him in every country that lead the phoenixes in said country."

I nod like I have any idea what he is saying. I am so lost and on top of it I'm not even paying attention.

"So the mythology is that in the very beginning, the griffins pulled the chariots of Apollo and the phoenixes were the symbol of Apollo. The griffins felt slighted. They thought they were the more superior of the creatures and therefore should be the symbol and not the pack animals. They were jealous of the phoenixes and broke away from Apollo.

"They then went and joined Nemesis, the Goddess of vengeance. She let them be her symbol and they felt powerful. Then they came after Apollo and the phoenixes. For vengeance. Needless to say, they lost. Nemesis was defeated and Apollo punished the griffins giving them far inferior bodies. Human bodies. Apollo then rewarded the phoenixes with anything they wanted, for standing by him and never wavering. They chose human bodies. Who would have thought, right? But that's just the mythology. Who actually knows how our transformation came to be. I have never learned. I suppose I probably should."

Somehow, in the middle of Logan's storytelling, we wind up downstairs. Currently I sit on his recliner. The one I sat in when I first learned he was a phoenix. And just like that night, he sits on the arm of the couch. Tonight reminds me so much of that night. How much I learned. How I came to realize that things I never would have thought could be real, are in fact, real.

"What does any of this have to do with why Xander hates you?" I ask, more confused than ever.

Logan looks at me like it should be obvious. "Xander is a griffin."

"What?" I ask. "No. No. This is way too much. You're telling me my dad is not my dad. I am a supernatural creature. My best friend is also a supernatural creature, but happens to be my mortal enemy. Like, what? How can any of this be real?"

"I don't know, Casslyn. But it's real."

I want to pass out again. I think passing out is like my coping mechanism. It lets me escape into myself until I can deal with the situation at hand.

"Don't even think about it," Logan says.

"What?" I ask, twirling Nash's bracelet around my wrist. As much as I've been doing it in the last hour, I'm going to break it or rub my skin raw.

"Passing out. That's what you were going to do and I won't let you. You can find a way to deal with this without passing out."

"Jeez. Be mean about it."

"I'm not being mean. I'm trying to make you stronger."

"I don't know how to react to any of this. I don't know what to do with any of this. What do I do with this? How did you react to learning you're a phoenix?"

"I've known my whole life. I was bread for this. I can't even imagine what it is like to find out like this. I'm sorry."

"So you're saying that Xander, my best friend for my whole life, Nash's best friend, is the one who killed him?"

"No," Logan says. "Xander didn't know what you were. Did you see how he reacted to finding out you were a phoenix?"

"Yeah. I saw that. So who killed Nash? Do you know? I want to know. I'm going to hunt them down."

"That's a lovely gesture, Casslyn. But I don't know who killed Nash. And right now you are not a phoenix and won't be for months. So until then there is nothing you can do about it. Nothing I am going to let you do about it. You are not strong enough. Your life would be in crazy danger."

"Fine. But one day I'm going to kill them," I say, walking into the kitchen. I am so thirsty my tongue feels like sandpaper.

I take a glass from the cupboard and pour water in it from the faucet. I drink until it is empty. Fill it again. And drink till it is empty. It is not enough. I set the glass down and reach for the whole in my shirt. My skin is perfectly unmarred. Like nothing happened. I absentmindedly run my fingers over it.

"One day."

"So what do we do about Xander?"

"I don't know. I need to speak with your father. Tell him you know. That Xander knows about the both of us. All of it. Would you like to speak with him?"

"No," I almost spit the word. "Why didn't he come protect me? Why did he send you?"

"He has other things to take care of."

"I'm his kid."

"I'm sorry. That sounded insensitive. But when you are the leader of an entire race there are things you need to handle. You can't always be tied down."

"Tied down?"

"I am obviously not explaining this properly. Would you just accept that he can't be here right now and that if he could he would be?"

"Fine." I walk back to the living room and lay down on the couch, suddenly overwhelmed by all of this. How could someone want to kill us? Nash and I were just kids. We'd never done anything remotely bad to anyone and yet we were the targets of people we'd never met before because of a father we've never met before. It's all too much.

"Are you okay?" Logan asks.

"Am I a bad person?" I ask him, feeling that somehow I am missing something. Maybe I did something in a past life to have this brought down on me. "Did I somehow deserve this? Am I being punished?"

"Don't you think that for a second," Logan says, crouching down in front of me on the sofa. "You are not a bad person and you are not being punished for anything. You're a good person who bad things happen to and I am so sorry for that. But instead of letting that badness cripple you, you need to use it. You use it to make you stronger. You use it to fight. You use it to live better and love harder. Do you understand me?"

Logan stares at me until I nod my head that yes I understand.

"Good. Now, would you like to stay here tonight?"

All I can do is nod, so that is what I do. I am beyond words at this point.

"You'll be okay, love," Logan says, using the nickname he gave me on his first day here. "I promise."

Twenty Six

There is no going back to normal for my life any longer. Not after finding out that I am a mythological creature and practically immortal, that my best friend is also a paranormal creature, who happens to be my mortal enemy and the man I thought was my dad for my whole life is in fact not my father. Stellar.

I don't even know how to process any of this. Do I get mad? Do I cry? Should I be happy? Sometimes I feel all of them at once. And sometimes I feel nothing at all.

I don't know how Xander is processing this. And despite the fact that he is my mortal enemy, that he tried to kill the guy I love, and almost killed me, he is still my best friend and I still care about him. There are so many things wrong with that sentence. So many things run through my head. I wonder if he still loves me, or even thinks of me as a friend any longer. Does he hate me? Would he really throw away everything we've been through just because of what I am? And if he would, should I care? I also want to know how he feels about being a griffin. How long he has known about it. I've realized that after his birthday when I noticed changes in him, that it was really him changing into being a griffin. I wonder if he feels different, because I don't.

I've tried to call him. Tucker has tried to call all of us. He has somehow picked up on the tension that is worse than ever. I say somehow but really it is Tucker, he picks up on everything. It's so hard to keep this from him. Besides Nash, I did tell Tucker and Xander absolutely everything. And after Nash died, Tucker and Xander were told even more than they had been. I know Tucker would accept me. He'd accept Xander too. But I'm not sure on the rules of this being a mythological creature and from all the books I've read, it's mum's the word. Absolutely no telling of the deep, dark secret that is your whole life, to people that don't happen to be the same as you. I feel like I'm leaving Tucker out of so much of my life. I know it's for his safety and for my safety, but that doesn't stop it from hurting.

I've tried to call my dad, or who I thought was my dad. He's still my dad, even if not biologically and I want him to know that. I still love him. Why can't he love me back? My mom is never home. I want to talk to her about lying to me for my whole life, lying to my dad, lying to the whole world.

I wonder if she knows about my father being a phoenix or me being one for that matter. I could really care less about my biological father. As far as I'm concerned he has known about me for at least nine months now and has not tried to reach out once. If he doesn't care about me why should I care about him?

I also wonder if my mom knows that Nash was murdered and not just killed, if she knows that I was almost killed twice. And if she does know, how could she just let it go so easily?

Logan does what he can to help me with the phoenix stuff. He is still baffled as to why I regenerated when Xander stabbed me when I have not yet come of age. I wonder that also. But besides being baffled by it, I can see that he is worried. He tries to hide it from me, but I can see it in the dark circles under his eyes, the stubble that has grown longer on his chin, the way he drifts off in thought. He tries to help, he tries to give me my space, he does everything he can for my comfort. I could not be more thankful for him. But as he worries over me, I can't help but worry about him. He needs his sleep. I need him to get back his resolute strength and control. He is the one that is always unwavering at all times, I need him to get that back so I can feel safer. I desperately need someone to talk to and I feel like he is the only one I can talk to. However, I'm afraid to bring some of my fears to his attention, in fear that doing so will only make him fear and the both of us will be crippled by our fear.

My world has turned upside down but instead of feeling

angry or sad or happy, I feel confused and curious. I try to sleep as often as I can to have the chance of getting a dream with Nash in it, but as of yet I've gotten radio silence. I miss him more than ever. I keep thinking that if we had known we are phoenixes from the very beginning we could have protected ourselves. Nash wouldn't have been killed, and we would both be aging into phoenixes in a few short months.

That is another thing that is troubling. I can sit here and say I am a phoenix and it doesn't really sink in, but actually turning seventeen and my whole body starting on fire, reducing to ash, and me being reborn out of it scares the living daylights out of me. What if I burn to ash and don't rise from it? Is that even a possibility? Since I have already regenerated once will I even do it when I turn seventeen?

And worse of them all, I wonder if I will even turn seventeen. Will Xander try to kill me for real this time? Will another of his race try to kill me again? My mortality has never actually been a concern for me, even after both of my accidents. But now, knowing that people actually want to kill me, I have a new lease on life. Or maybe a fervent death wish. I have not yet decided.

All of this thinking has happened in the span of two days. My brain hurts. I feel stupid half the time. Like, there are three people in little Cedars, Nebraska out of three thousand that are part of this elite group of fiction that is actually real but if anyone found out about it they would think we were completely mental. But at the same time, I feel like there are only two people here that know what I'm going through. That one of them is exhausting himself doing everything he can to get me through this and keep me safe at the same time. And the other won't have anything to do with me. I'm caught in the middle and it is a really hard place to be in.

New Year's Eve is in three days and Tucker always has a party for he, Xander, Nash, and I. We make homemade pizza and ice cream. We have popcorn and drink as much Mountain Dew as we possibly can without throwing up. We watch Dick Clark's New Year's Rockin Eve with all the musical performances and cement our bestfriendship even deeper. Then, just before Midnight and the ball is about to drop, we take pieces of paper and write our predictions for the New Year. After the ball drops, we take out our previous year's predictions, read them, and see how well we did.

Despite our crumbling friendships, Tucker is still having his New Year's Eve party and has asked Xander and I both to attend. I want to. I want to go have a fantastic night with my two best friends, and eat a bunch of junk food, and write predictions that will actually come true. But at the same time, I am so sick of doing things that I used to with Nash, without Nash. Every holiday, every day is another day without Nash and even though people say it only gets better, it hasn't yet. Also, who knows if Xander will show up. I really hate fighting with him. I hate this tug-of-war we have between being friends and enemies.

But that is three days from now, in the meantime, I need to have a chat with my mother, about my two fathers. I'm sure it's going to go swimmingly.

I try calling her. She doesn't pick up on her cell phone and when I call the hospital she says she is busy. When I tell her that I need to talk to her and that it is important, she blows me off and says that she will be home late and not to wait up. But that is what I do. She will not escape me this time.

When she gets home I am waiting for her in the kitchen, in the dark. She jumps when she turns the light on and I am sitting at the island waiting for her. Serves her right.

"Casslyn, you scared me."

"Sorry," I say, not meaning it.

"What are you doing up? I told you not to wait up for me."

"And I told you that I need to talk to you."

"Can't this wait till morning? I'm exhausted."

She moves for the stares but I stand up and run to block her path. "No, it can't. If I let it go till morning you will be gone before I will get the chance. We are going to do this now. Whether you like it or not."

"What is this about, Casslyn?" my mom asks, crossing her arms over her chest like a petulant child.

"My dad," I say simply.

"I told you we are not getting back together."

"Oh, I know that," I say, raising my eyebrows and my tone. "And I know why."

"What do you mean?"

"Don't play dumb with me. I know that you had some

affair, got pregnant with Nash and me and then married dad and told him that we were his. And I also know that after our accident you needed my real father's blood to save my life and that dad found out. That's why you split up, and that's why you're not getting back together. You betrayed him, you lied to him, and you lied to me and Nash for our whole lives. Nash died not knowing who his real dad is."

Instead of apologizing. Instead of groveling. Instead of denying it, my mom says, "How do you know that?"

I deflate, expecting more. "Is that all you have to say? My dad is not *my dad* and all you have to say is how I found out. God, mom, what has happened to us? To you? I don't even know you."

My mom takes a deep breath, her shoulders rising and falling heavily. "What do you want to know?" she asks.

"Did you cheat on dad?"

"Your dad and I were having problems. That's when I met your *father*. We fell in lo-"

"Stop," I say, holding my hand up. "I didn't ask about your relationship. I asked if you cheated on my dad."

"We weren't together at the time it happened, but I guess you could consider it cheating."

"How could you?"

"While we were apart, your dad met someone and I felt like I had to do the same to get back at him. But then I met your father, he was special. He made me feel special. I loved your dad very much, I still love him, but we betrayed each other and I don't think we can fix it. I'm sorry sweetheart."

"How could you lie to him about us being his? How could you not tell my father about us? How could you lie to us about it?"

"It was a hard decision to make, but I was about to have babies. I had just gotten your father back and I wanted to keep my family together. Can you fault me for that?"

"Yes."

"Casslyn, don't," my mom says, eyeing me. She seems to think about something then asks, "Would you like to know about your father?"

"No," I say, recoiling at the thought.

Logan asked me the same question and I reacted the same way. I don't know what it is about the situation, but I have no want to know my father. I have a dad, one that I know, and one that I love. He may not want me right now, but I will not stop loving him, not stop trying to receive his love in return.

"Casslyn, he is your father."

"But he's not my dad," I say, turning around and walking up the stairs to my bedroom, effectively ending the conversation.

Twenty Seven

Trying to contact my dad has got to be the most challeng-
ing thing I've ever done. He doesn't pick up his phone. He's
never home when I go to see him. He doesn't have an email
address, Facebook or Twitter account, and he won't text me
back. I'm tempted to get in trouble at school again just so he
can pick me up, but I promised Logan that I wouldn't stoop
to such a low, not to mention the fact that we aren't back in
school for another week. Short of committing a felony, I'm
not sure how to get in touch with him. I'd ask my mom, but
I'm sure my dad would be less inclined to answer her than
me.

I'm not sure why he is trying so hard to ignore me. I get
the fact that I am not his biological kid and that is devastat-

ing, but he raised me and I am still his daughter. I will not be ignored.

I've decided to camp out at his house until he returns. Surely he can't stay away forever.

I still have a key to his house, that is, unless he changed the locks. And as far as I know, my mom hasn't told him that I know he isn't my father.

I set my plan in motion. I don black sweat pants, a black hoodie, and black beanie. I even go as far as putting a thick layer of black eyeliner around my eyes. I will sneak into my dad's house if I have to. Covert ops, mission impossible, if you will. I feel all sorts of bad ass.

Unfortunately, my bad ass levels plummet when I get to my dad's house, the lights are on and his car is in the driveway. Oh well, there's no way for him to get away now.

I run up to the door and knock ferociously until I hear footsteps on the other side. My dad opens the door then stares at me like I am a lunatic.

"What's going on, Casslyn?" he asks me.

"I need to talk to you and you won't answer your phone and you're never home," I huff through heavy breathing.

"I'm sorry, sweetheart. Why don't you come in and we can talk."

He moves so he is not blocking the doorway, leaving a path for me inside. That's where I panic.

"I know you're not my father," I blurt before I can stop myself.

My dad's mouth drops open, then slams back shut. His

eyes narrow and he stares at me long and hard. Finally he says, "Come in, Casslyn."

I blink back tears that are already building in my eyes and follow him into what was once my living room. He sits in his recliner. I sit on the edge of the couch. My knee bounces and I can't help the constant movement of my hands; clasping, rubbing the tops of my knees, kneading into the couch, intertwining. My dad just watches me. I'm not sure if he doesn't know what to say or is trying to decide how to word what he has to say.

"How did you find out?" he finally asks.

Why is the first question, maybe the most important one, how did you find out? Why? Who cares how I found out, I found out, and that is what should be discussed. Not to mention the fact that Logan was the one that told me and telling my dad that a guy I've known for a few months and who my parents have never met, was privy to this information, would not go over well.

"I found out and then mom confirmed it."

"I see."

My knuckles knead into the tops of my knees. I feel a sob coming on and swallow hard to keep it away. The welling tears threaten to spill over. How can my dad be so cavalier about this? Our relationship or lack thereof has been tearing me apart for the last nine months and he can't seem to care.

"Why didn't you just tell me?" I ask, my voice shaky. "I thought you hated me. That you didn't love me. I thought you blamed me for Nash dying like mom does. Why didn't you just tell me? Instead you just abandoned me. Do you know how alone I felt?"

My dad's jaw quivers. He too is close to tears. But it's all his fault. He left me. He stopped loving me. The only thing I wanted, when I had nothing left, was to know that I wasn't alone.

"Casslyn, I don't expect you to understand. But please let me explain," he says, then pauses, for a really long time, before going on. "My greatest achievement in life was you kids and your mom. Then I found out you weren't mine. I didn't know what to do. I felt like your mom betrayed me. I felt for some reason like I didn't deserve you. I felt like once you found out, that you would want to know your real father and cast me aside. I'm so sorry I abandoned you. Believe me, I am. *But I didn't know what to do.*"

It's a nice speech, but it's not enough. Not after all this time.

"Good excuse, *Dad.* But if you think I'm going to accept it, think again."

He takes a deep breath then sighs heavily. "I said I am sorry. I know that is not good enough, I'm sure it will never be enough. But I meant it. If you will let me make it up to you, I would like to try."

My eyelids can no longer hold back my tears, which freely spill down my cheeks. "That's all I've wanted for the last several months. Why would you try now? Because I've finally stood up to you? Because I finally know why you abandoned me? Why now? And what if it's too late?"

"Why now? Because I miss my kid. I love you so much, Casslyn. I've missed way too much of your life in the last several months, I don't want to miss anymore."

"I miss you dad," I say, more tears streaming down my cheeks. "I miss you so much. And I miss mom. And I miss Nash, so much. My heart aches without him. I just want to scream it hurts so bad."

My dad folds his hands together then pulls them apart and runs them down his face. Then of all the things this moment might require, he smiles. "Did we ever tell you the story about the day you two were born?" my dad asks.

"No," I say, wondering where he is going with this.

"Your mom was in labor for hours and hours. The doctors were so worried that if they didn't get you out the three of you could be in real trouble. But your mom insisted that you would come when you were ready. And then you did. You came out first. Then Nash. They put you in different bassinets to clean you up. The second you were separated you both screamed and screamed until they put you together. Then you were so still. So still they had to make sure you were still breathing. The two of you were still together. Always. We always said you were two halves of one whole. And then you lost half of your whole.

"I don't know how you are going to live without him. But I promise, you will. Just scream as long as you need. One day you will both be together again. You will be whole again. And you will be still. Casslyn, I know how much your brother meant to you. But now he is gone. And that's something we all have to deal with. He may be your brother, but he was my son. I miss him too. And, for what it's worth, I miss your mom, too."

"I know you do," I say, "I'm pretty sure she misses you, too."

"So what do you say, kid? You want to let your dear old dad back into your life?"

"You're the one that left," I remind him.

Before I leave his place, my dad and I make arrangements to go to the bowling alley, grab a bite to eat, and play pool. It's not a grand gesture, but it is a start. I've missed him so much I would settle for a Lunchable and a ride home.

The botched Christmas plan made me realize that my family will never be the same. We will never be the family we were. Too much has happened. We have lost too much and can never gain it all back. But maybe we can be a different kind of family. I'm not going to try to get my parents back together. I'm not going to try to make them love me in the way that I think I need, but let them love me in the way that they can give.

Twenty Eight

I've tried calling Xander every day since he stabbed me. Several times a day. I've left him messages. Messages he either isn't listening to, or that hold no sway over him. I've texted him. Texts that he will not return.

I think I've lost another best friend and I feel nothing. I am numb to it. Losing my brother broke my heart. Losing Xander now feels inevitable. I just wonder when I will lose Tucker too. It would seem as though I am cursed, or maybe just meant to lose the ones I love the most. My life is not turning out the way it should have. The way I imagined it.

I still love Xander the same way. I still want to be his best friend. I didn't even have to think about forgiving him for stabbing me and almost killing me. So why can't he do the same? Why can't he even talk to me?

Tucker has called me twice today and it is barely noon. I've avoided him twice today. I know he wants to make sure I am coming to his party tomorrow. I know he knows there is something going on between Xander and I that is worse than it ever has been. I can't bear to tell him that our friendship is over. I don't want him to have to pick between Xander and I. I don't want their friendship to be over just because of me.

I sit at the island in my kitchen, laying my cheek against the countertop, hoping it will have some calming, soothing affect. I am not rewarded. I am a phoenix and we do not register temperature change. I guess being the symbol of Apollo would be a little warm seeing as he is the sun god. Not being able to feel how hot the sun is would be mighty handy.

My phone vibrates right next to my face. I don't want to answer it, no matter who it is, but I raise my head anyway and answer it.

"Casslyn Evans, you are my best friend and therefore entitled to tell me what the hell is going on between you and my other best friend," Tucker yells through the phone. I have to pull it away from my ear he is so loud.

"We just had a fight, Tucker. I'm sure it will blow over," I say. I have stooped to lying to my best friend. You aren't supposed to lie to your best friend. What have I become?

"Don't you dare lie to me, Casslyn. I called him to make sure he would be coming tomorrow and he said he wasn't because you are going to be there and he wants nothing to do with you. He said he won't talk to you. That he can't even stand to look at you. Now I will ask you again, what the hell happened?"

Here I go again, lying. "He was jealous of Logan and they got into a fight. He's mad at me because I took Logan's side."

"Again, you are lying to me. You have never lied to me, ever. Neither has Xander. I don't know what is going on with the two of you but I am getting tired of it."

"I'm sorry, Tucker. Believe me I am. But I promise you it is for your own good."

"Yeah, whatever. That's what Xander said."

"See, at least we agree on something."

"Really? Do you both agree that treating your other me like shit is the thing to do? Has either one of you stopped to think how I feel in all of this? I am so sick and tired of trying to keep us all together. I know you lost your brother and I am sorry. But it is hard work trying to be your shoulder to cry on. It sucks that Xander loved you so much and I was the only one he could talk to about it. It's become pretty much impossible to keep you two from fighting or trying to kill each other lately. But do I ever hear a thank you? Do either one of you stop to ask how I feel in all of this? Do either of you ever ask who I am in love with? Do either of you try to hold the three musketeers together with everything that is inside of you that you get so sick you don't want to get out of bed? Do either one of you force a smile on your face when you are screaming on the inside?"

And there I've done it. I've lost my last best friend.

"Tucker, I'm sorry."

"Save it. If you are really sorry you will both be at my party tomorrow. You will both have fake smiles plastered on your damn faces. You will both eat and be merry. And you will both make me happy even if it kills you."

Before I can say anything, Tucker hangs up the phone and I am left to listen to white noise. I take a deep cleansing breath before I can get mad at him. He has every right to feel this way. He is right, neither Xander nor I have once stopped to think about how he feels. I was afraid I would lose him as a friend but I thought it would be because we didn't spend enough time together or he couldn't handle Xander and me fighting. I didn't think it would be because I didn't think of his feelings, and that may just be worse.

My phone call from him made me feel like a terrible friend. My life may be spinning out of control, but that doesn't mean I can be like my parents and abandon those who need me.

I swipe the screen on my phone, pull up Xander's number, then hit send. I know he will not answer me, but he may listen to my voicemail. Who knows. I've heard that miracles do happen.

The phone rings and rings until I hear, "Hey, this is Xander, you know what to do."

I absentmindedly rub my fingers over the spot where Xander stabbed me. It's become a habit. There is no scar. I don't feel any pain. And yet I can't seem to leave it alone. "Listen Xander, I know you and I are having our issues. Believe me, I am aware. You stabbed me for goodness sakes. And sure we may be mortal enemies, but we also share a best friend. And right now he needs us. He basically gave me an ultimatum today. If we don't go to his party we will lose him. And I don't know how you feel about that because obviously you don't care about losing me as a best friend, but I will not lose Tucker too. You will be at that party or I will come find you and drag you to it. Do you understand me? See you tomorrow," I say then hang up my phone.

I feel huffy and jittery. I feel like doing a head/desk maneuver but settle for laying my cheek against the countertop again. I feel myself dosing off when I hear a knock at my front door.

I don't want to get up from my comfortable spot, but I also don't know who is at the door, so I would feel safer answering it than just telling them to come in.

I swing the door open and am met by the most beautiful blue eyes I've ever seen. "You don't have to knock, you know. You can just walk in like you used to," I tell Logan.

He is certainly a sight for sore eyes. Although I saw him the other day, it feels like it's been too long since we spent time together.

"Hello to you too," Logan says.

I smile at him and say, "Hi," moving away from the door so he can enter.

He makes his way to the living room and sits down, patting the spot next to him for me to sit down. I oblige and immediately feel the warmth spread through me that only

Logan can ignite.

"So what's wrong?" he asks.

I narrow my eyes at him, wondering how he could possibly have known that something is wrong.

"Your pulse is quick and you looked stressed. What is it?"

How about that. He can tell a person's mood just by how quick their heart is beating. Or maybe just mine. It's a nice thought that it may just be me. That he may be so in tuned with me that he knows how I am feeling at all times. Romantic even.

"How can you hear my heartbeat but I can't hear yours?"

"You haven't aged yet. Don't change the subject," Logan says, narrowing his eyes right back at me.

"Tucker called and basically told me that our friendship is over if Xander and I don't start paying more attention to him," I say and then recant to him everything Tucker said. Then I tell him about the message I left on Xander's phone.

Logan stiffens beside me.

"What?" I ask.

"I don't like the idea of you and Xander being together. He's a griffin, Casslyn. He may have been your best friend at one time, but now he is your enemy. He may try to hurt you. He already almost killed you. And if he doesn't, what if he has told one of his buddies about you? Or what if he brings one of them with him to kill you?"

I'd never thought about any of that. I don't even want to think about it now. But I also don't think Xander has told anyone about me. If he had, I'm sure I wouldn't be sitting here having this conversation with Logan. And I also don't think that he would bring someone with him to hurt me. Xander may be my enemy, but he is still my best friend. We grew up together. I'm sure that a lifetime of friendship is stronger than being enemies for a week.

"Logan, I'm doing this for Tucker. I will not lose him. If you're so against it, why don't you come with me?"

Logan thinks on this. He is silent for a short time before he says, "I shouldn't. If it is just you and Xander, alone, neither one of you should feel threatened. But if I come then Xander would look at it as a threat and then get one of his griffin buddies and it would turn into a whole mess. Which I don't want. I'm sure you don't want that. And I don't think it would help your chances with Tucker any." He takes a deep breath, holds it in, then releases it slowly. "I don't like it. But you can go."

"I'm glad you feel that way, but I wasn't about to not go simply because you don't like it."

"Casslyn, you may be afraid of losing Tucker, but this is your life we are talking about. I don't think you know how serious this is. I was sent here to protect you and that is what I am going to do." Logan reaches a hand out to me and places it on my arm.

I cross my arms and lean away from him. "So do your job. Protect me. But I am not losing Tucker. I've already lost too much."

Logan pats my leg and leans back against the couch. He

lifts his arm up and rests it against the top of the couch. Then he looks at me and nods at the crook in his arm. My heart rate picks up. I know he can tell because he smiles. It's not a happy smile, but a smile that means he knows how I feel and understands. It's a sad smile. I lean back into him and rest my head on his shoulder. His arm sweeps down so it is resting along the side of my body. I close my eyes and wish for what could be.

Logan still says we can't be together, though everything we feel, every touch, every look, every movement between us tells us we should be together. It seems to be killing both of us, but if Logan is not willing to give in, I can't let myself feel the things for him I feel, if they will not be reciprocated. It is achingly sweet to be this close to him and not be able to call him mine.

Logan said it is my father that would not allow us to be together. But the more I think about it, I feel as though it may be Logan keeping us apart. And how he feels about himself. His sense of duty. Him taking his job seriously. But besides that, I'm not sure if he feels like he is worthy of me.

How could he ever think that he is not worthy? He is more worthy that any person I have ever met. He is the most extraordinary person I have ever met, and that is not just because I live in small town Nebraska. And I don't just mean extraordinary physically, which he is. I've never seen anyone with a body like Logan's. But there is more to Logan than a hot body. And I wish he knew that.

I've thought about bringing it up to him. I want to ask

him how he could possibly think he is not worthy of me. How he could possibly think I am better than him. Or better off without him. But I'm afraid that if I talk to him about it he will shut down, shut me out, and be driven even further away from me.

I fall asleep in Logan's arms, my thoughts surrounding me like a vicious shroud.

Twenty Nine

I get to Tucker's house early, hoping to brace myself for the impending loss of another friend. Brace myself from the hatred I will surely feel if and when Xander decides to show up.

Tucker invites me in with a smile but there is a tension behind his eyes that I feel all too well.

"Happy New Years, Tucker," I say, giving him a hug.

He tenses but hugs me back. How could this be what our lifelong friendship has become? A perfect friendship between four people, dying. Maybe it was too perfect for too long. Maybe this is the universe's way of balancing itself out. Or maybe it's the universe's sick joke. Whatever it is, it sucks major donkey balls.

"Happy New Years, Cass," he says solemnly. Nothing like the Tucker I know and love.

"Cheer up, Tucker," I say, slapping him on the arm. "This is going to work."

"I hope you are right."

"Enough of this sad talk. Let's get our party on."

Tucker smiles. It is almost a real Tucker smile. Then he says, "There is Mountain Dew in the fridge. Help yourself. And be prepared for a lot of groveling and doing as I tell you tonight."

A smile cracks on my face and I make for the fridge.

I finish chugging down my version of liquid courage when the doorbell rings. Apparently Xander does care about keeping Tucker as a friend. I wasn't sure. Tucker looks at me with raised eyebrows. He must also be surprised Xander came. Before winter break, Xander had been spending a lot of time with Ashley and her posse. We'd thought he'd abandoned us for good. Maybe Tucker and I haven't lost our Xander after all.

A chill runs up my spine and I am suddenly nervous, which I've never been around Xander before. A flash of him stabbing me runs through my head. *He was aiming for Logan*, I tell myself. But it does nothing in the way of easing my panic. What if Logan was right and Xander will try to hurt me? No. This is Xander I'm talking about. He may be my enemy, but he was also scared out of his mind when he stabbed me.

I don't know how he will react when he sees me, and

I'm not all too sure how I will react when I see him. I'm suddenly afraid of him. Not only of what he could do to me, but what he could do to Tucker. I retreat into the kitchen, waiting for him to find me. Maybe if our sighting isn't too abrupt we can at least be civil.

I don't know what he thinks of me any longer. I haven't seen him since he stabbed me and found out I am a phoenix. His mortal enemy. He must see me differently. I know I see him differently. If he has known he was going to be a griffin his whole life, it must be ingrained in him to hate me. Despite the fact that we have been best friends for our whole lives, something that has been taught to him his whole life plays a part in how Xander feels about me not as a person but as a species. I can't change that. I don't think anything can. It's almost impossible to change a belief system. Ask anyone who has fought in a religious war.

I hear footsteps closing in on the kitchen. Maybe the food center of the house was not a good place to hide from growing teenage boys. I lower my head and wait for what is about to happen.

"Hi, Cass." His voice is so familiar and yet now so strange. He sounds reserved, maybe just as nervous as I feel.

I swallow hard and wait three heart beats before I look up. Xander looks about as bad as I feel. There are dark circles under his eyes, which are bloodshot. His hair is longer and tousled like he ran his hand through it and decided to call it good. His clothes are tighter than normal. As much of a mess as he looks to be, there is still this hauntingly beautiful quality to him that is all Xander.

I want to say hi back. To tell him I missed him. That I am sorry for everything. That we can get through this. But it all gets caught in my throat. So I just stare at him, hoping my eyes can convey at least some of what I wish I could say. Long moments pass between us, no one saying anything. Then Xander nods and everything is okay again. If only for the time being.

Tucker chimes in and says, "At some point tonight the two of you will have to kiss and make up." He looks between the Xander and I. His cheeks turn red, embarrassed, something Tucker is not ever. "Um. Well. You don't have to kiss, but you will make up." His shoulders slump and through a sigh he says, "If it kills me, you two will be friends again."

"We're fine," Xander says, patting Tucker on the shoulder for effect.

"Are we?" I ask, almost mad. How can he just ignore me for the past few days and then tell Tucker we are fine. He's the one that stabbed me and left me for dead.

"Casslyn, don't start with me," Xander says, taking on a bigger stance.

I'm frightened of what angering him might do, but I'm mad too. He has no right to use my fear against me. To use it to his advantage. "Don't start?" I ask then breathe heavily. I glance at Tucker who has a pained look on his face. This feud with Xander really is destroying him. "Fine. I'm sorry. Shall we grab some food then start watching New Year's Rockin Eve?"

Tucker smiles but it is strained, almost like he is on the verge of tears. Xander has turned hard, a scowl on his face. He just nods and turns to the table full of food.

I take a deep breath, exhale, and follow his lead. There is so much food. Pigs in blankets. nachos, pickle wraps, spinach dip, little smokies, little smokies wrapped in blanket. Nothing healthy. Everything delicious. We pile our plates high then return to the living room.

We each find our own seat, separate from each other. Tucker and I each take a recliner while Xander spreads out on the couch.

Carson Daily shows up on screen and introduces the first performer. We settle into the show and eat our food in silence. We go back to the kitchen for more food and drinks. We arrange ourselves on our respective furniture trying to find a comfortable position and eventually trade and share furniture. That is, Tucker and Xander share, and Tucker and I share. Xander and I make sure to keep our distance.

It hurts to be this emotionally distant from someone I've been as close to as siblings for my whole life. Xander may have felt like I broke his heart when I couldn't love him back, something that I had no control over. But he is breaking my heart for hating me simply because of who I am, which he is entirely in control of. It hurts that as a group we never missed a beat when it came to Tucker being gay, but the second Xander finds out I am not who we all thought I was, he drops me like I'm hot.

I am also so confused as to how I could have missed

Xander keeping such a massive secret from us. I'm sure Tucker knows nothing of this. Besides the fact that we tell each other everything, Tucker has been blessed with the gift of gab and would not be able to keep a secret such as his best friend being a mythological creature from his other best friend. Nash knew nothing of it. He most definitely would not be able to keep a secret like this from me.

I would give anything if Nash were still here. If I could talk to him about all of this. It would be so different if we could be phoenixes together. I honestly believe that if Nash were still here, Xander wouldn't hate us for who we are and that we could still be friends. Before Tucker was the one to keep up together, to keep the peace, Nash could seamlessly, effortlessly smooth things over. Not that there ever were things to smooth over. At least nothing more important than what movie we would watch or how many bags of popcorn we would need. I never would have believed Nash was the center of our group if he weren't gone from us.

Sometimes I have to wonder if we, or at least Tucker, are working too hard to hold something together that no longer has any business being together. Like if it is this hard to keep us together, then maybe we aren't meant to be friends.

About halfway through the New Year's Rockin' Eve Celebration Tucker gets this mischievous gleam in his eyes, sits up, and says, "Because the both of you are here because of me, and because you will be doing anything you can to make me happy, I want the two of you to dance together to the next performance."

I want to protest, and I can feel that Xander wants to protest even more strongly than I do, but Tucker is right. We are both here for him and we will do what he wants to keep his friendship.

I've danced with Xander before. It's not something I'm too worried about. However, Xander may be a different story. He is the one disgusted by me. He is the one who loved me unrequitedly. He's the one holding the friendship card.

I look to him, sitting on the couch, and see a rigid posture. Xander has never been like this. He was always the laid back one. The musketeer who didn't let things bother him. The one who let things happen organically. Now that he is a griffin he has changed in more ways than he may even realize.

And that's when I realize that maybe it is I who should be holding the friendship card. Xander is the one who wanted me to choose between him and Logan. He is the one who continually told me Logan was dangerous and could have killed me trying to prove it to me. He is the one who has changed from who he is to who these griffins want him to be. He is the one who shoved me, sending me flying across the floor. If I can't get the old Xander back, I'm not sure I want to be friends with the new one.

I also realize that I need to learn more about these griffins. Logan told me they are dangerous and that they want to put an end to Phoenixes. And while I believe him, I need to know more about them. I need to know what, other than vengeance, drives them. I need to know how they train. How they plan on waging this war against the phoenixes. I need to know far more than I do so I can have a leg up and not be blindsided again like I was with Xander placing a knife made of ice through my chest.

"Whatever you want, Tucker," Xander says, breaking me out of my thoughts.

Carson Daily and Jenny McCarthy finish their back and forth and present the next performer. Of course it would have to be a singer who chooses a slow song. It's like Tucker is psychic and chose this moment for Xander and I to dance.

We stand up and join in front of the TV.

Tucker jerks back into the recliner, shields his eyes, and says, "I don't want to see it. I just want you to do it. Go in the back of the room."

Xander and I move to the back of the room and awkwardly join together to dance. He grips my right hand in his left and places his other hand right above my hip. Other than feeling a bit nervous and frightened I don't feel anything. Not like I feel with Logan. Just being near Logan sends shivers up my spine, but the slightest touch of his skin on mine burns through me like wildfire. This is simply one of the reasons I could never love Xander the way I love Logan. There is no fire, and sadly, not even a spark.

"Where is he?" Xander asks, venom spewing from behind his teeth.

"Not here, so leave it alone."

"You're not going to kiss him at midnight?" He doesn't look at me when he asks this, but his grip on my hand tightens.

"Xander, I'm warning you. But, if you must know, I am going to his place when I leave here."

"What are you going to do? Light me on fire?"

"I can't do that and you know that," I say, stepping on his foot.

Finally, he looks down at me and there is a hurt in his eyes I did not expect to see. "Why didn't you tell me, Cass? How could you keep this from me?"

Through my teeth I say, "I didn't know about it until you placed a knife through my chest. So maybe I should be thanking you for alerting me to who I really am."

Xander breathes heavily in and out but does not say anything.

We sway to the music, putting on a show for Tucker, who we know is certainly watching us and not the TV.

"But I'm guessing you've known your whole life who you are, right? How could you lie to me for our entire lives? To Tucker? To Nash?"

Xander lowers his head so he is eye level with me and says, "I was trying to protect you." There is conviction in his eyes. He truly believes what he said.

But I am still angry. "You should have been protecting me from yourself."

He shakes me. It is not hard but it is frightening. What if I make him so angry he snaps and does hurt one of us? "If he hadn't come into town you would never have found out."

"He was protecting me. If he hadn't come to town I

would be dead several times over. Which is the better pay-off? But you're right, if he wasn't here I'd never have found out would I? You should have told me. I thought you were my best friend. Didn't you think I could handle it?"

"So you're saying that we should both tell Tucker what we are?" Xander asks, cocking his head to the side in a you-know-I'm-right look. He doesn't let me say anything before he says, "If he wasn't here-."

I don't let him finish the sentence before I say, "What? We'd be fine? Logan being here doesn't change the fact that I am a phoenix. I'd still be one if he didn't come to town. And we'd still be enemies. Are you trying to say that's not true?"

"I don't think I would have stabbed you," he says dead-pan.

I try to jerk out of his arms, to escape this ugly back and forth, but Xander holds me in place and continues to sway to the music. I swear this is the longest song ever. Only until I realize a new singer is performing.

"What if I wasn't a phoenix, Xander? I could have died. You stabbed me. And then you left."

He looks down at me with a hallow expression. One that turns quickly into remorse. I know he feels bad about that night, but he needs to. What he did was wrong.

His eyes turn dark as if he is haunted. He says, "I will never be able to tell you how sorry I am for what happened that night. I know that I can never take it back and that you may never forgive me for it. But I am truly sorry."

"You practically spat your hatred at me. Then you *left me.*"

Again Xander's grip tightens, but this time it is not because he is angry, it's because he is afraid he's losing me. "I don't know what to say, Cass."

"Say you don't hate me."

There is a resolve in Xander when he says, "I could never hate you."

I feel a sob rise in my throat, but I force it back down, and instead opt for placing my head on Xander's chest. He rests his chin on my head and we are quiet for a time. A calm settles over us. Maybe an understanding.

Xander places his hands on my arms, pulls me away from him, and says, "Do you maybe want to go on a short walk and we can talk some more?"

"What about Tucker?" I ask.

Tucker chimes in and says, "Just go. This night was more about stopping the fighting between you two than it was about me. But you better be back in time for the ball drop."

I break away from Xander, rush Tucker, wrap him in a bear hug, and squeeze. "Tucker, I love you. You are my best friend and you mean more to me than I show you."

"I know you do, Cass. And no matter what I said, I will never stop being your friend."

I pull away from him, hold him at arm's length, stare deep into his eyes, and say, "I promise I will be a better friend to you. New year, new beginnings right?"

Tucker smiles at me and nods. "Now go. Make up with your other best friend."

"Be right back," I tell him then head for the door.

Thirty

Xander shivers as he walks next to me. I'm wearing a coat but I don't need it. Just one of the perks of being a phoenix. I'm not yet a full-fledged phoenix, but Logan and I think that because my father gave me some of his blood and that he is a true phoenix, that my phoenix powers may have been kick started. But every time I think about it, I can't help but feel like the night Xander stabbed me was not the first time that I regenerated. When Nash and I crashed the bike, I swear I was on fire. Everyone told me I couldn't have been because the bike did not catch fire and my clothes had no signs of burning. But I know what I saw and what I felt. I know I was on fire that night.

"We can go back if you are cold," I say to Xander.

"I'm fine," he says a bit sharply.

I could let it bother me, but I choose not to. He has a lot of issues that he needs to work on. One being the fact that he seems to be okay with killing people. I doubt that he would kill just any ole person, but just because a phoenix is not entirely human, doesn't make it okay to kill one of them.

We walk farther in the dark and cold until we reach the town's park. It is snow covered and deserted. It feels haunted and peaceful at the same time.

"Do you want to swing?" Xander asks. His voice echoes in the darkness. I shiver which has nothing to do with the cold.

"Yeah, sure," I say.

Xander wanted to take a walk to talk and so far neither one of us has said anything worthwhile. When we get to the swings, Xander brushes the snow off of one for me. I sit down with him behind me. He takes hold of the chains, pulls me back, and pushes me forward, then takes a seat on his own swing.

Xander laughs out of nowhere, which scares me, then says, "That was hard for me in there."

"Why?" I think he may mean because of Nash no longer being with us. I know I certainly feel his absence. But then again, when do I not feel his absence. I think it is one thing to lose a sibling, but when that sibling happens to be your twin, your equal in every way, it is so much harder. Sometimes when I think about it I also think of *Harry Potter,* how George Weasley felt after losing Fred.

"Because I knew that in a few hours we would be reading last year's predictions and I'm not sure if I can handle that."

"Why?" I ask, thinking I know where this is going.

Xander doesn't look at me when he says, "I wrote that at some point this year I was going to tell you that I am in love with you. And then tonight I would be kissing you at midnight. But this year has gone to shit. We're barely friends. We're mortal enemies. And while I want to hate you, I am still so in love with you."

I don't know what to say to him. Do I tell him I'm sorry? Do I say we can fix things? I'm struck dumb by the fact that he still loves me. I am not sure how he still could when so many things have happened in the way of thwarting his love for me. I am flattered. I am confused. I feel bad.

"You don't have to say anything. I just didn't want you to be blindsided."

"Thanks," I say, not knowing what else to say.

Silence falls between us for what seems like the hundredth time. I push myself back and forth in the swing with my foot. Xander digs a whole in the gravel with his.

"Listen, Xander, I know we are trying to work on the whole friendship thing. And I think we can stay friends. But I also think we need to talk about our respective . . . species."

"I can't." His answer comes swiftly and short.

"Well, we have to. Now, I don't hold you responsible, but your kind killed Nash, and I'm not about to let them do the same thing to me."

Xander's head whips around to face me.

"What are you talking about? That was an accident. They don't even know you are a phoenix."

"It wasn't an accident. Just like me wrecking your car wasn't an accident. My father had to come give me blood so I could survive."

"Your dad's not a phoenix. I would know."

"No, my dad is not a phoenix. But he is also not my biological father."

"What?" Xander asks, shock all over his face. As far as I know, Xander has known he is a griffin his entire life. Shouldn't he have known all along that I'm a phoenix and that my dad isn't my father? Shouldn't he have known everything about me?

"Yeah, I don't want to talk about it. I haven't even told Tucker. So don't you dare. But as I said, I'm not about to let them kill me like they did to Nash. And also, I will be getting my revenge. If your people think they can get away with killing my brother, they can think again."

Xander stands up from his swing. He is getting angry. Maybe I should too, but I am in a constant state of anger, so doing so would serve no point.

"They didn't kill Nash. I would know."

"Would you? It doesn't seem like you are very well informed."

He is about to say something when someone yells, "Yo, Xander."

Xander freezes in his spot. I look to where the voice

came from and spot three guys I've never seen before. They are big but they don't seem like much to fear, which is precisely the look on Xander's face.

"Xander?" I ask cautiously.

"Casslyn, I lied to you. I am so sorry. I know they suspected you as a phoenix. But they said they weren't going to do anything about it until they could prove it."

The whole time he speaks my ears fill with blood, making it hard to hear. The three guys that yelled his name are closing in on us and I feel a panic ripping up my body. These guys are griffins. And I am in big trouble.

I look around me for a way out of this. An escape route. But I know they will be faster, stronger, and I have nowhere to go.

"Casslyn, look at me," Xander says, but I struggle to do so. When I finally reach his eyes, the group is only feet away. "I didn't tell them. I swear to you."

"Hey, Xander," the one in front calls when they finally reach us. "What do we have here? A pretty little angel?" Up close they look like mangy dogs. Their hair is unkempt. Their clothes could rival those of gang members. And their eyes are crazed like a predator that smells its prey.

Xander's facial expression turns to one of calm. "Nothing. I've got it under control, Colt. No need for you guys to stay and waste your time."

"Who says we're wasting our time? This is the one everyone's talking about, right? Your little bestie?" The guy, Colt, smirks when he says this.

"Not anymore," Xander says. I know he is just putting on a show for these guys, group allegiance and all that, but it doesn't keep it from hurting.

"What, did you have a falling out?" the one to the right says.

"I don't associate with people who could be their kind," Xander practically spits the sentence out.

The one on the left cocks his head and says, "It looks to me like you are associating with her now."

"Jake's right, Xander, why are you here with her?" Colt asks.

There is a Jake and a Colt. Not knowing their names put me on edge. I thought knowing them might comfort me in the slightest, but it doesn't. At least it gives me two names to use when I go after my brother's killers.

"I thought I could find out for sure what she is and then bring her in," Xander says, crossing his arms. It seems as if Xander has no authority with these guys and I wonder why that is. He froze up when he heard them call his name. And now he is trying to assert his dominance but these guys are giving in to nothing. They hold all the cards.

The one on the right, the one I still do not have a name for, pulls something from his pocket, and says, "Why don't we find out? You'll oblige, won't you angel?" He flicks open the blade of a knife.

My blood runs cold. My vision blurs. And my chest compresses. I can't breathe. I am about to be killed and there is nothing I can do about it. And nothing Xander is going to do about it.

Xander doesn't panic, which scares me. He just says, "I told you, I've got it handled."

Colt steps forward, into Xander's personal space, and says, "Now, come on, Xander. She was your best friend for seventeen years. We know you will go soft on her. You don't think we can let you get away with that do you?"

Through his teeth, Xander says, "If she is one, I would never go soft on her, no matter who she is."

"So prove it," Colt says, producing a knife of his own.

He hands it to Xander who flicks the blade open. Xander turns to me, mouths *I'm sorry*, closes his eyes, pulls his fist back, and lands a punch to the side of my face. If I hadn't already been in two car accidents, almost died, and lost my twin, I might be able to say I've never felt such intense pain before. The side of my face is on fire, not literally thankfully, but it hurts like I Hell.

I realize then that these guys are going to beat me bloody until they can prove that I am a phoenix. And then they are going to kill me or take me to the other griffins. Either way I am a dead person. If I regenerated when Xander stabbed me, I am bound to regenerate now. There is no way for me to stop it.

I right myself and try to get away from them but one of them grabs me. I twist around to see that it is Jake. He hauls off and punches me in the mouth. The force of it blinds me with a white light, lands me on the ground. I scream, which hurts my lips. I touch my fingers to my lips and pull them black, bloody. This would generally be bad, but in this case it is good. If there is blood, it means I didn't regenerate. Maybe if I didn't now, I won't and it will save my life.

"There," Xander says. "You see. There's blood, no fire. Maybe she's not a phoenix."

"Are you defending her?" the one without a name asks.

"No, I'm just saying. They regenerate. If she doesn't, then she isn't one."

"Then why don't you use your knife instead of your fist and find out for sure."

Xander's shoulders fall ever so slightly. He walks towards me and closes his eyes again.

"Please don't do this," I beg him.

He grabs my arm, shoves the sleeve of my coat up, takes a deep breath, and places the blade of the knife on it. It is ice cold on my skin. I close my eyes and pray that my skin doesn't catch fire and heal itself. Xander slices the knife down, opening up my skin. I clench my teeth to keep back the scream that wants to burst through. It hurts so badly and I wish so much that Logan was here. His job is to protect me. I stupidly told him I would be fine. I told him I wouldn't leave Tucker's house. That I wouldn't be in danger. Maybe he will just know that I am in danger and come to my rescue. He has been able to tell before when I have been under duress. Maybe he will now. I can only hope.

"Damnit," one of them says.

I am still on the ground, in a vulnerable place. I need to get up and get away from them. I begin to crawl away, but am grabbed again, and punched in the side.

"Don't move, bitch," Colt says.

I am in so much pain and it has to only be the beginning. I curl up in a ball and try to make myself as small as possible, to give them a small target to wound.

I scream and writhe when a second blade opens the skin of my right leg. I feel blood pour out of it. Good. I am not re-generating. But they will not give up. More punches, kicks, and knife blades lay into me. I see limbs move around me, blurs. My head feels heavy from the loss of blood.

"Please, stop," I scream.

How can no one hear me? Why is no one trying to help me? Why is Xander letting this happen? I can't even see Xander. I only see three bodies around me. I am on the ground, surrounded by frenzied griffins. I feel like a gazelle carcass surrounded by starving lions.

"I think she's had enough," I hear Xander say.

Thank god.

"Are you still trying to defend her?" Jake says.

"No. Get off that trip. I'm just saying, she hasn't regen-erated. Are you going to kill her? Leave her here for some-one to find? She's lost a lot of blood and it's cold out. It's one thing to kill them, but it's another to kill an innocent person."

If I wasn't in so much pain, I would be happier to learn Xander's stance on death. While my torturers decide what to do with me, I lie on the ground and for the briefest of sec-onds, hope that I die of blood loss so I can see Nash again. If I were to die, I could be with him again. But that is a stupid thought, one that I regret instantly. I am not going to let these people destroy me.

"She's seen us, we can't just let her get away," Colt says. No wonder he is the leader. He seems to be the smartest of the group.

"I will make sure she doesn't speak a word of this," Xander says.

"You better," Colt says.

I close my eyes, praying that the torture is over. I yell out when one of them kicks me in the back. He may be stressing the point of Xander keeping me quiet. Or he may be getting one last kick in to show his badassery, but either way, he does not break my resolve. I will not let the griffins destroy me. They will only make me stronger. Stronger in my resolve to live. Stronger in my need for vengeance. I will not let them destroy me.

My eyes, along with my head, are heavy. I want to fall asleep. I move around on the ground. It is sticky, the snow covered in my blood. I wonder how Xander is going to hide that. Speaking of Xander, I don't see him. The other three griffins have left, but so has Xander. I can't believe he left me for dead. Again.

Fine. So be it. I will take care of myself. I have been for the last nine months.

Thirty One

I take a deep breath, try to steady myself, center myself. It is hard to do through pain that is everywhere. I lost track of how many times they cut me. How many times they punched or kicked me. I feel bruised deep down into the core of my body. Those guys may not have looked like much, but like Xander, they had muscle that packed a hard punch.

I move myself so I am at least on my hands and knees. It takes almost all of my strength.

"Oh my God." It's Xander. He actually came back.

"What?" I ask, looking up at him.

He is looking at the ground around me. As I suspected, the snow is covered in my blood, but it is so much worse than I thought. It looks like a murder scene.

"I'll go get my car and take you to the hospital," he says.

"No," I say. "Go get my car. And just take me home."

"Casslyn, I really think you should go to the hospital."

"I don't care what you think," I say. I want to yell, to put more force behind my voice, but I am too week. "Just take me home."

Xander pauses for a time, wondering if he should go against what I want and take me to the hospital, then decides and says, "I'll be right back."

He turns to leave then doubles back and says, "What do I tell Tucker?"

I forgot about Tucker. He is going to be heartbroken. If he knew the truth it might not be so bad, but he doesn't know the truth, so he is going to hate me.

"I don't know. Tell him I fell on the ice or something."

"Be right back," he says and this time he leaves.

Maybe I shouldn't have sent him away alone. Tucker's house, and my car, are only a few blocks away, but those guys could come back, and without Xander trying to stop them, I may end up losing my life. Ugh. This sucks. I am bleeding out in the snow, only semi-conscious, and yet I have to worry about defending myself against would be attackers.

I lick my lips, not remembering that they are split, and taste the metallic, rusty, taste of my own blood. I want to spit it out but fear that would take too much energy.

In minutes Xander is back with my car.

"Sorry it took so long. It took just about every play in the book to keep Tucker from coming with me."

"What, you didn't want him to see what a monster you've become?"

"That's not fair, Casslyn," Xander says, kneeling down beside me, doing his best to avoid the blood covered snow.

I do my level best to glare at him, which I think comes off as a look of indifference, and say, "Isn't it?"

"I swear to you I didn't tell them. And I had no idea they would be here. I promise. I may not like what you are, but I would never hurt you on purpose."

"Whatever, Xander. Just get me home."

Xander helps me to my feet, but when my legs buckle under me, he picks me up in his arms and carries me to my car. Then he sets me in the passenger seat, gets in the driver's seat, and drives to my house. The drive is painful and far too long. Every bump in the road sends shock waves through my battered body.

Every time I try to nod off Xander yells at me. "Stay awake, Casslyn. You hit your head, you may have a concussion."

"What do you care?" I ask, resting my head against the passenger window.

Xander doesn't reply. He knows I'm mad. And he knows I have every right to be.

The silence in the car gets to be too much and my anger spills over. "Twice now you have offered peace, friendship, and then ripped it away. *Twice* you've given me a small piece of mind that maybe we can be okay. Then thrown it back in my face a thousand fold. Why?"

"I told you I had nothing to do with those guys attacking you tonight."

"Except for the fact that you were the first one to punch and stab me."

"I had to. If I didn't they would know that I was protecting you and it would be my ass on the line."

"So you offer up your best friend as a lamb to the slaughter."

"I will never be able to tell you enough how sorry I am. But I promise you I am sorry."

When we make it to my house Xander wraps me in his arms again, pulls me from the car, and takes me inside.

"Where would you like me to take you?"

I want to climb straight into bed, but I know that is not an option without getting my bed covered in blood.

"Bathroom."

He carries me up the stairs, into the bathroom, and sets me on the toilet.

"Do you want me to help you?"

I've reached my quota of need for Xander and wish for him to leave. And I'm not about to be kind about it.

"Get out of my house Xander. And leave my car."

"I *am* sorry, Cass," Xander says before he leaves.

I sit on the toilet seat for a minute or two before I can work up the courage to do anything. I need to take my clothes off to get into the shower, but some of the blood has dried, making them stick to my skin. Those griffins actually cut me through my clothes.

I take a deep breath but let it out quickly. *I can do this.* *I can do this.* I take hold of one of my sleeves and pull. The pain is stabbing and excruciating. I bite my lip to keep from crying. But I forgot about my split lips. I close my eyes and tears roll down my cheeks. *Oh this sucks. I can't do this.*

Maybe I do need Xander's help. But I wasn't about to tell him that, or accept it.

Just rip the Band-Aid off, Casslyn, I tell myself. The trouble is, the Band-Aid covers my whole body.

I pull my arms out of my sleeves as slowly yet quickly and carefully as I can. As I pull the last sleeve down my arm, blood trickles down my hand and runs around my fingers. I stop taking the coat off just to watch it. I move my hand in front of my face only to watch the blood make a new path around my wrist.

I shake out of my reverie and yank the sleeve the rest of the way off. It hurts like I can't believe but it is over. Except for my shirt, jeans, and underwear. Christ.

My head is heavy yet light at the same time. My breathing is rapid and shallow. If I don't get my clothes off soon, I'm going to pass out.

I think about cutting my shirt off so I don't have to pull it over my head. It's already ruined anyway so why not cut it off? But that would just take more time. Not to mention the fact that it would require me to find a pair of scissors.

With the help of another deep breath, I pull my shirt over my head. My muscles protest as well as my torn skin. But I did it. I got it off without passing out. My jeans are next and I don't think they will be as bad. I just have to pull them down. And luckily I didn't choose skinny jeans tonight.

Once I am completely devoid of clothing, I turn the water in the shower on and look at myself in the full length mirror. My body is so much worse than I thought it was. I must have blacked out when I was being attacked because there are so many more cuts that I remember. There are angry red marks on my arms, my legs, under my chest, around my neck, and over my stomach. Some of them still bleed and look like running paint. The places where they punched and kicked me have turned a deep purple color. It is all ugly and hard to look at.

When I can no longer look at my bruised and battered skin I step into the shower and let the hot water wash away everything it can. There is no washing away Xander's betrayal. There is no removal of hate both given and received. There is no way to take away a hurt and a fear that I didn't know I was capable of. It doesn't take long before the moisture on my face changes from shower water to tears.

When Logan told me about the feud between the griffins and the phoenixes I believed that I knew how dangerous it could be. I believed I knew what being someone's mortal enemy entailed. But standing here in the shower, my blood running off of my body, I have a new understanding. A new outlook. And a new anger.

Through the tears I can see the water run red at my feet then escape down the drain. How can something so important to the human body as blood be so easily washed away?

The washcloth I use feels like taking more blades to my skin but I can think of no other way to wash myself and actually get clean. Before long I get dizzy and worn out and have to sit on the edge of the tub. I wish more than anything that this night was over.

Normally when one gets a cut and then cleans it, they then put some sort of antibiotic salve on it then bandage it. The trouble is, I don't have Band-Aids big enough to cover everything, nor do I have a number of Band-Aids enough for my whole body. I don't have gauze, wraps, tape, butterfly Band-Aids, liquid stitches, nothing. When I used the last one after the accident on my birthday, I threw them all out, hoping I would never have to use one again. Be careful what you wish for.

When I get out of the shower and dry off without ripping my skin off, I thank God my bathroom is on the second floor so I don't have to crawl up the stairs. The three-foot trek from the bathroom to my room takes a minute a foot and is terribly tiring. Besides the fact that it opens up my wounds.

I pull on a pair of underwear, forgo the bra, and find a loose fitting sweatshirt and pair of sweatpants to sleep in. I shut my bedroom light off then ease myself onto my bed. My body shudders as it tries to relax. A case of the shakes sets in as the tension gets to be too much. My eyes drift shut, my lids too heavy to keep open. I steady my breathing, which has calmed some since the attack, and try to fall asleep.

My body wants to crash but my mind is screaming. The

war between the two finally wears me out and I feel myself drifting away. I welcome it.

"Casslyn?"

I scream and jerk in my bed. Xander's back and he's brought those guys with him. They are going to finish the job. I'm too weak to defend myself.

Thirty Two

"Casslyn, calm down, it's just me," Logan's deep, booming voice lulls me into a sense of security.

I stop writhing on my bed. I forgot about hanging out with Logan tonight. He must have been worried. I feel stupid. He had every right to be worried.

Logan moves in the doorway.

"Don't turn on the light," I say to him. My voice is scratchy, broken. My whole body hurts from the fright of Logan and jerking around on my bed agitating my wounds. I can feel blood soaking through my sweatpants.

"Casslyn, what's wrong?" Logan asks before he turns on the light anyway.

The brightness of it hurts my eyes. I cover my face with

the blanket, both from the light and so Logan can't see my face. Of all the wounds on my body, my face looks the worst. Both of my eyes are a deep purple color and my lips are both split, bloody, and swollen. I barely look like myself and I don't want to freak Logan out.

"Nothing," I say from under my comforter, "I'm just tired. I was sleeping. I'm sorry I forgot about hanging out with you tonight."

"Don't you dare lie to me, Casslyn," Logan says, his voice getting closer until his weight collapses the mattress. "Did something happen with Tucker and Xander?"

He tries to pull the blanket away from my face but I have as much of a death grip on it as I can handle. He cannot see my face.

"Don't, Logan. I'm fine. I just want to go to sleep."

My muscles quiver from exerting the strength to hold on to the blanket. Logan pulls on it again and rips it from my grip. When he sees my face he recoils away from me and leaps from the bed.

"Who did this to you?" he asks, his voice hollow. The look on his face is far worse.

"Nobody," I say, turning away from him. "It's nothing, I just fell."

"You fell. Into what? Someone's fist?" Logan again sits on the bed. Gently, he takes my face in both of his hands. He cocks his head to the side and looks as if he might cry. I've never seen Logan like this before. It scares me. His voice is more firm when he asks, "Casslyn, who did this to you?"

I want the griffins to pay for this, and for killing my brother, but I also don't want to sell out Xander. I would never have done what he did, betray a friend like that, but I also don't know what being a griffin entails, so I don't know his reasoning. Maybe he is just too far gone to be my friend anymore. Maybe he is too far in with the griffins to protect. If he wasn't about to protect me, why should I protect him?

"Xander and I were taking a walk in the park when we got jumped by three griffins. They wanted to know if I was a phoenix." I don't need to tell him the rest.

Logan's eyes blaze like I have never seen before. I think he may jump from the bed to go find Xander and those other guys, but then he looks at me and the caring look is back.

"How badly are you hurt?"

"It's just my face," I tell him.

"I told you not to lie to me."

"They cut me a few times."

Logan stands up and away from the bed. "Show me."

I pull the covers from on top of me and am about to force myself off the bed when my phone rings on my bedside table. Logan grabs it before I can. When he reads the display his face turns murderous and I'm afraid he will throw my phone against the wall. Xander.

"Just ignore it," I say.

"There are fourteen missed calls. All from him," Logan says through his teeth.

"Just ignore it," I repeat.

I struggle to push myself up into a sitting position. My

arms shake and threaten to collapse under me.

"Do you need help?" Logan asks.

"I can do it."

My cuts burn from brushing against the sweatpants when I swing my legs over the edge of the bed. I stand in front of Logan and begin to pull a pant leg up to show him one of the cuts.

"No," he says. I think he might want to do it himself, or maybe he doesn't want to see them after all. But then he says, "Take off your clothes."

"Excuse me?"

"Take them off, I want to see it all."

"I'm not getting naked in front of you," I say. Not like this.

"I've already seen you naked. And besides, it's not like that. Not this time."

"That was without my knowledge, or consent. It's not the same thing."

"Casslyn, please," Logan says. He closes his eyes tight and rolls his shoulders back and around.

I ease my sweatshirt off over my head then pull my pants down. It hurts like a mother. With one arm over my chest, I stand in front of Logan in nothing but my underwear.

His breath falters then picks up double time. Then something happens that I would never in a million years have expected. Logan falls to his knees in front of me. He looks up at me with pure defeat in his eyes. His breaths come out ragged like he can't get enough oxygen. He begins to speak several times but nothing comes out. I am surprised by his intensity. Surprised more by how fiercely he is affected by this.

My phone rings again. Logan squeezes it in his hand so tight I think it might snap. Again he looks at the display. I am about ready to tell him to ignore it when he answers it. "I swear if you try to call, text, come here, see her in school, or in any other way try to contact her, I will put a dagger through your two hearts," he says, then hangs up the phone and tosses it on the bed.

"How could I let this happen to you?" Logan breathlessly says.

"It's not your fault," I say. My lips protest with every word I say.

"But it is. The only reason I am here is to protect you. To keep you safe. And I have failed. I am the worst guardian ever." Logan's head falls to his chest. He believes he has failed me and I don't know if I can make him think otherwise.

"Don't you say that. I am alive. And in a week or two I will be healed and we can forget this ever happened. Logan, you have given me more than I could ever have asked for. You are so much more to me than my guardian. But, if you feel the need, I will let you make it up to me."

His head pops up and he looks at me with so many questions in his eyes. But the one he asks is, "How?"

I reach down, take his hand in mine, the other still covering my chest, and pull him to his feet. "I would like to cash in my Christmas gift," I say, knowing he will only grant me this because I am injured.

The way he looks at me is more intimate and intense than any touch he could give me. His eyes burn with a passion I have never seen before in anyone. He takes his hand out of mine then places it on my cheek, the other hand following suit. I shudder when his thumbs brush over the bruises by my eyes and on my cheeks. My eyes close when his thumb moves to my lips and brushes the cracks. Then his lips press against mine so gently it's almost as if they aren't touching at all. His kiss is sweet and tender and filled with so much I could drown in it. Then he pulls away and a wetness hits my lips. And just like when Xander stabbed me and my skin knitted back together, I can feel my lips heal and stitch back together. It is only when I press my fingers to my lips and feel no cracks, no puffiness, no blood do I realize what Logan has done.

"You can't," I say, pulling away from him.

"Please let me do this for you," Logan pleads with me.

"You can't. If you heal me they will know. They will know that I am a phoenix if I can heal myself. Or they will know you are one, because you healed me with your tears. I have to heal naturally."

"Damnit," Logan yells, throwing his hands up. He walks away from me then throws his fist into the wall. I've never seen him this emotionally distraught. He splays his hands on the wall on either side of him. His shoulders rise and fall rapidly and heavily. "I'm so sorry."

"You have nothing to be sorry for."

Logan turns around sharply and charges at me. "Look at you."

I turn my head at him, smirk, and say, "You don't think I'm pretty?"

His eyebrows knead together and he comes closer to me so our bodies are nearly touching. He looks down at me with those smoldering eyes of his and says, "I think you are beautiful. I think you are more beautiful than I deserve to look at."

"Why are you so hard on yourself?"

"Because if I fail, it means losing you. I can't lose you."

The air escapes from my lungs and I can no longer breathe. "Why?"

"I was just supposed to protect you. I wasn't supposed to fall in love with you."

No way did he just say that. Did he say that? He said he wasn't supposed to fall in love with me. Does that mean he did? Oh God, I hope he did.

"What?"

Logan smiles a sad smile and says, "I love you, Casslyn. I am so in love with you."

That is the precise moment my heart melts out of my chest. It is everything I have wanted to hear from him since the first time we kissed. It is everything I knew I wanted, but didn't know I needed. I knew Logan felt something, but I didn't know the extent of it. I thought that it would be one sided with us. I would love Logan and he would just forget to love me back. But knowing he loves me is almost more than my damaged heart can handle.

Tears well up in my eyes then spill over. I can't believe I am crying. They are certainly happy tears, but tears nonetheless.

"Don't cry, love."

"You're not just telling me this because I got the shit beat out of me, are you?"

Logan smiles like he is about to laugh and shakes his head. "I'm telling you this because I should have told you a long time ago. And because I am tired of keeping my distance from you. I want to be with you more than you can imagine."

I bark out a laugh and say, "I can imagine."

Logan leans forward and catches my lips with a kiss that is more fierce than the last one. His hands grip my arms and agitate my cuts. As good as his kiss feels, the rest of my body is screaming in pain.

"Ah, that hurts."

"That's the thing about pain. It demands to be felt," Logan says but he's not talking about my cuts. The meaning behind his statement is so much bigger than my injuries.

Thirty Three

Logan and I wake in my bed several hours later. It hurt for him to hold me but he wasn't about to leave. I woke up many times during the night. Logan's massive body took up most of my twin sized mattress, not to mention the fact that I toss and turn in my sleep. So every time Logan touched my wounds or I rolled over and agitated one of my wounds, I would wake up resulting in me not getting too much sleep. And though he pretended to be asleep every time I woke up, I know he was awake, hating himself for the fact that I got hurt. Even though he has nothing to blame himself for.

I wake up to him kissing every part of my body. Every spot he moves to, every cut, every bruise, he brushes with his thumb and then plants a light kiss. Something in his kiss sooths my damaged skin.

"I could get used to this," I say.

"Every day," Logan says, looking up at me. There is so much love in his eyes I'm not sure how I missed it before. So much devotion. "You deserve it."

"I don't know about that. But I will take it."

When he finishes with all the cuts and bruises on my body he moves to kissing my lips and I am so glad. His lips are so soft and warm they start a fire within me that I hope never goes away. I want to take hold of him and kiss him until we can no longer breathe. But my body still aches leaving me to take what I can get.

"All I wanted to do last night was hold you, comfort you, make your pain go away. But I knew that touching you would only hurt you. You have no idea how hard it was for me," Logan says, resting his head on my shoulder.

"The fact that you were here was comfort enough," I say to him, trying to ease his unease.

Logan pulls away from the kiss and stares deep into my eyes for many breath taking moments. He says, "I want to be with you. I want to be your boyfriend. I want to take care of you and love you like you deserve."

I'm pretty sure I've died and gone to Heaven. I'm also pretty sure this is what my Heaven would look like. Logan making out with me, telling me he loves me and that he wants us to be together. Yup. This has to be Heaven. But then I adjust on my bed and my body reminds me that in no way is this Heaven.

"For as long as I've wanted to hear you say that. And for as good as it makes me feel, I have to wonder why you would want to be with me. I am a colossal mess."

Logan chuckles that deep throaty chuckle of his and says, "You're a mess. But you're beautiful. And you're my mess. If you will have me."

As a response I kiss him deep on the mouth.

He smiles and says, "I'll take that as a yes."

"Yes you will, boyfriend."

Logan kisses me again, igniting an all-out boyfriend/girlfriend blissful makeout session. I can't believe I could be this happy after the year I have had. But today is the start of a new year. And if it kills me, I will make this a good year.

I pull away from his kiss and say, "You know, I'm glad you finally gave in. You were a major grump. And so impatient with me. It was getting old."

Logan drops his head, sighs heavily, then looks up at me and says, "It wasn't that I was impatient with you. It's that I was frustrated with myself. I knew that I couldn't be with you. But I wanted it so badly that I allowed myself to have you a few times, let myself forget my position, my duties, and just be with you. But when I remembered I'd get mad at myself for giving in, and I took it out on you. I am so sorry. You deserve so much better."

"I deserve exactly what I have," I say before continuing to kiss my boyfriend.

When our lips get tired Logan makes me take a shower. He says he will never forgive himself if my wounds get infected because they do not stay clean and I won't let him heal me. I think he's being slightly over protective, but hey, if it helps him, I'm all for it.

When I'm in the bathroom I stand before the full length mirror and stare at the ugly, ugly cuts that will turn into even uglier scars. They will definitely be hard to hide in the clothes I like to wear. Even harder to hide will be the bruises that cover my face. If they are not gone by the time school starts again, I will have a lot of questions that I will not be able to answer.

Ugh. School. I *so* do not want to go back to school. It seems somewhat trivial in the scheme of what has happened to me in the past few months. I don't want to go back to face the even farther gap Xander has put between us. I don't want to go back to Tucker's disappointment over a broken friendship. I don't want to go back to Ashley's ridicule. Luckily I will have Logan with me to shoulder some of the burden.

When I get back to my room I grab my phone from the bedside table. I have three missed calls; one from my dad, and two from Tucker. I send Logan to his house to shower and change his clothes, assuring him that I will be fine while he is gone. Before he goes I tell him not to shave when he showers. He laughs but nods his head then heads out the door.

When he leaves, I lay back down on my bed, relishing the warmth he has left on it, as well as his unique scent. Logan smells like he has spent hours standing in a rain storm, clean and fresh, renewed. His scent lingers on my pillows, my sheets, my comforter, and it is all I can do to keep from smothering myself.

I use the time he is gone to return my missed phone calls. My dad wanted to make sure I know he still loves me and to set up a lunch date before I go back to school. That could be tricky, seeing as how my body doesn't like to move at the moment. Not to mention the fact that my face looks like a punching bag. Maybe it will be healed enough by the time I go back to school that I can wear concealing clothes and still be able to spend time with my dad. I could not be happier that I have my dad back in my life. My parents haven't talked yet, but that is to be expected. You can't exactly fix something as big as finding out your kids aren't your kids sixteen years later in a few days. I don't ever expect them to get back together, but it is nice to know that they don't hate each other.

I call Tucker back not knowing to what extent he is going to hate me. But he surprises me by asking me how I am feeling. That throws me off because I know Xander wouldn't tell him that he helped three guys beat me up. But then I remember that I told Xander to tell Tucker that I fell on the ice. I tell Tucker that I am fine, just sore and bruised. Then he goes into this speech about how happy he is that Xander and I were able to make up last night and how the three of us will go back to being best friends like we were before all of this ugliness started. And as he is talking I feel so bad that none of it is true. And I can't bear to break his heart and tell him. I just listen to him and tell him I can't wait to see him when school starts again.

I hang up the phone with a heavy heart. Tucker is so innocent in all of this. Maybe he would be better off if he found new friends. Maybe I should stay away from him so he stays safe. Woe is me to start the year off with three best friends and to end it with none. I feel like a special kind of awesome.

I don't know how else to protect him. I couldn't even protect myself.

Logan said he was my dad's best soldier. Even a phoenix soldier must know how to defend themselves. Besides the fact that Logan is a giant of a guy, my dad sent him here specifically to protect me. Surely my dad thought he might get into a scuffle, therefore he would have had to send someone who knows how to fight.

An idea clicks in my brain. Logan can teach me to defend myself. If I know how to defend myself, I can stay friends with Tucker and be able to keep him safe.

Not ten minutes after he left, Logan is back, showered, dressed, and trimmed stubble. At least he left some of it for me. It is the perfect time for me to ask him. It's not like he's going to say no.

Logan walks into my room and gently lies down on the bed beside me. But then he is above me, his face close to mine, his arms making a cage around my head. His presence is intoxicating. I pull my head up to meet his for a kiss, but he pulls back.

"Not yet," he says.

One of my eyebrows raises clear to the top of my forehead. He grins that devilish grin I love to hate. He's being mischievous and it will only prolong my pleasure. Then he leans down closer to me, teasing me. My pulse quickens. My breathing becomes heavy. His scent fills my nose. I could breathe him all in and it would not be enough. All I want is a taste and he will not give it to me. Logan wrinkles his nose as a way of saying *haha* and pulls away.

I take his shirt in my hands and try to pull him to me. He is much stronger than me and does not budge.

"Please," I say, not above begging.

He leans down so his mouth is at my ear and says, "Not . . . yet."

"Ugh," I growl. I, as well as my lady parts, am frustrated.

He flicks his tongue behind my ear then blows his hot breath on it. My eyes close involuntarily, a shiver runs up my spine, and a noise escapes my mouth that is very unlady like. Logan laughs that deep throaty laugh in my ear practically unnerving me. I am putty in this man's hands and he knows it.

"You're taking to this boyfriend thing very quickly," I say.

"Mmh hmm," he agrees. "I have been waiting too long for this. It's time I got to enjoy it."

Logan's mouth moves to my neck where he nibbles ever so slightly. Then licks. Then blows. It is all too much. I sigh in pleasure. He definitely knows what he is doing.

"What about my father?" I ask, remembering that he was one of the reasons Logan refused to be with me.

"You're ruining the mood," Logan rumbles into my ear.

"Maybe you should kiss me and shut my mouth."

Logan smiles, an actual smile, and says, "You'd like that, wouldn't you?"

I wrinkle my nose like he did, raise my shoulders, and roll my eyes as if to say, *maybe-maybe-not*. But he obliges and his lips meet mine in a kiss that makes me forget to breathe. I could lie here all day, every day, kissing my boyfriend. The only part of him touching me is his lips and yet that is enough to drive me wild. Pure bliss is not even close to describing how Logan makes me feel. It makes me wonder how I make him feel. That is when Logan growls in pleasure and I have my answer. I rest back into the bed and continue to kiss my boyfriend.

Logan lies back down beside me and we stare into each other's eyes. His are the calmest I have ever seen them. No burning, no smoldering, no dancing flames. Just calm. It is a sight to see.

"I love your eyes," Logan says.

"Please," I say, "I have coal eyes. Black. It's like it's all pupil, no iris. You on the other hand, it looks like you have dancing flames. You have no idea how beautiful they are."

"Is this that cute honeymoon phase everyone talks about?"

"God, I hope not. Also, I have something to ask you and I don't think that's part of the honeymoon phase."

"Ask me anything," Logan says, propping himself up on his elbow.

"Well, it's more like two questions. First, I want to know everything you know about the griffins. Everything. What motivates them. How they train. How they find out who the phoenixes are. How they find out who other griffins are. Everything."

"I can do that," Logan says. "Next?"

"I want you to teach me to defend myself. Teach me to fight."

"I cannot do that. I will not do that."

"What?" He didn't just say no, did he? What? Why would he say no? Wouldn't he want me to be able to defend myself?

"*I'm* here to protect you."

"But what if you're not there?"

"Casslyn, I will always be there to protect you," Logan's eyes begin to smolder. I don't understand why he doesn't want to do this.

"But you weren't there," I snap. I regret the words as soon as they are out of my mouth. He blames himself. He is so upset with himself. How could I make him feel worse? "I'm so sorry. I didn't mean it."

"It's okay, Casslyn," Logan says, but I can tell that it is not. The light in his eyes is gone.

"I'm so sorry."

"It's okay," he says again. He kisses me but it is a sad kiss.

There is no way to fix this, but I must try. "I have no doubt that you will always keep me safe. I just want to be able to do it for myself. You know, I am woman hear me roar, feminism and all that stuff."

Logan smiles but it doesn't reach his eyes. I've really hurt his feelings. I totally suck as a girlfriend.

"I'm sorry, Logan," I say again. I wish it was enough.

He places one of his big hands on my cheek and says, "I know, love."

"I really want to learn to defend myself. I never want to feel that helpless again. Being that weak was debilitating. Please. I will find someone else if I have to."

Logan closes his eyes, and sighs as his head falls back. I know he would roll his shoulders back if he wasn't lying down.

Two hours as a couple and I've broken him. Maybe there is something wrong with me. Maybe I can't make any relationship work be it sibling, friend, or romantic.

"Alright," Logan says. "I'll teach you to defend yourself. But I promise you it will not be easy. It's going to be long hours and really hard work. I am going to make you push your body to the limits and then some. You are going to hate me. Do you understand?"

I almost laugh. He isn't serious, is he? But he stares at me, unwavering, and I know he is serious. Well, it is what I asked for.

"I understand. I will not hate you though."

"Oh, you will, I promise."

"When do we start?" I ask.

"When your cuts are mostly healed. I don't want you getting sweat into them"

"Gross."

Lying next to Logan my eyes scan my bedroom, seeing it in a new way, a way Logan might see it. Boxes are still piled along one wall, still unpacked. Now that I know my parents won't be getting back together any time soon I might as well unpack. Plus, with Logan living next door, living here might not be so bad. My heart plummets when my eyes rove past the open door of my closet and I notice the dress I got for the dance. The dance that happens to be next week. There is no way my skin will be healed by then. There is no way I'm wearing that dress to the dance, putting my shredded skin on display. Now that Logan and I are together, the dance would have been the perfect place to showcase our relationship. And now that is not going to happen. Just one more price to pay for being a phoenix. With the tally as it stands, I'm not sure being a phoenix is worth the price of admission.

I look out my window and notice the sun is setting. How could I stay in bed all day? It felt good. My body probably needed it. But I've never really done it.

I want to get back to the boyfriend/girlfriend portion of the day, but Logan has that distant look that says I'm getting nowhere with him anytime soon. It's my fault. I hurt his feelings. I have no room to talk, Xander and I can hold a grudge with the best of them. I couldn't possibly expect Logan not to. I just wish that I hadn't screwed up. I feel the need to tell him I'm sorry again, but I don't think it would do any good.

Logan and I remain in my bed, my head resting on his shoulder, our hands and fingers interlocked. The moments could be awkward and uncomfortable, but instead they are calm and almost peaceful. Then my stomach growls and the peace is broken by our laughter.

"Hungry?" Logan asks. I can hear the smile in his voice.

"Maybe a little," I say sheepishly.

"Do you want to stay here while I cook or do you want me to carry you downstairs so you can watch while I cook?"

I smile at him and squinch my nose then say, "Definitely downstairs. I want to watch my sexy man make me food."

"Dork," Logan says, grinning.

"You love it," I say, teasing him.

"I love you."

"I will never get tired of hearing that. I love you."

Logan pushes himself up and off my bed. He pulls the covers off of me then gently places his arms under my back and knees. My skin still tingles every time he touches me. I will never get tired of his touch. I love everything about Logan. I hope I never get enough of him.

Thirty Four

My skin itches so badly. I have never, ever itched this badly. It is like there is a fire underneath my skin that will not go out. Everything itches. The more I scratch it, the more it itches. But if I don't scratch it I am in agony. There is no winning.

Logan chastises me every time I scratch, telling me I'm going to scar. I tell him he can't possibly know how badly I itch and am in pain so he should let me do what I want. It doesn't get me far. He may now be my boyfriend, but that doesn't mean he is any more lenient on me. If anything, he is now more protective.

I want to heal so badly. Simply for the fact that I'm sick of hurting and itching. But I also want to heal so that I can have a real make out session with my boyfriend. He is always so careful with me now that almost every inch of my skin has an evil red mark on it. But what I so desperately want is a kiss like the two before Logan declared his love for me. Our first kiss, where he held me up against the wall of the bowling alley and growled his pleasure into my mouth then dropped me on my ass. Or our second kiss, where his control slipped and he ravaged me on the couch. Other than the fact that my skin itches because it is healing, it itches with the want of Logan's touch. That fire our skin on skin contact ignites.

For that reason, I am almost glad to be back to school. It is a distraction. It helps me take my mind off of my romantic frustrations, as well as everywhere else my mind likes to wander. The closer it gets to the ten month anniversary of Nash being gone, the more I think about him and how much I miss him. I haven't seen him in a dream or any other time since I found out Logan is a phoenix. I miss that contact, even if it wasn't real. I miss his take on my life and goings on. I miss him constantly being with me, never having to worry about ever being away from him. I know now that I took him for granted. I never had to worry about being alone, until I was. Nash was my other half, my twin, my equal. The farther away from him I get, the more my equilibrium shifts, and I am not who I once was. I miss that girl. The worst part of all this, is that the closer I get to that one-year mark, the closer I get to being seventeen, Nash stays sixteen. Forever sixteen. And that kills me.

So maybe school isn't that good for keeping my mind off of things. I turn to my last best friend in need of a distraction. Mrs. Glass stands in the front of the class droning on about some war that I could care less about. It's the first day back and no one is paying attention. Therefore, she couldn't possibly get mad at me for not paying attention.

"Tucker, what's new? How was the rest of your vacation?"

"I should be asking you that," Tucker says. "I can't imagine how sore you must have been after falling on the ice."

"You have no idea," I say as Logan, who sits on the other side of me, places his hand on my leg. A warmth spreads through me that only Logan can unleash. But his warmth does a lot to calm me from a panic attack that merely thinking about the attack from the griffins can bring on. "But I asked about you. I told you I was going to start being a better friend, so you need to let me try."

"So sorry. The rents and I went to a movie and to the Olive Garden. It was fun. Xander and I hung out the other day. It was nice. He feels really bad you fell on the ice. I told him he shouldn't feel bad. It was just an accident. But you know how Xander is," Tucker says flippantly.

Logan's hand on my leg squeezes. After the attack, Logan's view on Xander skyrocketed from tolerance to the purest form of hate. I'm sure if I let him, Logan would have no problem killing Xander. I don't have a problem with Xander being a griffin. I really don't. I just wish that our two species weren't enemies. I don't understand why anyone ever has to be enemies. If people would ignore others, forget about others, leave others be, we could all live in peace. Yes, I know how delusional I am. I just want peace so badly. More than that, I wish the griffins didn't care that I was a phoenix so I didn't have to worry about my safety or mortality. Shouldn't someone who is immortal never have to worry about mortality? One can only wish.

"I do," I say, then immediately feel the need to change the subject. "Any new love interests?"

Tucker shrugs as if it is no big deal, but I know better. Cedars is a small town and even if there was another gay guy in town, he would never own up to it. There are some people in Cedars who still don't accept Tucker. They tend to get a mouthful from Xander and me if we ever hear about it. "Nah. But it's no big deal. I'm holding out hope for college," he says. "But speaking of new love interests, I'm so glad you and Logan are together now. And don't worry, I'm not mad that you didn't tell me the minute it happened."

I smile at my best friend, loving him more than anything. When Nash died, Tucker and Xander had to pick up the slack and they did a very good job. Unfortunately, I didn't realize I needed to do the same thing for them. I am learning.

"Tucker, stop changing the subject. We are talking about you now."

"My bad," Tucker says, scrunching up his face in his most innocent look. "There really is nothing new with me. I promise. You know when there is, I do tell you."

"I know. I was just checking."

"Miss Evans. Mr. Fleming. Would you do the class the honor of paying attention?" Mrs. Glass says.

I haven't gotten in trouble this past year unless I wanted to. My teachers are very lenient on me after my whole birthday debacle and the losing my brother thing. Tucker and I talking now may get us called out in class, but it isn't about to get us detention or sent to the office. I'm just glad I'm talking in class, and not screaming myself out of a daydream.

"Sorry, Mrs. Glass," Tucker and I say together.

"I'm sure," she says in answer.

Tucker and I share a look, smile, then turn back to what is left of class.

Mrs. Glass's reprimand was nothing compared to what I receive when I leave class. Luckily I had been able to avoid Ashley and her group for the beginning of the day. However, we have a run in when I leave the history room.

"Well, well. Look who decided to show her face," Ashley says, striding toward Tucker, Logan, and I from down the hallway.

Sometimes I really wonder how intelligent she is. Why wouldn't I show my face? I still have to go to school. It's not like I can just skip it for the next two years. And I'm not quite sure what it is I should now be cowering from. Maybe she knows something I don't.

I decide not to give in to her tormenting and continue to walk. She stops right in front of me, however, her posse surrounding me and I have nowhere to go.

"Nice face," she says. "Did your boyfriend beat you for mouthing off? Or did Xander beat you for stepping out on him?"

My blood threatens to boil. Why does she always bring up the things that bother me most? Maybe she does know things about me that others don't. Maybe she has some inside source. I swear if she goads me about Nash I may punch her in the face and mess up her perfect little nose.

If Logan still intimidates her, she does not show it. Instead, she looks up at him and smirks. I can feel him stiffen beside me. His job is to keep me safe. And while I am not in any immediate danger, the subject matter infuriates him. But there is something else. Another reason why he has gone rigid. Maybe Xander is nearby and Logan can hear his heartbeats. Maybe there is another griffin in the school we didn't previously know about. I plan to ask him about it when we are alone. But whatever it is, Logan's anxiousness has me on edge. If he is nervous, I am in danger. Forgetting Ashley for the time being, I look to Logan's taut jaw line and statuesque form. There is definitely something wrong.

Ashely attempts to make some other comment that I choose not to listen to. Instead, I take Logan and Tucker's hands in mine and walk through Ashley and her friends.

When we reach an empty section of the hallway, Logan leans down close to me and says, "Do you still want to learn to defend yourself?" His jaw is tight, so serious.

"Yes," I say, more adamant now than before.

"We'll start after school today," he says. He does not say

what set him off. He just takes my hand and leads me to my next class.

When we get to the gym, Logan stops me before I can head to the girls locker room. He pulls me to him, holds me tight, and kisses me deep. It is a deep, possessive kiss that takes my breath away. I would fall to my knees if he wasn't holding me so tight. As quickly as he kisses me, he pulls me back, still holding me in his arms, and looks deep into my eyes. He seems more worried than ever.

"I love you, Casslyn. I'm never going to let anything happen to you," he says, now cupping my face with his large hands.

"Logan, what is going on?" I asked, worried because he is so worried. I realize that, now more than ever, the griffins suspect that I am a phoenix and that my life is in danger. But I wasn't about to let it bother me because Logan is here solely to protect me. And if Logan doesn't think there is anything to worry about, I have no reason to worry. But the farther Xander gets into the griffins, the more we worry what he could be telling them. And the more worried Logan becomes, the more I have to worry about my own safety. I hate it. Before I learned of my real parentage and heritage, I had somewhat of a life. I had freedom. And while I love Logan, and love spending time with him, he is becoming a bit overprotective. Before we got to know each other, Logan protected me from the sidelines. Now that I am his girlfriend, a part of his race, and his charge, he has taken his job to a whole new level. The gleam in his eye when he asked if I still wanted to train to fight was as if he wished it was his idea.

"Nothing, can't a guy just tell his girlfriend how he feels?"

"He can when he is not lying to her," I say, pulling my hand from his and placing both of mine on my hips.

"I'm not lying to you," Logan says. He tilts his head as if he is confused or offended.

"Hiding things from me is like lying. Withholding the truth is like lying. You promised you would never lie to me again."

Logan's eyes start to smolder as he begins, "The griffins are planning something. I don't know what it is. I've tried to get inside, to gather information. But they are being very tight lipped. As much as I hate to say it, Xander really had no idea you were going to be attacked. They don't tell him much. They don't tell any of the new griffins much. Getting inside is hard. But they are planning something big and it scares me. Something could happen to you and I might not see it coming."

I pull Logan away from the gym doors and from prying eyes and ears. I really miss the masculine, undeterred Logan. The guy who was afraid of nothing. The guy who was the intimidator. I don't want to be the reason Logan is weak. I don't want to be a distraction for him. If something happens to Logan because he is more worried about me than himself, I don't think I will be able to live with myself.

"Logan, nothing is going to happen to me. You are here to make sure of that. I have complete faith in you. You have already saved me more than once. You don't have to worry so much."

"You don't understand," Logan says, his eyes burning with something akin to agony.

"Then tell me."

"I am terrified of losing you. I love you more than I have ever loved another person in all of my lives and it scares me to death to think I could lose you. Would you *please* let me be a little overprotective, until you're seventeen? Then you'll be a little more durable, and I'll back off. I promise."

"Okay," I say.

"Okay? What? You're not going to fight me on this?"

"No.

"No? You, who fights me on every meal we make in Home Ec.? You, who has no issue fighting Xander and Tucker on anything. You, who call out Ashley on all of her bullshit. You're not going to fight me on this?"

"No. I trust you. And I value my life just enough to listen to you."

"I do love you, Casslyn."

"I know, baby. I love you, too. But I am way late for class."

Logan chuckles, but it does not settle deep within him. He leans down, kisses me on the cheek, and walks away from me. My cheek tingles as I run to the locker room.

One day, when all this griffin stuff is over, if it is ever over, I want to see Logan return to the way he was when I met him. A fierce man who excites me, but instills a calm so profound. I want Logan to be free, not worried about duty, honor, or failure.

Before I can reach the locker room, I am caught by the arm and spun around. I am never getting to class. The hand clasping my arm is tight and hard, almost mean.

"What do you want, Xander?"

"I want to talk to you."

"You might want to leave. Logan just left. I'm sure he can hear us. I don't think you want to know what happens if he sees you with me."

"I need to talk to you. I'm so sorry, Cass. What happened the other night . . . It is killing me," Xander says. His eyes are wild and frantic. "I am *so* sorry. I don't know what I was thinking."

"You chose sides, Xander. That's what happened," I tell him. I didn't know what I would say to him if confronted about the other night. At first I wanted to hate him. Then I felt bad for him. Then I was just mad. And now I'm more focused on more important things.

"You are the most important person in my life. I don't ever want you to feel like I'm not on your side. I am always on your side."

I stare at him, trying to discern whether or not he is sincere. He seems to be, but he has duped me before. Fool me once and all that.

"You can say that, but we both know it's not true."

"It is true. I will prove it to you."

"Xander, you are a griffin. I'm a phoenix. And while

neither of us should hold that against each other, I just don't think we can be friends right now."

"Don't say that," he says.

"You're the one that-," I begin but am interrupted.

"Ms. Evans. Mr. Grosvenor. If it doesn't inconvenience either of you, would you care joining the rest of the class?"

Xander sighs heavily beside me while I say, "Yes, sir. Sorry, Mr. Kneifl."

"I'm sure," Mr. Kneifl says.

Why do teachers always say they are sure? It's like teachers have a set vocabulary when it comes to dealing with delinquent students.

I race off for the locker room and finally make it.

Thirty Five

My muscles scream at me. It's quite laughable how much I thought they hurt after I was attacked. They just hurt then. Now, they burn. I thought I was somewhat athletic, somewhat in shape. But the workout Logan is putting me through has me realizing I don't even know what being in shape meant. He told me I would hate him. I also thought that was laughable. Boy was I wrong.

The stretches he had me do before the workout, were more of a workout than I've ever done. I am in big trouble.

I stand, hunched over with my hands on my knees, my breathing heavy, in Logan's basement-turned-gym. Yet another thing I did not expect from this house that was once thought to be haunted. The floor is concrete but covered in some sort of rubber mats. There is a pristine Stairmaster, elliptical, treadmill, abs machine, and weight bench along one wall. Jump ropes and weight belts hang on hooks behind them.

We've been at it for half an hour and already I'm ready to quit. But according to Logan, we haven't even begun. Ugh. And besides exhausting me physically, he is exhausting me mentally. After all, I did tell him I wanted to know everything there is to know about griffins.

"Okay," he says once I've finished my required twenty minutes on the elliptical, "You do twenty pushups while I tell you the geniality of the griffins." Apparently he thinks that if he talks while I work out, it will take my mind off of my burning muscles. He is wrong.

I glare at him before lying on the floor for more torture. The first five pushups aren't so bad. It is the rest that kill me.

"Phoenixes are a patriarchal society. Our genes are passed on through the father. The griffins, however, are matriarchal. The mothers pass on the gene. Now, that being said, the phoenix fathers have all the powers every phoenix has. The griffin mothers, well all females, pass on the gene but have no powers."

I stop in the upright position of my tenth pushup and say, "What?"

"Exactly what I just said. Keep going."

I go down to the floor, push back up, and ask, "Why don't the females have any powers?"

Logan, who has his arms crossed, raises an eyebrow and

says, "I don't know, I'm not a scientist. Ten more."

"Yes, sir," I say with as must sarcasm as I can muster. It is difficult though when my arms waver and threaten to give out from under me. I'm not the skinniest girl in the world, but I'm nowhere near overweight, and my body feels like it could weigh a ton. Every pushup becomes more difficult, my arms hating me with every up and down. Who does this for fun?

While I do my pushups, I can't help but think about Xander being a griffin and all the female griffins who don't get to have powers like the men. As a girl who has a slight I-am-woman-hear-me-roar complex, I would be pissed. Especially if I was in a case like Nash and I, if Nash was still alive, and he got powers and I didn't. I would be way pissed. Something clicks as I think about this. Something that never really clicked this whole time. Xander's mom, who I have known my entire life, who has been like a second mother to me, is a griffin. What if Xander's dad is a griffin? Do they know that I am a phoenix? Are they the ones who told the griffins about me? Do they want me dead like the rest of the griffins? This sucks. The farther into this life I get, the more people from my old life I lose.

Logan does not skip a beat when I have reached twenty. "Alright, one hundred abs. Go."

"I'm pretty sure I just asked you to teach me to defend myself," I say, so tired I want to quit.

"You have to be fit in order to learn to defend yourself. Actually you should be fit anyway. If you can't defend yourself, you should at least be able to run away."

"I'm not about to run away from someone who wants to kill me. Someone who might have killed Nash."

Logan's head snaps towards me. "Are you just going to let them kill you because you are too stubborn to run away?"

"No," I say quietly, feeling like I have been scolded. But in no time I find my nerve, "That's why we are doing this. I will find the one who killed Nash, and I will kill them."

"I'm not going to teach you to fight just so you can go kill someone. If you want that, why don't you just go buy a gun?"

"Maybe I will," I say, crossing my arms.

"Abs, now," Logan says, dismissing my comment.

I sit on the abs machine and get to work. Around the seventy mark my mid-section burns, but this time I don't mind so much. When I am finished, Logan throws me a bottle of water. I down half of it in one gulp.

The second I finish it, Logan says, "Jump rope. Fifteen minutes."

How much more could he possibly make me do?

I don't even regard him when I reach for the jump ropes behind him. A rubber rope in hand, I move to the open part of the floor and begin to jump rope. It takes me a couple jumps before I get a good rhythm but then it is just jumping and my mind goes blank. I don't see the basement around me. I don't hear the slapping of the rope against the rubber mats. I don't notice the sweat pouring down my forehead and running into my eyes.

I catch my foot in the rope and fall to the floor when Logan says, "Casslyn, are you listening to me?"

"Obviously not," I snap. "Thanks for scaring the shit out of me."

Logan laughs but comes to my side to pick me off the floor.

"Where was your head?"

"I spaced out. What do you want?"

Logan cocks his head to the side and bites his tongue. He either wants to yell at me, laugh, or roll his shoulders back.

"Are you going to be like this every day?"

"Maybe."

"May I remind you that you wanted this," Logan says.

"You may, but it doesn't mean it's going to get you anywhere."

Logan picks me up off the floor, plants me firmly on my feet, then steps away.

"You are just a peach, you know that," he says, running his hand over his face.

"Yeah, but you love me and you already said it so you can't take it back," I say in my best five-year-old voice.

Logan laughs that deep throaty laugh that I love and takes me in his arms. "I do love you," he says then plants his lips on mine. The kiss is salty from my sweat, but is sweet nonetheless. Logan's hands on my sides does crazy things to my brain and when they slip under my shirt and ride up my ribs my brain short circuits. I could definitely get used to this. Then he pulls away and says, "Jump rope. You still have ten minutes.

"Ugh."

"Hate me yet?" he asks, and smirks.

"Yes," my voice is snarky.

"Good."

When I have finished the jump rope and everything else he makes me do he says that I should be warmed up and that it is time for a run. My mouth drops open and I have to pick it up off the floor. What the hell were the elliptical, stair climber, and treadmill for? Nevertheless, we put on light jackets and head out for a run. I'm pretty sure if anyone sees us running in light jackets, in the dead of winter, they are going to think we are crazy. I think we are crazy. Logan anyway.

"Okay," Logan says as we start out our run. "I've already told you about the griffins being spurned about the whole Apollo thing. Which really is the reason they hate us, don't believe otherwise. But what any griffin will tell you, is that the reason they kill us is because we are a danger to humans."

I don't say anything in answer to Logan. He takes it as confusion, but it is merely from lack of oxygen. "You see, in some myths, legends, whatever you want to call them, griffins are believed to be the king of the creatures because they are half lion, half eagle. King of the beasts. King of the air. So because of that they were considered the most revered of guardians. Now, in those legends, they guarded kings' and gods' gold and other treasures."

The feeling in my legs is a mix of the jello feeling, and the screaming pain feeling. More sweat then my body has ever produced rolls down my head, my arms, my legs, in places I don't want to mention. I feel so gross. Most people who run in the cold like it because the wind and the chill cool down the sweat. I do not get that luxury. The cuts that still cover my body become itchy from the sweat. But worst of all, I have this stabbing pain in my side that makes my breathing difficult.

"In later years they guarded a person's most priceless possessions whether that be materialistic objects or people. And then, when gold and treasure was a thing of the past, those priceless possessions became people. Because a person's life has no value. Therefore it is the most valuable."

I stop running because I want to address this, but also because I want to stop running. "You're saying that griffins say they kill us because they say we are a danger to humans? That makes no sense. Why would any phoenix want to kill humans?"

"Humans kill humans all the time. There are bad seeds in every race. Sometimes a phoenix does it for fun, sometimes because their lives are in danger. And sometimes it is an accident. If you don't know that you are a phoenix and you burst into flames, some bad shit goes down."

"But," I start to say and don't get to finish.

Logan pushes me in the back to make me run again and says, "Learn to talk while you run."

I turn around to look at him incredulously. "You do know that I am not yet a phoenix and that I am not yet as strong as you or as fast as you. And so on and so forth."

"Mind over matter," he says and turns me back around.

"Yeah, okay, Obi Wan," I say, rolling my eyes.

We begin to run again. We turn left at an intersection. If we turn left again, Logan must be making me fun four miles, since gravel roads are divided in square miles. Logan stays with me. I know there is no way, with his long legs, extreme physique, and even breathing, that I could possibly be keeping up with him. I am in so much pain. I want to quit so badly, but I know I can't. I won't let myself. I won't let myself down. I won't let Logan down. And I certainly won't let Nash down. I may be doing this for myself, but I am also doing this for him.

It is dark when we turn left for the last time and run past my house. I feel a sense of relief. We are almost home free. But I also feel a sense of accomplishment. I did it. I ran four miles and did all of the workouts Logan made me do without crying, pulling a muscle, or passing out. I consider that a win. That is, until Logan takes me back to the basement and makes me do it all over again. I'm not sure if he is trying to make me stronger or kill me.

I down another bottle of water then check the time. My heart sinks. We have been at this for three hours. Good thing none of my teachers gave homework on the first day.

When I replace the jump rope on the wall, Logan says, "Ready for the good stuff?"

I'm really not, but why else am I here, and what else am I going to do tonight?

"Bring it on," I say, half determined, half ready for a nap.

***

"Oomph," is the noise that escapes me, as well as all the oxygen in my body, when Logan slams me to the floor. And I do mean slam.

Logan has spent the last hour beating me up. He isn't holding anything back. Well, maybe a little bit, but who could tell when your body feels like a punching bag. Because that is what it has been the last sixty minutes. Logan punches me, uses his hand to simulate a knife across my neck and into my heart, kicks my legs out from under me, picks me off my feet and slams me to the ground, like he has just done.

Frustration clouds my actions as I feel like I am not getting anywhere. Over and over Logan defeats me. I realize he is twice my size, but I should have quickness on my side. No. I have nothing on my side. The more I get defeated, the more I become frustrated. Forget about asking for a mile, Logan won't even give me an inch.

"Pay attention," Logan barks. "You have to watch for my movement. You are trying to defend yourself, so defend. Don't focus on where you are going to hit or how hard you are going to hit. You have to move out of the way or be prepared to block blows."

"Yeah, I'm working on it," I bark back.

I know he is trying to help me, but it is hard to see that while he is beating the crap out of me. My body is tired. My mind is tired. And my heart is tired. I just want to be done for the night.

"Again," Logan commands.

Begrudgingly, I get to my feet and stand at the ready like Logan showed me. I take notice of his hands and his feet. He shuffles around, crossing his feet as he moves in a circle. My eyes flick between his hands and feet. He is going to attack. He always attacks. I need to pay attention like he told me to, and maybe I can prevent it. If he strikes with his hands I can use my arms to deflect it. If he tries to kick out with his leg, I can jump over it. He makes a quick move to the right and an even quicker one to the left. I lose track of him and am instantly sorry for it when his hand makes contact with the side of my face. It isn't hard enough to bruise, but he got me again.

Logan takes advantage of my disorientation by wrapping his arms around my legs, picking my off the ground, and slamming my back to the floor. This is getting so old. Then, like the boyfriend he is, he leans over me and extends a hand to help me to my feet. Without his help, I spring to my feet and slam my hands into his chest, shoving him backwards. I follow his rear movement and slap him across the face. It feels good to let out some of the frustration but does little in the way of relieving it.

Logan rubs his cheek with his hand and laughs at me.

He laughs at me. What a jerk. "Feel better?" he asks.

"Yeah. Don't laugh at me," I snap. "And would you take it easy on me? I'm not going to learn any of this if you kill me."

Logan's expression turns from amusement to anger. "Did those guys who beat the shit out of you take it easy on you? Do you think any other person who wants to harm you is going to take it easy on you? No. They won't. You need to be ready."

"And you think you beating the shit out of me is going to make me ready?"

Logan opens his mouth as if to say something, then closes it. His face changes in an array of expressions. He looks sad, mad, frustrated, guilty. After a minute of struggling with a feeling, his face is still. Expressionless. Finally, he says, "We are done for tonight." Without another word, he turns on his heal and walks up the stairs.

"Excuse me?" I say to the now empty basement.

I look around the basement, confused, angry, sad. I want to kick something or hit something, or punch something. Maybe throw something. My eyes land on a medicine ball lying on the floor. I stalk over to it, pick it up, and hurl it against the wall, letting out a yell of frustration. Logan can't just walk away during an argument. And I'm not about to let him.

"Hey," I yell when I get upstairs. I move around the first floor looking for him. "Logan," I yell and I move from the vacant living room to the empty kitchen. "Logan!"

The fact that he knows I am looking for him and won't answer me makes me mad.

"Logan," I yell when I get to the second floor, opening the bathroom door to find it empty.

Unless he left the house all together, he has to be in his room. I turn the knob and shove the door open. Logan stands by his closet pulling his pants down his legs. When he kicks them off, he stands there in only his boxers. My heart skips a beat, and I know Logan can hear it, but I don't care. The man in front of me is manly perfection. Bulging muscles. Six pack. Tan. That v that starts at his stomach and travels down to a place I only dream of. My brain is suddenly foggy. Why was I mad when I came up here? Was I mad? His body is so tantalizing and covered in a thin layer of sweat I want to lick off. Wow. What am I thinking? I am staring, but I can't help it. Before I know it, all of his perfection is standing inches in front of me, in a pair of boxers. It is all too much.

It takes many moments before I can pry my eyes away from his chest to look at his face. When I manage it, he is looking at me with the classic Logan smirk on his face. And then I remember why I came up here.

"What are you doing?" I bark.

"I'm going to take a shower," he answers in equal amounts of snark and cynicism.

He goes to move past me but I stop him by placing a hand on his bare chest. A spark flares where my hand rests and turns into a flame that burns up my arm and through my body. There is no denying that Logan and I have a connection. Instantly our bodies and mouths crash into each other. He tastes like loving and letting go. Like burning passion and fiery desire. I love him and I want to devour him. Logan must agree. He growls in the back of his throat then flicks his tongue against mine. It makes me light headed and dizzy. My heart pounds in my chest. I have never felt so alive.

Logan's hands move to my hips. I wrap my legs around his waist when he lifts me up. The warmth from his skin travels from my legs to the rest of my body. Then his hands move to my butt and my vision goes dark as my eyes roll to be back of my head. Logan carries me to the bed and lays over me. My body shakes with want and anticipation.

I can't help my hands from roaming his body. My fingers trail the ridges and dips of his muscles. I press my pointer fingers into the dimples above his butt. His reaction is to bow his hips deeper into my legs. I let out an embarrassing sigh of pleasure and almost lose my shit.

His lips move to my neck, planting kisses as he goes. My breath falters in the best kind of way. His kisses trail back up my neck to my ear. He licks behind my ear then blows on it like he knows drives me wild.

"Are you still mad at me?" he whispers into my ear.

I can barely breathe but manage to say, "No."

"Good," he whispers. Then, the jerk removes himself from above me and walks out of the room.

I feel cold when his warmth is gone.

I follow him into the bathroom and demand, "What are you doing?"

Logan looks at me like I am a lunatic. "Taking a shower," he says as if it is the most obvious thing.

"But you . . . and we . . . and you . . . ," I stammer.

Logan laughs at me. He is lucky I don't slap him for it. "You're welcome to join me," he says.

My cheeks flame in a blush causing Logan to laugh harder. "You should do that more often. You're so cute, love."

"Yeah, shut up," I say to him and retreat to his room.

When he is finished in the shower, I take my turn, then meet him in the kitchen. Whatever he is cooking smells amazing. I sit at the island as he sets a plate piled high with spaghetti in front of me.

I stare at the plate in awe then look up at Logan. "Um," I start, "I can eat, but I don't think I can eat that much."

"Soon you will. And you'll need the energy the carbs give you for the workouts."

I raise my eyebrows and nod but do not say anything. He is right, I am hungry, and it smells so good. I dig in without another word. It tastes even better than it smells and I shovel it in. I'm sure it's quite attractive, but I don't care.

"Are you staying over tonight?" Logan asks. "Or is your mom going to be home?"

"She is on call this week. She thinks it's more practical to stay there than to come home and to have to go back."

"So that is your long way of saying . . . ?"

"Yes, I will be staying tonight. You, however, after what you pulled today, will be sleeping on the couch or on the floor."

Logan places a hand over his heart and feigns pain. "You wound me," he says.

"Back at you, buddy."

Thirty Six

All week Logan has tortured me with his workouts, running, and body slamming. All week my body has grown weaker and stronger at the same time. I have never been so tired, sore, and worn down, and yet I have never felt so energized, built, and powerful. My legs are more defined. My stomach is flatter and more toned. And I actually have some muscle in my arms.

The workouts have become easier, though the better I get at them, the more Logan makes me do. Running has become comforting and rhythmic. It helps to take my mind off of things. And though Logan still kicks my butt when it comes to sparring, I have gotten better. Luckily I haven't been attacked since New Year's Eve.

Because Logan has spent the week torturing me, I thought today was time for payback. I dress for today's workout in Logan's bathroom then head for the basement.

Logan is already there, lifting weights. I could watch him press the bar up and down forever, his muscles swell and bulge. His breathing is strong and he makes this funny noise when he pushes the bar up and brings it down.

"Get to work," he says.

"Yes, sir," I say moving to the wall where the jump ropes hang. I take off my sweater and sweat pants and stand in a sports bra and tiny spandex shorts. Even with scars covering most of my body, I don't look half bad. I smile when I hear the weight bar clang against their resting place.

I stand in front of Logan and the weight bench and begin jumping rope. Logan watches me, tries to push the bar above his head, then looks back at me, and almost drops the bar on his chest. Clearly distracted, Logan moves on to the abs machine behind me. I let him get a few abs in before I let the rope fall out of my hand and bend over to pick it up. The machine slams forward when Logan tries to get a better look. I laugh inwardly, not wanting Logan to catch on to what I am doing. When he realizes he's not going to get anywhere with the abs machine, he moves on to a treadmill. That is when I sit on the floor to do my stretches. He starts out in a jog. I start out with toe touches. It's probably mean to divert his attention around dangerous work out equipment, but he's a tough guy, he can take it. I bend over to touch my toes and make sure Logan gets a good look down my bra. I know I've succeeded when I look up to see him trip over his own feet and the treadmill belt. This time I let out a good laugh.

"Okay," he says, letting out a heavy breath, "I can't focus. But I expect you to."

I look up at him with confusion and say in my most innocent voice, "I am focused. What's your problem?"

Logan smirks at me then says, "Very funny. Get back to work."

I smile, knowing I have succeeded.

I continue to stretch, this time actually stretching. I can still feel Logan's eyes on me. It does a lot for my self-confidence. I move to the treadmill and begin a jog that will turn into a run. I can actually run a mile without feeling like I might pass out. It is a miracle.

When I have gotten into a good run, Logan stops jumping rope and stares at me. "What?" I ask, now able to talk while I run.

"Go take a shower," he says so earnestly.

I trip over my feet and almost slam my face into the treadmill screen before I catch myself. "Excuse me?"

Logan laughs at my mishap then says, "You've worked hard this week and I wanted to reward you by taking you out. I've been a good trainer, but not such a good boyfriend. I figured I should rectify that. So go shower, get dressed, and we'll go."

"Can I ask a favor?" I ask, thinking this is the perfect time to hatch a plan I've been formulating.

"What's that?"

"Can Tucker come?"

"You want to take Tucker on our date?" Logan asks, crossing his arms and cocking an eyebrow.

"I want you two to be friends and I think tonight would be a good place to start."

"Are you saying we're not friends?"

"Are you saying you are? You never talk to him. You never spend time together," I say. When he just stares at me like none of what I have said proves that they are not friends, I say, "Let me guess, you are one of those guys who thinks if you don't hate each other you are friends."

Logan shrugs his shoulders.

"Oh, you poor thing. You are so cute."

He gawks at me then says, "Thank you for thinking my social ineptitude is adorable."

"What am I here for, if not to make fun of you? So what do you say? Can Tucker come?"

"Yes. Did you actually think I would say no?" Logan asks then says, "Don't answer that. Where do you want to go, on our date, with Tucker?"

"The bowling alley."

"Are you being serious?"

"Yeah. A, I love bowling. B, I'm going to kick your ass at pool. And C, it's reminiscent of our first non-date, date."

Logan has a faraway look on his face that suggests he has an early start on the reminiscing. "Wear something revealing," he says.

I think about the short t-shirt dress I wore that night. I

360

think about how Logan picked me up, spread my legs to step between them, then placed his warm hands on the backs of my thighs. I get goose bumps just thinking about it. But then I remember that all of my body is covered in ugly, red lines.

"What about Tucker?" I ask.

Logan turns his head to the side, clearly confused, and says, "I thought he was gay."

I laugh, finding it funny that he would even think that Tucker would check me out. "He doesn't know about my scars."

"Oh," Logan says, his face suddenly turning dark. "Then forego the revealing clothes. But go get ready. If I have to stare at you for one more second in those nonexistent clothes I might lose my mind."

I hop over to where he is standing, place my hand on his tight chest, lean up, and kiss him on the mouth. "Is that so?" I ask in my most sultry voice.

"Please, woman," he says, closing his eyes.

I smile and walk away from him, sashaying my hips as I go. I hear him sigh loudly.

I text Tucker on my way back to my house. *Logan and I are taking you out tonight. Be ready in twenty minutes.*

His answer is almost instant, *are you serious?*

Yes. See you in twenty.

I am so excited!, I get as a reply when I walk into my house.

"Hello, Casslyn," I jump at the sound of his voice.

He leans against the couch in the living room. He looks

just like he did at school, but behind those walls I felt safe, like he couldn't get to me. Now, alone in my house, I am frightened of him. Of what he might do. Of who he might notify. Of who could possibly be hiding here waiting to strike.

"What are you doing here?" I ask, nervous. "If Logan knows you're here . . ."

"Just please, hear me out."

"Xander, you can't be here."

Xander looks at my face, almost pleadingly. Then his eyes roam over the rest of my body. I forgot to put my sweatshirt and sweatpants back on and stand before him in my shorts and bra. His expressions turns from pleading to horror.

"Oh my God," he says.

The bruises that covered my body are now very light shades of yellow. The cuts that adorn my body are now scars. But when the griffins cut me, they didn't care if they were clean cuts and many of them are jagged and ugly. Not once since the attack had I given any thought to how they might appear to anyone else or how I might feel with their eyes on me. But now, with Xander's gaze upon me, I feel self-conscious, ugly, and contemptible.

I cover what I can with my arms and look around the living room for a sweater or something to put on.

"I'm so sorry, Cass," he says.

My head snaps to his direction. There is repentance written all over his face, but it doesn't appeal to me. "Is that all you have to say for yourself?" I ask. Hate boils in my throat and spews out as venom, "You punched me in the face. And then you *cut* me for your sadistic friends. Do you want to see it?" I ask. I thrust my arm out at him and point to the scar he created above my wrist.

He flinches back and looks as if I have slapped him. "I don't know what else to say. I am sorry."

"Why don't you just leave?"

"I need to talk to you. The griffins are planning something."

"Which I'm sure you are helping with."

"Would you just listen? I don't know what they are planning and I don't know when they are going to carry it out. They are going to attack you again. It's not going to be just a few of them. Our leader is convinced you are a phoenix. He never gets into anything this deeply. Why you? Why are they so interested in you? I don't get it, but you need to be ready. You need to be careful. I'm scared for you."

"It's too late for that. It's no longer your place to be afraid for me. Now, you need to leave before Logan gets here."

Xander stands in front of me and stairs for a long time. After many long moments he drops his head and walks towards the front door. He places his hand on the knob but does not twist it. He turns to me and says, "I love you, Casslyn. I do. Please be careful."

I watch him leave then head for the bathroom. I don't have enough time to dwell on what he's said before Logan gets here and we have to go pick up Tucker.

The head honchos of the griffins really must not tell the peons anything because Xander seems not to know that my real father is the leader of all the phoenixes. I swear I mentioned to him at the New Year's party that my dad isn't my father, but he must not have listened to me. Not surprising as of late. Though I still don't understand how the griffins know that. There has to be someone who knew my mom and father when they were together before I was born and informed the griffins. Who could that possibly be? Xander's mom is an obvious option, but I still don't want to believe that the woman who has treated me like a daughter my whole life would give me up. It's especially hard to think about there being more supernatural beings in Cedars than Logan, Xander, Xander's mom, and I. But there has to be. There has to be a whole community of griffins here. Besides Xander, there were three of them who attacked me on New Year's. And if their leader is getting involved, he must be here. Could their headquarters be here? It is all too much to think about. The terrifying thing to think about, though, is that there are only one and a half phoenixes here; Logan and I. If a multitude of them attack us, I fear that we will not be able to defend ourselves.

I turn on the shower and get ready to hop in when there is a pounding on the door. I scream. The person on the other side of the door stops pounding only to break the door down.

"What's wrong?" Logan asks, rushing me and taking me into his arms. "Are you okay?"

My heart is pounding in my chest. My head throbs.

When I calm down enough to speak I say, "I'm fine."

"There was a griffin here. Was it Xander?"

"Yeah. I made him leave. I'm going to get in the shower now."

"Casslyn," Logan says.

"I'm fine," I say a little too loudly.

"No, you're not. And that's okay. I'm here. Let me in, love."

I open the door to the bathroom and allow him entrance. "It's all too much, Logan. My best friend is my worst enemy. My other best friend doesn't know who I am. My twin is dead. My dad is not my dad. I don't know my father. My mother neglects me. I'm a paranormal being. I can't take it all," I say. I rest my head on Logan's chest and sob into him.

"I don't have the words to comfort you," he says, "because I don't know what you are going through. Anything I would say would be meaningless. But please know that if I could, I would take it all away. I would give anything to see you smile. I love you so much. It kills me to see you in so much pain."

"Would you just take me out tonight, be friends with my friend, and take my mind off of it? Would you do that for me?"

There is an unfathomable amount of love, heartbreak, and yearning in Logan's eyes as they flame in front of me. His chin quivers as he says, "There is very little I wouldn't do for you."

I smile a sad smile, reach up to kiss him on the cheek, and turn away from him to get in the shower.

Thirty Seven

"So tell me, Logan," Tucker says, dead serious. "Do you have any gay friends you want to hook me up with?"

"I'll tell you, Tucker. Just tonight my lovely girlfriend was so gracious to inform me that I have no friends," Logan says. He looks at me and wrinkles his nose.

"Oh my *goodness*," Tucker says, placing his hands over his heart in an inflated gesture. "You two are so cute."

Tucker, Logan, and I sit at a table in front of the lanes eating fried food. I've told Logan before that I am not one of those girls who is a dainty eater. Or a girl who doesn't eat in front of guys. I like bacon cheeseburgers and fries and cheese balls. Tucker has the dainty eater thing down for me. Though tonight he has to settle for a grilled chicken sandwich. The bowling alley doesn't serve spinach salads.

We ordered our food, bowled, and are now eating and talking. I was really afraid that Tucker would monopolize the conversation, or that Logan wouldn't talk at all, or that they would have nothing to talk about. Unfortunately, I happen to be one of their topics of interest. They spent a good fifteen minutes on the clothes I used to wear to school.

I finish my burger then stand up and walk towards the lane we are using. "Okay guys," I say, addressing Tucker and Logan. "I think tonight is my night. I think I'm going to break a hundred. I can feel it."

"Casslyn, you've said that every time we've bowled since we were ten."

I tilt my head at Tucker and smirk. "I really mean it tonight, Tucker."

"You've also said that every time we've bowled since we were ten."

"I get it, Tucker. Thank you."

"Here to help," he says and smiles.

I take my ball from the ball return and stand in front of the lane. I line up my feet, bring the ball up in front of my face, and close my eyes. Taking a step forward I open my eyes, bring the ball down, walk towards the lane, swing the ball forward and release. It hits the floor and begins to roll. It swings to the right and my heart sinks knowing it's going to go in the gutter. But then it swings back to the middle and strikes the front pin which consequently knocks down every single other pin behind it. Strike.

I turn around and look at my boys at our table, smile, and say, "Suck on that, Tucker."

Tucker stares at the fallen pins in awe. Logan laughs. And for the first time in many months I feel alive. For the first time as an only child I don't feel so alone.

Tucker picks his jaw up off the floor to bowl. He knocks down seven pins then gets the rest in a spare. Logan stands up to bowl and knocks down three the first time and two the second time. Tucker and I make sure not to laugh at him. A guy as manly as Logan could easily get his ego hurt for failing at something as common as bowling.

It is my turn again. I compose myself enough to throw the ball down the lane and get another strike. I shriek in joy and run up to Logan. He has his arms open so I throw myself into them. He hugs me tight and kisses me on the forehead.

The third time I go I get another strike. A turkey. Never before have I gotten a turkey in bowling.

"I told you tonight was my night," I say to the boys.

But after my turkey, it would seem my streak is over. I only knock down seven pins the next time and five the time after that. But by the end of the game, however, I have reached one hundred and three points. I stare at the automated score board in shock and awe. Logan kisses me on the cheek and Tucker claps me on the back. I've only broken one hundred points in bowling and yet it feels like a victory much larger than that. It feels like a life victory. Like I've accomplished something I never thought I could. I feel like I could climb a mountain or possibly fly. Either option sounds plausible at this moment. I feel so good and it has so much to do with the two men I stand with.

"Now," I say, smiling from ear to ear, "who wants to get their ass kicked in pool."

"No way," they both say together.

"Come on," I say, "I like this winning thing."

"No," they say shaking their heads.

I stick out my bottom lip and fake pout to both of them. "Fine. I'll just go play by myself."

I start downstairs to the arcade and hear both boys in tow. I get to the table and start racking the balls. "Why don't the two of you play," I tell them.

"No way," Logan says. "I'm not embarrassing myself in front of him."

Tucker says, "I am not getting my ass handed to me if I beat him."

"You two are ridiculous," I tell them.

With a little cajoling, I play a game with Logan, a game with Tucker, and then the two of them play together. I beat the both of them and Tucker lets Logan win. There is a lot of laughter. There is talk and smiling and pure joy that I have so missed in my life.

When we head up the stairs at the end of the night, Logan shakes Tucker's hand and says, "You're alright, Tucker. Now I get what Casslyn is always going on about."

Tucker looks as if he is about to cry. He turns to me, envelopes me in a hug, and says, "I love you, Casslyn."

"I love you too, Tucker. You know that."

I look over Tucker's shoulder to Logan and give him a look that I hope says, I-love-you-thank-you-so-much-you-win-the-best-boyfriend-slash-friend-award. He smiles a knowing smile at me and nods.

When Tucker pulls away from me he shakes Logan's hand and in an offhand tone says, "Well, I guess you're alright."

The three of us burst out into laughter as we leave the bowling alley. When we walk out, I notice how empty the street is for a Friday night. There are usually cars everywhere, their drivers bar hopping through town. But not tonight. Tonight the town is too quiet. Deadly quiet.

Almost immediately after the door closes behind us, Logan's laughter cuts off. He stands stock still, his posture rigid. Something is wrong, way wrong. Like I had the feeling I was going to reach one hundred in bowling, I have a feeling something truly bad is about to happen.

"Get in the car, Casslyn. You too, Tucker."

Tucker becomes anxious almost instantly. "What's wrong?"

"Do what he says, Tucker," I say.

I turn to him to make sure he does so only to scream when he is hit on the head from behind. The guy from New Year's Eve, Colt, stands behind him. He doesn't even catch Tucker when he is knocked unconscious.

Colt stands in front of me with a grin on his face that can only spell out danger. Out from behind him steps Ashely Steffen, the person who I always believed to be my mortal enemy. She can't be a griffin. Can she? No. She can't. Then again, Xander told me how many times that he didn't tell the griffins about me. Maybe it was Ashley. She has known all about my family and ridiculed me about it. I always wondered why she hated me so much. Now I know. She hated me because I truly am her mortal enemy. Maybe she also hates me because when I come of age I will get all of the powers that come with being a phoenix and as a female of her race, she gets nothing but to carry on her race. That must suck.

She runs her hand down Colt's arm, smiles up at him, then kisses him on the lips. If I wasn't so afraid right now, I might vomit. When she detaches herself from his face, she looks at me and smiles a more vindictive smile than ever before.

"I hate you," she says to me.

"Right back at you," I say, smirking back at her.

From behind, Logan grabs me and pulls me to him. It would seem as though Ashely and Colt are the only ones here, until we are swarmed on all sides be at least ten other griffins. They all hold a weapon of some sort in their hands; knives, bats, even a gun. My blood runs cold then begins to boil. This is not happening. It is not going to end this way. Logan and I have been training. I'm nowhere near ready to take anyone out. But I might be able to defend myself if it was absolutely necessary. Maybe I could hold one or two off until Logan can deal with the others.

Wait a second. Am I really thinking about ending their lives? I can't possibly be. But they killed Nash. They have tried to kill me several times now. I have vowed revenge. It's about time I take it.

"So nice to see you again, angel," Colt says, cocking his head with a smile.

"And if you're lucky, I'll be the last thing you see," I say, emitting hatred through my voice.

"Such ugly words for such a pretty angel," he says.

"Don't you speak to her," Logan spits through his teeth.

"Stop messing with them," one of the other griffins says. I look around the circle of griffins. I recognize some of them as people I've known for many years. People from my community. There are teens I know from school. Adults I know from my parents or businesses around town. How can there be so many griffins in this town?

"But it's so fun to play with her," Ashely says, "I would know."

"Yeah, let's just finish them," another says. I turn to get a look at this new speaker and am hit by a blinding light.

He is coming so fast. He won't get out of our lane. His headlights are blinding. But behind them sits a man I see for the first time. He isn't impaired by alcohol. His sadistic eyes are clear and sure. He is going to kill two teenagers on their birthday and he is happy about it. Nash swerves the bike, the man behind the lights turns in our direction, making sure we go off the road before driving off.

The man the police haven't been able to find for ten months. The man who has haunted my dreams for ten months. The man who ruined my life stands before me.

"You," I say through my teeth.

"Hello, precious," he says.

I shudder at his words. I recoil from his gaze. But beyond that, I am filled with such hatred as I have never felt before. It was easy before to hate him and not have a face to put to the hate. But now. Now that I know what he looks like, now that I know he actually exists, the hate is palpable.

My breathing has become heavy and erratic. My heart threatens to beat out of my chest. The throbbing at the base of my skull may just turn into an aneurism and kill me. My vision is a shade of crimson only seen in movies and video games.

"It's nice to see you, precious. Because of you, though, I got into a lot of trouble. You just wouldn't die. I've tried twice now. And you just won't die. I mean to correct that tonight."

Logan's hold on me tightens. He means to fight our way out of this. I can feel it in his stance. The defensive stance he has tried to teach me all week. I've never actually seen Logan fight so I am unaware of our odds on making it out of here. But if he's my father's best soldier, our odds should be okay. Speaking of my father, if he knew Cedars was so infested with griffins, why did he only send Logan, and not a whole army?

My father. He had two children he didn't know about and now he's about to have none and he'll never get to meet us. Lucky guy.

"Seriously," a female griffin says, "Can we get on with

this? I have somewhere to be."

I'm glad to know killing me and Logan is not very high on their priority list. We are just an item to check off their list before they go back to living their lives.

"Right," Colt says, "About that."

Colt raises an eyebrow, smiles at me, and shrugs his shoulders as if to say all-in-a-days-work.

They attack from all sides. I can feel Logan's presence beside me and that is comforting. I try to take the defensive stance he taught me and prepare to defend myself, not attack. Colt comes straight for me but Logan intercepts him. Colt gets a good punch to Logan's face, but once Logan has regained his composure, Colt is easy to take down.

I am grabbed around the waist from behind. I struggle against a rather small person behind me. It must be one of the women I saw. She is a bit taller than me though. She controls me enough to hold a knife to my throat. I stop thrashing in fear of making her cut me. This cannot be my end.

Think Casslyn, think.

What did Logan teach me about being grabbed from behind? Or was it maybe *Miss Congeniality*? Something about singing? I pick my foot up off the ground and step on the woman's foot. She screams from the pain and loses her hold. I take the advantage to hit her in the face. Somehow she goes down. My reprieve only lasts a second before another griffin is coming after me. Their speed is surprising. But then again, I knew they would be. Maybe that's why Logan stressed paying attention to the slightest movements.

Speaking of Logan, I have lost him in the throng. I don't feel as safe without him so near, but I can't rely on him right now. I have to help myself.

The guy with the gun stands in front of me, the gun pointed right at me. This could very well be my end. Logan didn't say anything about phoenixes surviving bullet wounds. Besides I'm not even a full phoenix yet. Logan throws one of the teenage girls at the man, knocking him out and the gun from his hand. I run for it but am knocked to the ground. I hit my head on the cement and almost lose consciousness. My head spins as I lie on the concrete trying to gain some sense. My head hurts really badly. I try to gain my footing but fall again. My stomach roils, threatening to lose everything I ate an hour ago. The dizziness does not help the standing.

But I have to stand up if I want any chance of staying alive. I get to my knees then start to stand when a foot connects with my side and sends me flying. I land on my other side and roll several times. A metallic taste invades my mouth. I am getting my ass handed to me. I wonder how Logan is doing. I look around me, momentarily more concerned with his well-being than my own. By the looks of it, and the bodies on the ground around him, he has dropped at least six of them. That leaves four, including the one he is currently grappling with.

I need to get up. I need to get up. That is all I can think. *I need to get up.*

I get to my knees again and start the grueling climb to

the top when I hear a tsk tsk of someone's tongue against their mouth. I look up into the eyes of the man who killed my brother. I am going to kill this man if it kills me.

He lets me stand up. I try to prepare myself for his attack. I try to watch his movements. But my head spins and I can barely see.

"Such a precious angel, aren't you?" he says then punches me in the nose.

I fall backward landing on my butt. Blood runs down my nostrils and into my mouth. I'm pretty certain he has broken my nose. This guy means business.

Get up, Casslyn. I hear a voice. It is not my own.

"Nash?" I call out loud.

"Your brother can't help you from where he's at. I killed him remember?" the man says. I don't even have a name for him. I only know him as the man who killed Nash.

Again he lets me get to my feet. This time I swing at him. I don't care about defending myself anymore. I'm going to kill this guy. I scream when he grabs my arm and swings it behind me. I can feel it about to pop. I slam my head back into his. He stumbles backward and releases my arm. I scramble around, trying to get some space between us. I need to find the gun.

I search the ground around me. I am nowhere near where I started. Nowhere near the door of the bowling alley. But that's where I look. And that's where I find the gun. I run for it. If you could call the limping I am doing running. Before I can get to it, I am tripped up. I fall face first into the street.

My hands catch most of the fall, saving me from killing myself. He has a hold of my ankle. I spin over on the ground and use my other foot to kick him in the face. Blood spurts from his nose. I stay on the ground and crawl to the gun.

I reach it before he can get me again, grab it, turn over, and point it directly into his face. He stops feet from me. He doesn't look frightened. He doesn't even look defeated. Instead, he smiles, blood soaked teeth and all.

Keeping the gun pointed at him, I get to my feet. He does the same. We stand in the street at a face off. If this was a western, I would be considered a cheater, but he would already be dead.

"Do it," he says.

I spit blood at his feet and say, "I'm going to end you, like you ended my brother."

"So the angel becomes the devil," he says smirking at me. How could he not be afraid?

How has my world come to this? Standing in the street after an attack by mythological creatures, pointing a gun at the face of a man who murdered my brother?

My hands shake holding the gun upright. My arms begin to tremble. Tears stream down my eyes, further impairing my vision. I look around me at the fallen bodies. The girls look worse for the ware than the guys do, but then again, they don't have the speed or the strength that the men have. I don't see Ashley. Maybe she got away. Maybe she really is the coward I thought she was. I'll get her one day. Because of her, I have lost my brother.

"Do it," he yells.

"Casslyn," Logan says. His smooth, calm voice breaks me further.

I tear my gaze away from the griffin to look at Logan. He is bloody and cut up but looks otherwise intact. His skin bursts into flames as he walks towards me. His body is healing itself.

"It's okay, love," he says.

"No," I say, thrusting the gun at the guy in front of me. "He killed Nash."

"I know he did. But you don't have to do this."

"Yes I do," I scream, tears running down my cheeks. "I have to do this."

He shakes his head and says, "No you don't. You don't want to kill him. You'll only be as bad as him, and the rest of them."

"But he killed Nash," I say, now weeping.

Logan walks towards me and holds out his hand. "Give me the gun, Casslyn. It's okay. It's over now."

I look back at the man who killed Nash. He looks tired, like he wouldn't fight back given the chance. I hate him. I want to kill him. I want to trade his life for Nash's, but I know life doesn't work that way. I want this to be over with. But I know I cannot kill this man. I don't have it in me.

My arms collapse to my sides. Logan takes the gun from my hands and kisses me on the top of my head. I feel defeated. I feel as though I have failed Nash. But if I had killed that man, I would have failed myself.

I look back up at the man to leave him with a warning that if he comes after me again, it will be the last thing he will do. But the instant I open my mouth to do so, a fist comes out of nowhere and smashes into his face. He loses consciousness and falls lifeless to the ground. I stare, stunned. Then the man is replaced by a new man.

He is tall and lean but built and looks vaguely familiar though I'm sure I've never seen him before. He stares at me without saying anything. He studies my face as if he is interested in me or maybe as if he is looking for something.

He doesn't seem like a threat, and Logan isn't attacking, besides I am too tired to fight another person. The adrenaline kept me up and going this long, but with the battle over, it has left me. My body finally registers this and decides it no longer wants to stay standing.

My body collapses in on itself. I am caught from behind and steadied. Logan holds me upright.

"It's okay, Casslyn," he says but his hold on me remains.

My head feels heavy. I wish I could go home, crawl into bed, and sleep for ten years.

"What happened here?" the new man asks.

"We were attacked," Logan says in a voice I haven't heard from him since his first two weeks here. "A civilian was knocked out before he could witness anything."

That's when I remember Tucker being knocked out.

"Is Tucker okay?" I ask through the fog that clouds my brain.

"He is safe. He will be fine," he says to me then turns

to the new man who stands in front of us, his arms crossed. "We fought with the opposition and escaped with our lives."

"Very good, soldier," the man says. He doesn't seem like much. Just a man. An average man.

None of this makes any sense. Why would he call Logan soldier? And why would Logan call Tucker a civilian? Maybe I have a concussion. I really just want to go to sleep. The man turns his gaze away from Logan and onto me.

"You are severely injured," he says to me.

"Gee, you think?" I say, somehow retaining my sarcasm.

I hear Logan release a sigh of relief.

"Who are you?" I ask.

He stares at me head on and says, "I am your father."

Laci Maskell grew up in Northeast Nebraska. Her love of reading began when her sister handed her the Harry Potter books. Laci spent her childhood telling hour long stories on half hour TV shows. She began writing not long after. Laci attended Wayne State College where she earned a degree in English Writing and Literature as well as Editing and Publishing. Laci has worked as a secretary for a physical therapy department, a tax firm, and a computer repair company. She currently works as a Subway sandwich artist and for a daycare when she is not writing her books. In what little spare time she has, Laci enjoys spending time with her family, listening to music, watching movies, and reading.

Follow Me:

Twitter
@LaciMaskell

Facebook
Laci Maskell

My Blog
Laci Kay With Words To Say

73398334R00236

Made in the USA
Columbia, SC
14 July 2017